Once
We
Were
Home

ALSO BY JENNIFER ROSNER

The Yellow Bird Sings
If a Tree Falls: A Family's Quest to Hear and Be Heard
The Mitten String

ONCE WE WERE HOME

Jennifer Rosner

FLATIRON
BOOKS
NEW YORK

ONCE WE WERE HOME. Copyright © 2023 by Jennifer Rosner. All rights reserved. Printed in the United States of America. For information, address Flatiron Books, 120 Broadway, New York, NY 10271.

www.flatironbooks.com

Library of Congress Cataloging-in-Publication Data

Names: Rosner, Jennifer, author.
Title: Once we were home / Jennifer Rosner.
Description: First edition. | New York : Flatiron Books, 2023. | Includes
  bibliographical references.
Identifiers: LCCN 2022039784 | ISBN 9781250855541 (hardcover) |
  ISBN 9781250855558 (ebook)
Subjects: LCSH: World War, 1939–1945—Children—Fiction. | Holocaust
  survivors—Fiction. | LCGFT: Historical fiction. | Novels.
Classification: LCC PS3618.O84513 O53 2023 | DDC 813/.6—dc23/
  eng/20220923
LC record available at https://lccn.loc.gov/2022039784

Our books may be purchased in bulk for promotional, educational, or business use. Please contact your local bookseller or the Macmillan Corporate and Premium Sales Department at 1-800-221-7945, extension 5442, or by email at MacmillanSpecialMarkets@macmillan.com.

First Edition: 2023

10 9 8 7 6 5 4 3 2 1

For my family
and for Kevin McIlvoy and Ruth Salton, in dear memory

Once
We
Were
Home

From primeval forest to ribboned tree, from stout trunk to husked log, I wait. Fine wood shavings drift and swirl, matting the floor like a page upon which stories will be written.

I might become a bird with ruffled feathers, a knight astride a whinnying horse, a top that spins around and around. I might become a boy's prized notebook, or a girl's tiny doll, solid to the core and brightly painted.

When I am released from the carver's hand, pink circles gloss my cheeks and flowers travel my red coat. My family's song sets the rhythm of my heart as I nest inside my mother, inside her mother, inside her mother.

1

ROGER
1946

In the hills above Marseille, in the Convent of Sainte Marie de Sion, Roger cups his hot, throbbing ear with one hand and stacks prayer books with the other. Palm flat, patting the edges, he straightens the piles so the books won't tip over and tumble. If they do, he'll get another ear twist or worse. At seven, he knows better than to bother Sister Chantal at lauds—but yesterday he couldn't help it, his ankles itched him to distraction and the question sprang from his mouth: "Why, if God is good, did He create mosquitoes that sting and bite us?"

Roger finishes his stacking, a final *pat pat* of the books, with the feeling of eyes at his back. He looks around for Sister Chantal—or was it God watching?—before he rushes out the door, ear still pulsing. He wishes he'd stayed quiet, held his question for Sister Brigitte, as she was always encouraging him to do. There is so much he doesn't understand.

Why are some potatoes purple?

Does a tiger's skin have stripes beneath his fur?

Can a person cry under water?

(This, Roger wondered before his baptism.)

He didn't want to cry. The babies cried, even though they were cradled in their parents' arms and held at the side of the basin, not dunked into it. Madame Mercier told him he was lucky baptism was possible at all, as he was born to parents whose religion killed

Jesus. Being baptized would "keep him ever in the Christian fold" and "secure his life in God's kingdom." He wanted that.

But on the morning of the ceremony, Sister Brigitte looked like *she* was crying, huddled with Father Louis and Brother Jacques. *Why?* he wanted to ask, but then Madame Mercier showed up with a crisp white robe folded over her arm and shuttled Roger to a church off the Sainte Marie grounds.

At the altar, an unfamiliar priest gripped Roger's shoulders and twisted him around, back to the font. Roger thought again of the babies on Sundays after Mass, water dribbling gently down their cheeks.

"Isn't baptism for babies?" Roger asked.

The priest, one slate-blue eye magnified larger than the other behind his glasses, flicked a look at Madame Mercier then back at Roger and answered, "By God's grace, it's meant to happen now."

Roger is sure he'll always remember the shock of cold water, the shiver he'd wished to conceal but knew he couldn't hide from God. Ears pooling with the holy water, he couldn't hear the priest's words, only saw him signing the cross, his big eye glinting. Afterward, soaked at the collar and dripping, Roger tried not to wriggle as Madame Mercier fussed over him with a towel, the expression on her face like she'd gobbled up the entire croquembouche she'd brought for the occasion.

Roger still didn't understand why Sister Brigitte was crying earlier, or why they waited the four whole years he's been at Sainte Marie's—and just weeks before his first Communion—to have him baptized. But he was happy for the sweet, caramelized ball of dough he got to eat. And he was happy to be saved.

Across the cobblestone courtyard. Past the cupboard with Mary inside, marble robes flowing to her feet. Around the stooping oak tree and up the stairs. Roger pulls open the heavy refectory door with both hands, releasing a flood of echoing chatter, and edges onto a crowded bench hardly wide enough to hold his bottom. He chews the morning's baguette, swallowing quietly, scratching at his stung-red ankles and stealing glances around the room. The other boys joke and jostle as their mouths move around their ration of bread. A new boy named Henri looks Roger's way and gives a small smile. His hair and eyes are golden, reminding Roger of the croquembouche. He smiles back.

After breakfast, Roger collects his lesson books from the dormitory room. His uniform shorts are too big for him; he has to wrap the belt twice around to cinch them. Then he wets his hands at the sink and pats down the cowlick at the top of his head so Albert won't tease and call him "hedgehog." All the boys rush so as not to be late. Roger heads down the hall, gripping the thick banister to steady himself. His shoes sound on the stone stairs, *slap slap slap*.

They cross the courtyard to class. Already, the day is hot and sticky. Some of the younger boys extend their arms like airplanes, swerving through the thick summer air, making noises with pursed lips. "*Sheeew!*" Roger joins in, veering this way and that. He misses Georges, his friend since nursery, who was moved to Saint Michael's after making up a game of dangling books, tied in their carrier straps like bombs. Sister Brigitte called Georges a prankster and reminded Roger that he can't afford to get into trouble. "You must keep to best behavior—I mean it, Roger."

Roger drops his arms now, bringing his books close to his chest. He has new questions that popped into his head last night.

Do bats have upside-down dreams?

Why do stars twinkle?

Does Heaven get full?

He spots Sister Brigitte, small in the folds of her habit,

pink-tipped nose and eyes like sea-blue marbles, standing outside the classroom building. Roger begins asking her his questions, and though she shushes him—"Not now, you'll be late for
lessons"—she pulls him in for a quick hug, fabric rustling, and
presses her soft cheek to his.

The schedule is always the same:

Wake up, lave, make the bed, and morning exercise
Lauds and breakfast
Lessons
Lunch and washing dishes
Afternoon rest
Arts and crafts
Chores by rotation
Supper
Vespers and bedtime

Roger has Sister Brigitte's permission to spend rest time in the
garden. Stepping-stones spiral like snail shells around tall stalks of
purple iris and white lilies. Beyond the iron-slatted gate, mounded
hills dabbed with wildflowers. Roger sits on the rock bench, looking past the gate, wondering who might come, and writing stories
on spare pieces of paper that Sister Brigitte saves for him.

He writes about a boy who wishes to do nothing all day long,
but in wishing to do nothing, he does something. He writes
about two friends, a moose and a deer, who believe they are the
same until they come to a lake and see their different reflections.
One day Roger writes about a girl—a real girl he spots carrying a
basket of dug-up plants over the hillside. In his story, she drifts to
sleep dreaming of planting a garden and wakes the next morning
in a full-grown flower bed.

After reading his latest, Sister Brigitte says, "Be proud of that wild imagination you got from your *mère et père*."

Roger wishes to write even wilder stories.

"Hey, sissy, are you writing in your diary?" Albert says, walking past, freckles splashed across his nose and cheeks.

The adults think Albert is angelic, but the kids know he is a bully. He's always mocking Roger for using the private stall in the boys' bathroom, and for turning around to undress, even as other boys chase each other, naked, hurling pillows. But Roger is doing what Brother Jacques, praising modesty, told him to do. He angles his paper away and continues writing.

The new boy, Henri, takes a seat at the far end of the bench. His shorts pouch like Roger's do, and he has nearly as many mosquito bites on his ankles. Roger keeps to his writing. Henri gave a smile earlier, but maybe he's fallen in with Albert.

"I like stories that are funny. Do you write funny stories?" Henri asks.

"Not really," Roger says.

Henri looks toward the chapel. "Have you noticed that Brother Nicolas's eyes are bloodshot?"

Roger looks up. "What's that?"

"When there are red lines in the white part."

"Like tiny lines of a map," Roger says.

"Like the roads to good and evil," Henri says, his voice pitched high in imitation of Sister Chantal.

Both boys laugh, then look around to be sure no one heard. Maybe Henri is a prankster, too, but he doesn't seem eager to get in trouble.

"I'll show you some of my stories anyway," Roger says.

Henri scooches closer on the bench.

There is only cold water at Sainte Marie's, so once a week Brother Jacques leads the boys through town to the public bathhouse. Roger and Henri walk side by side now, inhaling the street smells: fried fish, pipe smoke, garbage, the salty sea air. Brother Jacques, straight and tall like a tree, doesn't talk much, but he also doesn't quiet the boys as they chatter on their way. Henri knows lots of riddles, and he tells them to Roger. Roger doesn't know the answers to any of them, so Henri supplies them.

What goes up and down without moving?

Stairs.

What is as light as a feather but the strongest man cannot hold for long?

Breath.

Where can you find cities, towns, and streets but no people?

A map.

"With the roads to good and evil," he and Henri both blurt at the same time.

The boys clatter into the bathhouse, wriggling out of their coats and shoes, leaving them in heaps in the outer changing room. Brother Jacques ushers them along, quietly directing most of the boys to the showers, Roger and Henri to individual tubs. Roger feels lucky he gets a tub again. This is how he knows he must be Brother Jacques's favorite.

The first thing Roger does in the bath is dunk himself all the way under the water and cross himself, to make himself really clean. Then he soaks and floats, trying to think up riddles to tell Henri. He watches steam rise above the water like the Holy Spirit and adds his own warm breath to it.

Outside, hair hanging lank—not like in winter, when it dries straw-stiff, even more like a hedgehog—Roger and Henri keep to the back of the line to avoid Albert. Then, with their hands cupping their ears, elbows swinging, they take exaggerated jerky steps, pretending they've been boxed on both ears by Sister Chantal.

Roger's assigned chore for the week is peeling potatoes. He sits over a bucket, the musty smell of earth in his nose and on his fingers. Nuns scurry between the stoves, fretting over the watery soup. One constantly looks over to make sure the peelings land in the bucket, every scrap worth saving. Roger's hands turn red-raw as he peels one slippery potato after the next. Outside, the sun sifts through the clouds, splaying light beams as if from Heaven into the steamy kitchen. He thinks of the religious paintings that dot the hallways and wonders,

Are there really roads to good and evil?

Why did my parents take the wrong road, like Madame Mercier said?

Can I really be saved if they weren't?

2

ANA
1942–1943

Mira doesn't want to promise she'll watch over her little brother, but her mother's eyes are welling with tears, and this scares her into a cautious nod. This, and everything else about the strange morning. They went to the bathhouse early, as soon as the Rapoports and Kohns left, and her mother had soap, which she almost never had, not since they moved here. But then Mama bathed them so quickly, scrubbing and drying. No time for splashing or floating or dribbling water on Daniel's cheeks to make him giggle.

Now, back in the apartment, Mama keeps pulling shirts over their heads, more than they need for the spring day.

"I can't move!" Mira says, working to straighten her bunched-up, twisted sleeves.

Her mother hushes her, "Don't wake your papa," and darts about the tiny room, stuffing things into a satchel.

"Are we bringing all that with us shopping?" She doesn't understand why her mother is delaying. The Rapoports and Kohns left straightaway for the food lines. If they don't go soon, all the bread will be gone.

Her mother doesn't answer but instead lifts Daniel onto her lap and spoons something into his mouth. He barely turns to her. The violinist upstairs is practicing, and Daniel is in thrall. What three-year-old loves the violin so much?

"What are you giving him?"

"Shh, it's all right," Mama says.

In a few minutes, her brother blinks heavily, still reluctant to stop listening to the music. His head droops.

"Why is he going back to sleep? We just woke up."

"Come," Mama says. "I need you to carry the satchel." She lifts Daniel with one arm and takes Mira's hand with the other.

Mama walks them down the back stairs, sour-smelling and creaky, her sure steps at odds with her doubtful face. A truck idles in the alley; their friend Bluma is in the driving seat, her dark hair knotty, her eyes the color of hulled chestnuts. Mama opens the passenger's side and takes the satchel while Mira climbs in.

"Get in and crouch along the floor space, there," Bluma says, a bit brusquely. Mira looks at her mother.

"It's only for a little while, until it's safe," Mama says.

"*What's* only for a little while?" They were going to the market, and that's just a walk.

Mama leans over the seat, and as she hands sleeping Daniel over, she kisses his cheek, his shoulder, his side, his bottom. She holds on to his foot a moment, then lets go. Bluma wraps his body around her middle, and Mama spreads a thick-knit shawl over him, smoothing it across Bluma's lap. Bluma looks like she's wearing all of her clothes, too. Or else having a baby.

"Mira," her mother says, turning to look at her squarely, eyes flooding now. "You are my girl, and I will always, always love you."

"Mama, what's the matter? Where are we going?"

"Please, promise again you'll take care of Daniel."

"But we can't leave Papa!" When her father shivers, Mira is the one who pulls the blanket to his chin.

Bluma puts a hand on Mira's shoulder. "Get down. I'm going to cover you. We have to move."

"Mama, get in!" Mira says.

Her mother's voice is a choked whisper. "I have to stay with Papa while he gets better, and I need you to be safe until I can come get you."

Mira is scared of the way her mother's face is crumpling, so she huddles down, clutching the satchel. Bluma presses her lower to the floor. "Keep quiet, not a sound."

She is covered over with heavy blankets and cannot see. The truck jerks over the cobblestones, then stops. She hears Bluma say, "I have a permit to travel to the municipal hospital."

If they are at the ghetto gate, guards are there, soldiers. She has seen them.

"What are the blankets for?" A man's voice.

"They're from a sick house. I am incinerating them in case of typhus. Do you wish to inspect them?"

A grunt. "No, get going. Go."

The truck shudders along twisting roads. Mira grows more frightened with every jostle. *Where are we going?* Finally she peeks out from a tiny corner. She sees Bluma driving with one hand on the steering wheel, the other curled around Daniel's body at her middle.

As soon as Bluma stops the truck, Mira throws off the blankets. While Bluma unwraps Daniel—still asleep, his cheeks rosy, his hair slick—Mira scrambles out from below the seat and looks around. She is staring at a farm. Fields and a barn. A house with painted shutters, like others up and down the lane. Red poppies dot the side of the road.

"Bluma, where are we? Why are we here?"

"Your mama and papa need you to be safe," Bluma says. Her voice is soft and raspy now.

A couple are hurrying toward the truck. Mira recognizes

them. She knows them from the market. And the man came to their house once, before they had to move to the ghetto. Mira was little then, only five, but she can still remember him, tall in the doorway, pacing foot to foot. His wife was dangerously ill. She'd lost a baby and was still bleeding. "You'll need to watch Daniel until Papa gets here," her mother had told her, rushing around the kitchen, gathering herbs and leaving with the man. Later, he brought a chicken as payment. His wife sought Mama out at the market, frail, her eyes sad. Reaching with a quavery arm for a squeeze of Mama's hand. She looks better now.

"Come in, right away." The wife lifts Daniel out of Bluma's arms and ushers Mira toward the house. The husband takes the satchel and closes the passenger door. Mira whips around to face the road—she doesn't want this; she wants to be back with her parents. But Bluma is already turning the truck, driving away.

In a Polish farmhouse nestled among rolling green fields, forest woods, and a wide winding river, Mira stares about the kitchen, scrubbed clean. The walls are hung with bright embroidered linens and dark wooden crosses; high shelves hold decorative plates and a large box engraved with flowers. The air that wafts in from the open window smells of cows. No scent of drying herbs, as in their kitchen at home, or the rolled-together smell of earth and fire from her father's blacksmith shop. No ghetto smells, either.

"How long are we staying here? When will our parents come for us?"

The woman is holding Daniel, still asleep. "I am not certain," she says.

How could Mama send us away to strangers?

Fighting tears, Mira peers into the satchel. She finds clothes for her and her brother; Dani's nappies and toy bear; a small, framed photograph of their parents. Her mother looks young, a dark-haired beauty; her papa, healthy and strong. Mira is glad to have the picture, even as she puzzles over why her mother packed it. They weren't going to forget their parents' faces in a few days.

At the very bottom of the bag, her wood-carved spinning top.

The woman—scurrying between the kitchen and the table, hair in a braid, apron tied at her waist—seats Mira with a glass of fresh milk. Mira takes a small sip, thick and foamy, and her stomach practically jumps to get the rest. She gulps it down, its richness bringing a flicker of gratitude.

"I remember your beautiful hair," the woman says, putting a gentle hand to Mira's head.

"Thank you, Pani . . ." She trails off, trying to be polite, but not knowing the woman's name.

"It's best if you call me *ciocia*."

"But you're not my aunt."

The woman's cheeks go pink.

"You will call me Ciocia Agata. And I will call you Anastazja. This will be your name from now on, and your brother will be Oskar. These are the names of my sister's children, my niece and nephew. We'll say you're here because my sister, Jadzia, is ill. You mustn't, under any circumstances, use your other names. You're here to be kept safe. Do you understand?"

Anastazja nods.

"Good. Now would you like another glass of milk?"

"Yes."

"Yes?"

"Yes, Ciocia Agata."

An unsettled quiet. Anastazja stares at the colorful embroideries on the wall—red flowers on green stems, yellow-breasted birds with green feathers perched around the cheery words

Dzień Dobry—wishing it felt like a good day. She looks over at the closed door, wondering when her mother will arrive to take them home.

When Oskar wakes, he cries out. The sound sends Agata's eyes jumping to the window.

Anastazja stands to tend to her brother.

"It's all right. Drink your milk," Agata says, gently patting Oskar's back.

Anastazja nods and sits back in the chair.

"Maybe he's just wet?" Agata asks, a bit uncertainly. She's not practiced, like their mama. She unfolds a blanket and lays Oskar upon it. When she straightens his tucked-up legs to unfasten the diaper pin, she lets out a small gasp.

Anastazja looks at Agata. Her hands are raised to her cheeks. She hasn't even opened the diaper yet.

"Is there a spare nappie in your bag?" Agata asks, her voice a lilt higher. "I'll make a pile of them this afternoon—"

"He doesn't really need them anymore. It was just for the ride, for while he was sleeping. He's three," Anastazja says, then adds, "and I'm seven."

"Well, let's get him a fresh one for now, until he's comfortable."

Anastazja sees Agata slip something gold into her apron pocket.

Newly dry, Oskar reaches out his arms. When Agata picks him up, he folds into her, close.

"Shall I take him?" Anastazja asks.

"No," Agata says. Anastazja knows how heavy her brother is, but still, Agata keeps hold of him as she maneuvers about, as she sets the table for four.

At mealtime, Anastazja silently replays the prayers her father says over wine and bread, blotting out Józef's grace. Oskar doesn't flinch when they thank Jesus Christ for the food they are about to receive—but he wouldn't understand, would he?

When Agata places a bit of pork on her plate, Anastazja's hunger battles with the thought that it isn't kosher. She tries to think of the last time she ate meat. Months, at least, as her family has lived on watery soup and bread. She takes a bite, greedier than she intends.

Afterward, when Anastazja helps to clear the table, she notices a small tarnished cup tucked in the back of the dish cabinet. She wishes to reach out and touch it, for it reminds her of her family's Shabbos wine cup; also the engraved baby cup the Kohns brought with them to the ghetto, with a birth date and a tiny star of David carved on it, but no baby. She clenches her fingers and moves away.

At bedtime, they're led to a pallet laid with blankets. Everything in the darkened room is unfamiliar—the shadowed shapes of the furniture, the pictures on the wall—and the bedding has a strange, woolly smell.

"I won't be able to sleep," Anastazja says aloud.

But then Oskar is nestled beside her and the two of them fall into a sleep such as they can't remember, stomachs full and limbs warm beneath thick, quilted covers.

Next morning, Anastazja steps outside to a prepared basin of warm water. A soap block is perched on the metal rim. Tentatively she dips a finger in the water, her stomach hitching knots. Why hadn't she read *leaving* in her mother's desperate eyes, her quick movements at the bathhouse, scrubbing and toweling, the rushed gathering of her and Oskar's things?

Only now has she begun to perceive what hangs silent in the

air. Grief in the creases of Agata's eyes just before Oskar reaches for her; need in her elbows as she pulls him close. Fear in Józef's jaw whenever anyone passes by the farm, receding only when they're fully out of sight.

Anastazja hesitates, then climbs into the bath, her long white hair fanning out over her shoulders, the blue sky at her back. As the warmth loosens her, coaxing her to unclench, tears rise up and blur her vision. She sloshes, forward and back, with enough force to create waves but not send water over the edges of the basin. She feels small amid the splashes, too small for what her mother has asked her to do.

Finally, she stops her sloshing. It takes several minutes for the water to calm. Anastazja breathes in the scents of hay and earth. She may not forgive her mother for sending them away. But she will obey her.

"Ciocia Agata," she calls.

Agata opens the door and Oskar is there beside her, already tugging at his clothes, eager for his turn in the bath. Ana swings around, eyeing the nearest neighbors' houses along the lane, re-membering her mother's pleas to keep Oskar safe. "May we move the basin inside for Oskar's bath?"

Sunday morning, Agata brushes and braids Anastazja's hair and teaches her to recite the Our Father and the Hail Mary. Ag-ata gives her a cross to wear around her neck and describes the church service, instructs her on how to behave in case anyone is watching.

Everyone is watching. Anastazja shrinks from their gazes but speaks the words Agata has taught her. The priest wears a tall cy-lindrical hat with a veil of fabric in the back. His face is narrow and his nose is pointy. He paces back and forth upon the fancy red rug.

Anastazja is conscious of the tilt of her chin. She is aware of being attentive, and also of looking attentive, of playing her part. She has never been inside a church, and she tries to look around without gaping. Oskar appears to be mesmerized, too, his eyes not knowing where to rest. Gold-framed paintings span the front wall. A huge shining cross is arched by painted sunbeams. There are columns, swirled in white-and-gold paint, and gold crosses poised above sky-blue domes. The synagogue at home had a wooden ark, simply carved, and the Torah scrolls were wrapped in black velvet. That was all.

After the service, neighbors surround them, glances shuttling between her and Oskar. A sharp-featured woman named Pani Lis elbows her way in to be nearest. The smile at her lips does not reach her eyes. Agata lifts Oskar to her hip and drapes one arm over Anastazja while she's darted with questions.

"Your sister's children, you say?"

"You haven't mentioned she was ill."

"Not much family resemblance. Especially the boy."

"I thought I noticed a truck stop at your house early the other morning."

Agata's voice remains steady as she explains, over and over, the story of her niece and nephew's arrival. Two dollops of pink on her cheeks are the only sign of her distress.

"Ciocia Agata," Anastazja says, taking a handful of Agata's skirt in her hand, "I think Oskar needs his nap."

"Yes, I believe you're right. You see, I have an excellent helper."

Agata leads Anastazja and Oskar out of the swarm and, quickly, they walk back to the house. Inside, Anastazja sits folded, her arms crossed over the nervous cramp in her middle.

Agata warms a pot lid on the stove and wraps it in a cloth. "This is for your belly, to calm it a bit. Press it there, gently."

Anastazja holds the cloth-wrapped bundle to her stomach as

Agata rubs light circles on her back. She breathes deeply, feeling the warmth seep into her skin. "Thank you, Ciocia Agata," she says.

Late afternoon, Agata returns from another outing, flush-faced and holding tight to her purse. She leads Józef a few steps away from the table. Anastazja looks up from where she and Oskar sit, drawing.

"What did Father Laska say?" Józef asks.

"He agreed, the identification cards need to align with our story. An associate helped with . . . paperwork." Agata looks toward the table. Anastazja quickly lowers her eyes to her drawing. Agata is whispering now. "We have to register them at the Commandant's office and pray no one cross-checks the records forty kilometers from here."

Anastazja's cramp is back, gripping her tighter. In the ghetto, the Commandant ordered people away.

"I gave them paper and pencil," Józef says.

Agata steps toward them. "May I see your drawings?" she asks.

Oskar's is all scribbles. He accompanies his pencil flourishes with quiet "moos" and "baahs." Anastazja's page is a riot of squares, people crammed inside, faces overlapping, arms flattened at their sides, except for those with babies pressed to their chests. In the center square: a man and woman, huddled alone, dark-circled eyes staring out.

Anastazja feels Agata's firm hold on the back of her chair as she leans in and says, "Why don't I warm a bit of milk. That will be nice, won't it?"

In the evening, Agata teaches Anastazja her new surname, her birth date, her village.

"Tomorrow we'll sign you in at the registry."

"Isn't Oskar coming with us?"

"He's young enough, he needn't come along."

A quick rage flares in Anastazja. Why does *she* have to do everything, while her brother sleeps, or gets toted around in someone's arms? "That's not fair!" she shouts.

Agata's eyes fly to the window, and suddenly Anastazja feels afraid. Can the neighbors hear them from *inside* the farmhouse?

"I'm sorry, Ciocia," she says in a rush. Then, quietly, "Are you certain *I* have to go?" She is scared of meeting the Commandant.

"It will be all right. Just remember what I've taught you." She reaches out a hand to Anastazja's cheek.

When they arrive at the Commandant's office, Agata explains about her sister's children and produces the identification certificates. Anastazja watches the man's eyes shift between her and Agata, then settle on her. His hair is as white as hers, even his eyebrows and mustache.

"What is your name, young lady?"

She speaks out the name Anastazja Wójcik, not Mira Kowalski, and the parent names, Jadzia and Emil, not Chana and Zvi. She hopes he can't hear the roil in her stomach. She looks down at her feet.

He writes something in a notebook. "Very well, you're registered."

Anastazja meets his eyes now, and he gives a quick, nearly imperceptible wink, same as her papa when she'd look in on him at his blacksmith shop.

As they leave, he says to Agata, "Pretty girl. She looks quite a bit like my own niece."

Agata grips Anastazja's shoulder and guides her out into the street. Anastazja turns and looks back at the office. The Commandant is standing in the open doorway, lighting a cigarette.

The Dąbrowskis' fields run in long narrow swaths, bordering the neighbors' fields on both sides and backing up to a wooded area before reaching the river. The neighbors' boys, Paweł and Tomasz and Rafał, all with the same honey-colored bowl-cut hair, ears sticking out, show up at the farmhouse door, peering in without knocking. They're near to Anastazja's age. Oskar stands in the open doorway, staring at them solemnly, one hand fisted around a little wooden whistle that Wujek Józef gave him. The boys stare back.

"Who are you?" one of them finally asks.

Anastazja steps beside Oskar and says, "I'm Anastazja, the Dąbrowskis' niece, and this is my little brother, Oskar." She's thankful that Oskar is too shy to talk to anyone but her.

"You look like them," another of them says, pointing at her, "but he doesn't."

Anastazja shrugs. She remembers children back home saying that she didn't look like her family, because her eyes are blue whereas theirs are brown, and because her hair is shimmery and light. "Like a fairy's," her mother would say as she wove flowers for a crown.

Anastazja speaks low in Oskar's ear: "Don't pay them any mind, Oskar, they're just *gnojki*." Little snots.

Still, the boys want to play with her, and they even include Oskar in their games. They take exaggeratedly slow strides in tag so that Oskar can keep up, or else they pick him up and run with him, squealing.

Later in spring, she and Oskar are at the end of the lane, gathering up whirlybirds from beneath a maple tree, when they notice a patch of blackened ground, hay, and leaves. In the middle, charred beams like burned crosses piled in a heap. Oskar walks closer, squats down to touch the scorched earth.

Anastazja, smelling the ash now, feels a shudder of fear. "We shouldn't be here, Oskar." She tugs him by the arm in the direction of the Dąbrowskis.

When they walk past the Nowaks' field, Paweł and Tomasz see them and come out.

Oskar splays his ashy fingers.

Tomasz looks between Anastazja and her brother. "Did you see the burned-down barn?"

Both nod. "How did it burn?" Anastazja asks.

"It was set fire to," Paweł says.

"Who would do that?"

The boys exchange looks.

"Tell me," she says.

"Our parents said it was German soldiers," Tomasz says.

"Why would German soldiers burn a barn?"

"They didn't like what was inside."

A moment's quiet.

"What was inside?" Anastazja asks.

The boys don't know.

"Pan Lis said snakes," Paweł says, finally, "but our father said he was just trying to scare us."

Tomasz shakes his arms, as if trying to fling off snakes. Then he scoops up Oskar. "Race to the river!"

Anastazja wants to go straight to the Dąbrowskis, but she joins the chase.

On the walk back, Oskar tells her he has to pee.

He points around a tree. They've both seen other boys relieve themselves this way. He fumbles to loosen his pants.

"*No*. You can't!" Anastazja says, her voice a suppressed hiss.

"But, Stazja—"

Pulling him ahead of Paweł and Tomasz, out of earshot, she

says, "You can't pee outside, Oskar, ever. You have to wait until we're at the farmhouse, and always, only in the privy." Even then, Anastazja worries that the boys might come close, see in.

Oskar nods, obeying her, though she's sure he doesn't understand.

That night, she speaks to Wujek Józef. "There are gaps in the privy walls. Can we cover them, please?"

Of the adult villagers, Pani Lis and Pani Zając, her face doughy white with small blueberries folded in for eyes, inquire after Agata's sister the most. On walks home from church they pepper Agata with questions.

"How is she feeling? Any improvement?"

"What a long time to be apart from one's children."

Agata clutches her embroidered pouch, rosary beads inside.

Anastazja and Oskar dawdle up the lane, apart. The tall grass ticks in the wind; the trees whisper and creak. Pani Lis slows, pulling Anastazja aside.

"Your mama's not feeling well?"

Mama? For a moment, Anastazja falters: *Perhaps Mama has taken ill like Papa? Otherwise, wouldn't she have come by now?* But she steadies, fingering her necklace with the cross, and answers as she's been told she must: "Our Auntie Agata is taking care of us."

She sees there is no gladness in Pani Lis's eyes.

Early mornings Anastazja milks the cow, leaving the full buckets, as instructed, for Agata or Józef to carry out. Next, she heads to the coop to collect eggs. Oskar is already there most mornings, kneeling down, listening to the rustle and murmur, observing the chick who has bent feet.

"I can hear him purr, like a kitten!"

The stink doesn't seem to bother Oskar. Anastazja pinches

her nose. Sometimes, when her mother distilled black cohosh for tinctures, their kitchen would smell sharp like this, but without the burn of ammonia. Then, she and her mother would stand together, so close their elbows might touch, Anastazja handing her the washed bottles, one by one. Her mother would hold up a twine-tied flower bundle.

"What's this?" White petals, yellow center.

"Chamomile!"

"And this?" Gold clusters, bunched and drying.

"Yarrow."

She loved being quizzed, loved learning about the herbs and flowers that could help women to have their babies and heal afterward. Maybe she'd be a midwife one day, too.

Here, the herbs sprouting by the vegetable patch look to be for cooking, though Anastazja thinks some could be for healing.

When they help Agata with harvesting the vegetables, the tops of their hands redden and their fingertips stain brown as they dig for leeks and carrots. Oskar brings his hands to his nose and inhales the scent of the rooted earth. Since arriving here, Anastazja has taught him to recite Christian prayers, stamped out any hint of Yiddish—they're to speak Polish here—and now, she instructs him on numbers and simple math, using the cabbages for counting.

"Oskar, pay attention," Anastazja says.

"I *am* paying attention," Oskar answers. When he pulls his hands from his face, there's dirt on his nose.

"No, pay attention to *me*."

The math is mostly subtraction, as the majority of their yield is taken to a collection center for consumption by the German Army.

They make weekly outings, to market and to church. Oskar skips down the road, swinging the market baskets, asking Ciocia

Agata if they can walk past the field with the horse and along the stream afterward. Anastazja tries to appear calm and unflurried, though she's filled with dread. Even if she looks as if she belongs here, Oskar is a different story, and there's always someone staring or asking after their mother's health, their "home."

Months pass and the seasons change. Anastazja watches Oskar dart between trees, running his hand along the birches' peeling bark, new buds poking out from the high branches. Calling out the names of birds that swoop over the sunflowers, feathers glinting in the golden air. Gathering up red and yellow leaves, sending them cartwheeling again and again, and then, when the ground is carpeted with snow, gliding down the road like a skater on ice. *This* is the life her brother knows.

She and Ciocia Agata continue to hurry him along, skirting conversation with the neighbors if they can. When Anastazja spots a cat basking in a spot of sun, she thinks of how they gave Bolek to a neighbor when they had to leave their house and move to the ghetto. "He won't be safe with us," her mother had said. Oskar doesn't remember their parents' house, or the ghetto, or Bolek, either. When the three of them arrive at the farmhouse, Anastazja waits by the stove while Agata heats a pot lid for her stomach.

3

RENATA
1968

In Jerusalem, sacred ground of holy tombs and temples, ancient rock walls and vine-wrapped garden gates, Renata plops down her bags at her lodging, splashes water on her face, and heads out into the early evening. The air is thick and fragrant, the limestone buildings sponged gold in the waning light. She hurries past outdoor markets closing up, baskets heaped with dates and figs and olives of every variety.

She can't believe she's here, her first excavation outside the UK, after all the uncertainty—the politics of the region, her mum's long illness. Invited by the brilliant Professor Shomron, along with fellow Oxford postdocs Margaret, Linda, Ian, and Robert, to join a raft of highly accomplished Israeli students on the dig.

Her insides jitter.

Around a corner, the wafting scent of sweet-roasted nuts; up the block, a woman's purposeful gait. Renata slows, memories of her mum mingling with the thought that, if this dig hadn't come through, she'd be stuck in their flat, alone.

She stops to consult her map. People pressing past, a few men staring. She turns right, past tables mounded with spices: sumac, coriander, cumin, turmeric, za'atar. Two blocks farther, a glance between the wilted address and the number on a blue-painted door. *Here.* She scales a narrow staircase to the roof, lit up, lively, and booming.

She's never been one for bars. She always turned down her classmates' invitations to head to the pub, even when Professor Shomron, a visiting scholar at the Griffith Institute and closer to their age than to the dons', agreed to join them. That was before her mum got really sick and Renata spent her nights pacing hushed hospital corridors.

Her shoes stick to the floor as she weaves inside, people jammed at the bar. She'll have to squeeze past cluttered tables to find her group, keep her eyes peeled for Robert (a head taller than most everyone else), or Margaret's black bob, or Professor Shomron—

She spots the professor first, in a colorful dress, waving her over. Lustrous and assured, her dark hair reddish in the bar light. "There you are. How was your flight?" Quietly, just to Renata, "I was sorry to hear about your mother. I'm glad you're here." Then turning to a clutch of Israeli students, "This is Renata, one of the finest I taught while visiting at Oxford."

Renata's cheeks heat up. Just in time, Ian appears and hands her a glass. She's grateful to have a few Oxford mates here, collegial if not close after so many years in school together. Especially Ian, from her DPhil cohort, who has always gone out of his way to be kind. "How are you?" he asks her now.

The chilled glass is sweaty in her hand. Cold beer. She swallows it down. "Thanks, I'm all right. There was so much to sort out before I left; I couldn't get to it all. Still so many boxes."

"It'll all be there, waiting for you." A warm smile.

Quick introductions as they take seats at a long table, everyone talk-shouting over the noise. Ian slides pita and various creamy dips in Renata's direction. She takes small bites, tasting sesame, eggplant, and garlic.

After several rounds of beer, a few of the Israelis grow flirty. None rivals the one named Yonatan, who pins Renata with a stare—his eyes as intensely green as hers are blue—before she looks away. Later she'll hear that he asked Linda out in their first conversation and, when she declined, moved on to Margaret.

Professor Shomron asks Ian how fatherhood is treating him. Renata feels a pang of guilt; she's been so consumed with losing her mum that she hasn't asked after Ian's little boy, Mark. One of the Israeli students—who introduces herself as Irit—says something about the hardships of being away from family. Ian ducks his head, and Renata wonders if perhaps he's embarrassed by his excitement to be here on the dig. "At least you'll get some decent sleep," Irit says.

Robert asks about best falafel stands, and a debate ensues among the Israelis.

"El Wad's can be soggy and they add too much lemon."

"You can't have too much lemon."

"You can, and the balance of cumin to coriander is off."

Renata would love bakery recommendations but hesitates to break into the banter, and then the moment has passed. Professor Shomron stands and says, "Make sure you all get a good night's sleep because we're starting bright and early tomorrow." A collective groan, but the excitement is palpable.

Five A.M. at the dig site, they map and prep the work area, dividing it into squares. Professor Shomron ("*Please, call me Tamar*") is wearing pants and thick red lipstick—not at all the way Renata's Oxford advisor shows up for digs, drab in a skirt. The rest of them are plainly dressed, neat and tucked in. No dusty stripes down their noses, no dirt in their hair. Not yet. Renata relishes this anticipatory moment: ground tools and collection kits awaiting action; clean, crisp field notebooks in stacks. And this land with so much buried history, secrets waiting to be uncovered.

They're excavating an area of Jerusalem's eastern slope where the ancient city's boundaries remain unknown. Terraced wall segments of differing time periods have been found in the vicinity; their team plans to target an elevation believed to be the location of Second Temple construction.

Slowly, methodically, the work gets underway. They dig in a box grid system, focusing on stratified layers of soil, a process meant to yield fine-grained information for dating purposes. In addition to the tools provided, many have their own trowels. Since participating in a dig in Skara Brae, Renata also carries along a magnifying glass, something of her father's. Occasionally, she reaches in her pocket and wraps her fingers around its stiff leather case, still marveling that she's here, digging in Jerusalem.

Her mum didn't believe in revisiting history, not even a return to Tübingen, where Papa had died when Renata was six. *Why do you want to dig up the past? There's no point to it.* She could not, or would not, understand Renata's fascination with archaeology. Rushing back to their flat, thrilled by whatever new thing was on display at the Ashmolean Museum—an ancient Etruscan vessel, a five-thousand-year-old ostrich egg—*Painted, Mum! It was painted like the eggs at the Easter markets!* Straight-backed at the kitchen counter, her mum barely lifting her eyes from the frosting rosettes she was piping onto a cake.

Digging at ten-centimeter levels, seeking to isolate sediments in datable layers, Renata unearths various sherds of pottery, some with intact bases and rims. When she finds a complete vessel, she calls over her area supervisor. Others nearby crowd around and examine it. Then a dispersal, returning to work, meticulously sifting and sketching. The day's heat gathers. Renata dabs at her forehead, the back of her neck.

They spend the afternoon in the lab, washing pottery and

cataloging finds, thankful for the cool indoors. Toward evening, some of the Israeli students invite them out for drinks again.

"We have to help the Brits get their bearings," they tell Professor Shomron.

Renata's old reflex would be to beg off, claiming jet lag. But as tired as she is, she's excited, almost giddy being here, far from Oxford and her grief, among people as passionate about her subject as she is. A tiny nudge from Ian, and she's in.

The sun is tamer now, the city bustling. They get beers and settle themselves, already deep in conversation, around a large table. Moments later, Professor Shomron turns up, drawing an in-unison cheer and a noisy shuffling of chairs. She's traded her dust-covered pants for a flouncy skirt that shows off her muscled legs. After serious political talk, they turn to lighter subjects—the Beatles, Benny Hill, Elvis. There are a few impersonators at the table. Renata takes in the laughter and the warm press of the late-afternoon sun on her shoulders. It feels like a dream.

Next morning, back in the field, she listens to Margaret and Linda chitchat as they each work their assigned areas. Linda, recently engaged, is talking about how her mum has gone wedding-bonkers and wants to throw a late-summer engagement party when she's back home.

"We'll have been engaged for months by then," Linda says.

Margaret looks staggered by the idea that someone would pass up a party.

On the way back from the supply table, Ian touches Renata's shoulder. "Are you all right? You're bleeding."

She puts a finger to the back of her ear. There's a red droplet on her fingertip that she quickly smears into her pant leg. "Oh, it's nothing. Just my scarf rubbing against a little mole I have 'there." Her mum used to call it her "polka dot." She adjusts the scarf.

"You won't have seen Nigel all summer. You may want to have a party by then," Margaret is saying.

"My mum would've loved to bake for an engagement party," Renata puts in. *Especially my engagement party,* she thinks.

How are you ever going to meet a nice boy if you spend all your time ogling old, broken pottery? Renata shovels soil onto the sifting screen in search of old, broken pottery.

Mum always said she wanted Renata to be more social, to have friends and a boyfriend, but really, what would've become of her if Renata had stayed away after school, gone out with the girls at night, fallen in love? After Papa died, Mum was alone except for her. They were a team, and pretty cash-strapped at that. So she came home directly after school, spread her books on the kitchen table, and when the food shortages and rationing were finally over—eggs and sugar returned to the shelves and her mum's pastry-decorating business picked up—she gabbed as Mum wrapped her confections with fondant and piped flowers on top.

That intensity, the laser focus when she spun boiled sugar into candy shells or formed lace patterns with melted chocolate. But Mum could be playful, too—with her funny doll-voice and her surprise petit fours, thin layers of delicate cake covered by fondant whose decoration, like a wrapped-up box, gave no clue as to what was inside.

Why did you decorate this one with yellow tulips? It was frosted pale pink, and when Renata bit into it, there were layers of vanilla, hazelnut, and chocolate cake.

Because they're for cheering. Mum's velvet-brown eyes were soft then.

Renata had a cherished book all about the language of flow-ers. For thousands of years, across the world and in ancient texts, flowers were thought to have distinct meanings, used to send messages. She kept the book splayed open on the counter while her mum was baking. *If it's a wedding cake, you could add dahlias, for commitment.*

Oh, I'd like piping dahlias. But petit fours were Mum's favor-ite to make, and she was going to keep the inside layers a secret, no hints from the flowers on top. Before the flight here, Renata had covered her mother's grave with chrysanthemums, white, for mourning, for loss.

The time ticks by, flagged buckets filling with soil samples, collection trays accumulating everyone's finds to be processed and analyzed later in the lab. Renata sights a series of sherds that look to go together. They may even fit, edge to edge, like puzzle pieces, or like words placed side by side to tell a story.

On the plane, she read a journal article about an early illus-trated "book"—planks on the walls of a sarcophagus found at an ancient Egyptian burial site—meant to aid the deceased on the perilous journey through the underworld. A sort of ancient how-to guide to avoid demons and fire, written in hieroglyphics, red and black on wood slats. Having had enough of death, Renata flipped the page. No use, though. An article about Vermeer's use of carmine, the crimson pigment made from cochineal: crushed bugs.

There's a murmur in the ranks. One of the Israeli students has unearthed a length of pipe. Renata goes over to see. It's made of terra-cotta, with a pipe of smaller diameter nested inside the larger one. Robert brings over calipers and begins comparing the diam-eters of each. Blinking at the sight of the gleaming metal in his hands, Renata returns a finger to the back of her ear, remembering.

Lined up beside a little girl, Judyta, the same age as her, doctors were measuring them, elbow to wrist, knee to ankle. Their white coats smelled starchy and their polished instruments glinted in the light as they went about the room, sizing the children's heads with calipers, comparing their hair and eyes to colored charts. One doctor kept folding Renata's ear to measure something there with a small ruler. It tickled but she held still, not giggling, because the doctor's eyes, pools of blue water, were stern and serious.

Judyta wailed, "I'm not Jutta!" to a uniformed lady who told her she was. She had to sit in the corner while all the other children got lunch. After that she allowed herself to be called Jutta, and when she returned to sit with the group, the girls' cross-legged knees touched.

Then there was a boy who kept trying to take Renata's wooden doll. The smallest of a set of matryoshki, but she doesn't remember the others. She stuffed it deep in her pocket, checking often to make sure it was there. Later, when she was in her Tübingen kindergarten (or was it some time when she was older?), her mum's suggestion, in a lilting doll's voice: *Why don't you leave me safe on your bureau and I will wait for you to come home each day?* She let her mother peel the doll from her hand, the wood nearly bare of its red and black paint, and perch it on the bureau, a perfect waiting spot.

Where was her doll now? She can't think of the last time she saw it. Mum must have stowed it away for safekeeping. Maybe it's in one of the boxes at the back of her closet, all of Mum's clothes still hanging there.

She takes a breath, the taste of dust on her tongue. The heat is dizzying. It's all still there, waiting for her. She steps away from Robert, his calipers spanning one of the pipes, the team gathered round, their voices filling her head again.

Back at her area, reaching for her trowel, her glasses slip from her face and drop onto hard-packed dirt. Not broken; she dusts them off with the corner of her shirt. She'd have managed anyway. She always travels with a backup pair, the pink-and-white glasses she was swayed to buy when a clutch of old ladies at the optical shoppe remarked how "lovely" they made her look. But at home, appraising her bespectacled self in the mirror, she thought she looked to be about eight years old or else eighty-eight, but not twenty-eight. Compared to the pink ones, even Mum liked this new blue pair better, and she rarely liked things that set off the color of Renata's eyes. When Renata was little, she wondered if her mum wished she'd had the same brown eyes as her and Papa.

The team continues to dig. Renata drops into the work, searching for artifacts, noting her observations on field forms, sketching maps, drawing measurements. Meticulous, layer by layer of soil. The sun is fierce now. She's flushed, sweaty. She wipes her face on a sleeve. Again and again, returning her trowel to the earth, seeking clues to the lived past.

4
OSKAR
1943–1944

"Do you remember Mama and Papa, or anything from before?" His sister is always asking. Oskar doesn't, and he doesn't need to. Here, they have Ciocia Agata and Wujek Józef. They have the fields and forests, and birds who trill and chirp and thwack and whistle, keeping them constant company. They have the farm, and games with the neighbor boys, and sitting quiet in the coop with the smallest chicken.

Inside the house, on the high shelf, they have the carved wooden boxes that nest, one inside the other. Had they always been there? Or did he notice them now because he'd grown bigger? Ciocia Agata stood on a chair to bring them down to show him. The outermost box had a painted-red flower on top. Within it was a smaller, identically designed box; a smaller one within that; an even smaller one within *that*. All told, eight boxes!

Now, she has placed them on a low side table, and each night Oskar opens them, one by one, to reveal the tiniest one nested in the center. He lines them up, largest to smallest, builds a tower, then tucks the boxes back until only the largest one remains. He still can't believe that someone made them so snug, a set that belongs together, a perfect fit.

One evening, while he's lining up the boxes in a row, he asks Ciocia Agata if she might tell them a story.

"Hmm. Let me think. Do you know the tale of 'The Magic Box'?" she asks with a teasing smile.

"No."

"If you sit beside me, I'll tell it to you."

Oskar eagerly nuzzles beside her. Anastazja listens from across the room where she's seated on the wide floorboards, spinning her wood top.

In the place where the pine woods meet the beech forest, Agata begins, and Oskar is happy already, because the story takes place among trees, *there lived a couple who desperately wished for a child. One day, while peering into the hollow of a beech tree, the woman saw a Spirit with glistening white hair flowing down to her waist.*

"Like Stazja's!" Oskar says. His sister, whose hair looks to be lit by the moon, glances up, pleased.

"Yes," says Agata.

The Spirit's name was Matuja and she looked kindly upon the woman, saying, "Tell me what you desire and I shall fulfill it." The woman told her that, more than anything, she desired to have a child. So Matuja instructed her, "Find a round pumpkin and scoop out its seeds. Pour milk into it and drink every drop."

Oskar makes a face.

"If you do this," Matuja told her, "you will bear a beautiful and happy boy, and when he grows up, he will go out into the world and seek the fortune he is destined for. Here is a box made of beechwood—it may be useful to him."

Oskar points to one of the smaller, but not tiny, nested boxes.

"Just like that one, yes," Agata says.

The woman did as she was told, and soon she bore a sweet baby boy named Bachtalo.

When Bachtalo was nearly twenty, he kissed his parents good-bye and left the place where the pine woods meet the beech forest to seek his fortune in the world. He carried the beechwood box in one hand and in the other, a stick of beechwood to chase away fierce dogs.

"Oh no," Oskar says. He wouldn't want to meet fierce dogs in the woods alone.

One day, amid his wanderings, Bachtalo heard of a forest king who planned to bestow good fortune on one who would do something new for him, something that had never been done before. Bachtalo approached the king that afternoon, but he was scolded for interrupting him. "The king is not to be disturbed from five to seven, when he listens to the forest rustlings," a servant warned.

The next morning, Bachtalo approached again and said, "I am here to do something new that the world hasn't seen. Tell me what I am to do." This angered the king greatly, and he put Bachtalo in the dungeon.

"Why was the king angry?"

"He didn't like that Bachtalo *asked* what he was to do."

"But why?"

"Shh, Oskar," Anastazja says.

Agata smiles. "Do you want to sit closer, Anastazja?" His sister shakes her head and twists the stem of her top.

While Bachtalo sat in the dungeon's darkness, Matuja, with her long shimmery hair, appeared. "I promised your mother that you would be happy. I will help you now to find your good fortune. You have with you the little beech box?"

"I have it, but I don't think it is of any use to me," he said.

"And you have a beechwood stick?" Matuja asked.

"Yes, but I didn't meet a single fierce dog on my journey."

"Don't worry." Matuja calmed him. "Here's a lock of my hair. Fasten four strands across the open box and attach the rest to the beechwood stick, stretching it from the top to the bottom. From now on, the box will gladden or sadden people, according to your wish."

"Hmm?" Oskar looks at the box and runs his fingers through his hair, recently trimmed with Agata's sewing shears, outside, the bits left for birds to take for their nests.

He notices that Wujek Józef has come into the room and is listening, too.

Matuja held the box in her hands. First she laughed softly into it; then she wept, letting her tears fall inside. "Now take the stick and move it across the box over the strands of my hair," she urged Bachtalo.

From the box floated the most beautiful sounds. Matuja disappeared, but Bachtalo played on and on. The forest king heard Bachtalo's playing and ordered him removed from the dungeon.

Bachtalo said, "Listen, Your Highness, here is something the world has not heard."

First Bachtalo played a sad song. The king wept, and from his tears grew many mushrooms, as after a heavy rain. Then Bachtalo played a happy song, and the king smiled. All his family and even the forest smiled.

Bachtalo brought his parents from where the pine wood meets the beech forest, and everyone feasted. From that day on, Bachtalo played the loveliest of tunes. The king stopped listening to the forest murmur between five and seven because the music from the enchanted beechwood box was even more beautiful.

And that's how the violin *came into the world.*

Anastazja gives her top a spin. "That's a good story for Oskar. He likes the sound of violins."

Oskar doesn't remember ever hearing a violin. Anyway, his thoughts are on making a music box. He reaches up to touch a strand of Ciocia Agata's hair.

"No, Oskar—" She laughs.

He looks over at Anastazja.

"*No*—" Stazja's voice is gruff now, the way it often is when they're outside, in the woods, or passing by neighbors. Oskar thinks she nearly added "*ty mały gnojku*" but caught herself.

After morning chores Wujek Józef gives Oskar a pocketknife for his fifth birthday and sits with him beside a small pile of gathered branches, glinting silver and white in the sun.

"You want to go *with* the grain, not against it," he says, showing him how to whittle. "That's right. Small cuts often work better than big ones."

"Like this?"

"Yes, but watch your thumb. There you go. You're getting it."

Oskar cuts away at the tip of a branch. The raw wood smells sweet, like vanilla, like the cream Agata dollops on his apple cake. He works along the edge, shaping a spear.

"You can round it out, too," Józef, says, showing him how, and Oskar gets the idea to form an acorn top, like the ones Stazja used to collect in the woods. "Fairy boats" she'd called them.

As Oskar works at it, Józef nods and leans back, watching birds overhead.

"When I was a boy, I loved to know the names for groups of animals," Józef says.

"Hmm?"

"Like that group of sparrows is called a host."

"What's a group of cows?" Oskar asks.

"A herd."

"And chickens?"

"A flock. Those are common. But then there are the groups of exotic animals: a parade of elephants. A shadow of jaguars."

"What else?" Oskar asks.

"A prickle of porcupines."

Oskar laughs, and Wujek Józef does, too, the skin at his eye-
lids crinkling.

Later, they forage for branches of every type of wood: oak,
ash, maple, birch, linden, willow. Józef points out the wood's
burls, knots, and grains.

"If you keep your knife in your pocket, you won't lose it and
you'll have it when you need it," Józef tells him.

Oskar whittles whenever he has spare time, the shavings drifting in thin coils to his feet, the scents of moss and pine rising to
his nose. He makes more acorn tops. He carves a willow-bark
flute. Near the end of autumn, he fashions a wooden spoon for
Agata.

The days grow colder. The produce yield shrinks, and early one
morning, German soldiers appear at the door, ordering the
Dąbrowskis to give up their cow.

"The cow should have been registered at the collection center.
We only just learned of it."

Oskar wants to cry out *No*, but Ciocia Agata's face is terror-
stricken. He huddles behind her skirts, tears streaming down his
cheeks. She puts her hands back to hold him there, and Wujek
Józef reaches for Anastazja as the soldiers pull the cow toward
the road.

For days, the door to the cow barn hangs open on its hinges.
Oskar's chest heaves as he walks past it to the chicken coop. He
thinks of the cow's soft ears, her glassy brown eyes, her long
sides that sounded hollow when he patted her. He fears that the
chicken with bent feet—who has turned out to be a hen—could
be next.

Agata and Józef whisper nervously, fear clinging to the air

around them. "Who said something? What else might they say?" Oskar and his sister are kept away from the winter markets, where there is little to sell or buy anyway.

Without milk to drink at mealtime, Oskar feels hungry all the time. The nightly soup, with no dash of cream, is thin and watery, made from the meager vegetable stores they're permitted to keep: a few heads of cabbage, a handful each of turnips and potatoes. Oskar finds himself flitting about, restless after dinner, knowing there will be no more until morning.

One evening Wujek Józef brings out a board with wood figures, intricate and slender. "Come, I'll show you a game."

"Is that chess?" Anastazja asks, her fingers moving over the board's squares, dark wood alternating with light.

Józef smiles. "Yes, Anastazja. Have you ever played?"

She shakes her head, no. "But our uncle had a set."

"This was my grandfather's. You two are old enough to play now. Oskar, why don't you help me?"

Oskar is intrigued by the carvings: the terraced circles leading to the king's crown, the horse's fringed mane. Józef lets Oskar sit on his lap as he arranges the dark pieces in two lines in front of him. Anastazja sits across, arranging the same lineup with the light pieces.

"Do you know there are four *hundred* possible moves for a player and his opponent to begin the game?" Józef asks.

"Really?" Oskar reaches for a knight. He inhales the faint scents of wood and varnish.

"Yes, and you can start with one of your knights."

Oskar places the knight two spaces forward and one space to the left, as Józef directs.

Anastazja moves a center pawn one space forward.

"My grandfather told me a story," Józef says. They both stare at him expectantly. "Over a thousand years ago, a very poor but very smart man showed the Sultan this game. The Sultan liked it and asked what he'd like as payment. The man asked for one grain of rice for the first square, then double for every other square on the board. Two grains of rice for the second square, four grains for the third, and on like that."

"How much is that?" Anastazja asks, now counting the squares.

"I don't remember," Józef says, "I'm not as good at stories as Agata—and I'm not keen enough at math to figure it out. But it was enough to make a poor man one of the richest in the world."

Oskar holds up the second knight, studying its face. "The Lises have a horse," he says.

"Why do they still have their horse when we lost our cow?" Anastazja asks.

"That's a good question," Wujek Józef says.

Oskar likes to stand by the Lises' fence, watching how the horse's mane blows in the breeze, how she flicks her long tail. Wujek Józef's chess pieces have blunt faces, but that horse has a softness in her eyes. Her muzzle twitches when Oskar offers hay, and her ears fall back when she chews.

A chilly night, Oskar asks Agata for another story.

She thinks for a minute. "I know a story about a girl called the Sister of the Birds."

"Who calls her that?" Oskar asks.

"Come sit." She pats the pillowed bench.

Oskar sits on one side of Agata, and this time Anastazja sits on the other. Agata has given her a small embroidery hoop and has shown her how to stitch flowers into the white muslin. She practices now, with green and purple floss. A lilac. An iris.

Once upon a time, Agata begins, *there lived an enchanted girl who could summon birds of every color to come sing for her. All she had to do was tie on her yellow kerchief and the trills of golden orioles filled the air. When she wore her pink apron, chaffinches warbled in the trees. Her russet skirt brought the chirps of red-breasted flycatchers. A white blouse brought the honks of a wild goose, and a brown jacket summoned the tittering of skylarks and sparrows.*

Oskar flaps his arms like wings, this idea pleases him so. Ciocia Agata continues.

The girl's grandfather, who was blind, walked with a white stick cut from a birch branch, and he took pleasure in talking about colors. When he heard the songs of chaffinches and orioles, he'd say, "Ah, the Sister of the Birds must be on her way to me, dressed in her yellow kerchief and pink apron!"

One day, the Sister of the Birds met a boy along the forest path who seemed to be searching for something. "What are you looking for?" she asked him.

"Tales," he replied.

"Tales, like stories?" Oskar asks.

Agata nods.

"So far, I have not found a one," the boy says. "I've gathered some berries and a few mushrooms but I have not come across a single tale."

Oskar smiles at this.

"Accompany us as we wander in the forest," said the Sister of the Birds. "I am sure we will come across many tales. This time of year, the woods are full of them."

That evening, when the girl and her grandfather slept, the boy stared up at the sky. He noticed the stars were disappearing before his very eyes. He climbed to the top of a poplar tree to better see the cause of their disappearance. From there, he saw an immense black bird pecking stars from the heavens. The bird did not sing but squeaked like a broken branch.

"Why do you eat stars and squeak?" the boy asked. "Did the Sister of the Birds give you permission to do that?"

"I did not ask her," replied the bird. "It is nighttime, when the colors fade; the Sister of the Birds has no power now." Having said this, the bird pecked the remaining stars, so that it was completely dark.

The boy grew fearful in the inky black of night. He decided to build a fire to sit by until morning. But long before dawn, he found he had no more pine cones to feed the flames.

"Oh no," Oskar says, and nestles closer to Ciocia Agata, who smells of fresh hay and dug radishes.

What shall I do? the boy asked himself.

A voice answered him: "Take the blind grandfather's white birch stick and strike the fire with it seven times."

As the boy struck the fire, sparks flew upward to the sky, changing into stars. After the seventh stroke, the sky was filled with stars, while the grandfather's stick had blackened until there was not a trace of white on it. The fire soon died, but the night was light, the heavens studded with stars.

"Was the grandpa mad?" Oskar asks.

"Shh," Anastazja hushes.

In the morning, the grandfather, taking his stick in his hand, stood speechless with amazement. The scales had fallen from his eyes as the birch bark had disappeared from his stick, and he was now able to see the colors of the world.

The Sister of the Birds dressed herself in all the colors she had so the forest filled with the song of the orioles, chaffinches, titmice, robins, turtledoves, cuckoos, nuthatches, and every other sort of bird.

In bed that night, Oskar imagines the forest filled with bright colors and birdsong. Stazja there, all dressed up, singing. Next day, he begins whittling a bird. He practices, over and over, to shape feathery wings and a sharp beak. He whittles every free minute, out on the front porch no matter how chill the air, his fingers growing red and stiff.

In time he forms a variety of bird types. Sparrows. Robins. Finches. His best is a skylark, so he carves a whole lot of them—an *exultation*.

5

ROGER
1946

At Catechism, Roger hears the miracle of Jesus turning five loaves and two fishes into a meal for five thousand, and of making water into wine. Wonder lights the other boys' faces. Roger opens his mouth to raise questions but closes it before the words can form.

Later, sitting with Sister Brigitte in the garden, he asks, "Do you think Jesus really turned five loaves of bread and two fishes into a meal for all of those people?"

Sister Brigitte turns to him, her lips pressed into a tentative "Hmm" as she ponders. That's one thing he loves about Sister Brigitte. She doesn't act like she knows everything.

After a short silence she says, "We have to have faith that miracles happen."

Roger pictures the morning baguettes on the refectory tables. Using every bread ticket, they still run out, boys fighting over the hard ends. How could five be enough? He thinks about what he writes in the garden. "It sounds like a made-up story," he tells her.

"There are some who wouldn't be pleased to hear you say that," Sister Brigitte says, shifting on the bench.

"Sister Chantal?" he asks, but he worries she means God.

She snugs an arm around him. "You have a wonderfully curious mind, Roger—and that's a good thing in my book. Just, please, save your questions for me, all right? Not a word next week to Madame Mercier."

The following week, he is on his rock bench, watching as other boys are picked up at the gate. "No family coming for you," Albert says, his hair smoothed to his head, no cowlicks, as he's met by his parents. Roger turns away, wishing for a better view of the road. Wishing that miracles *could* happen. He'd picture his own parents, waving their greetings as they arrive. But he doesn't know what they would look like, and his sightline is obscured by the iron stalks of the gate. The next car to drive up is Madame Mercier's. The driver holds the door open. Roger has no choice but to get in.

He spends all the school recesses at her house. The mattress coils don't poke at his ribs and sometimes there is real butter, but still, he wishes he didn't have to. Sister Brigitte told him that he was just three years old when his parents placed him for safekeeping at the Saint Vincent nursery. From there Madame Mercier, the nursery's biggest benefactor, offered to "oversee" his care, arranging with Father Louis a future spot at Sainte Marie's. Word came that his parents were sent away, and that they died. "Otherwise, they would have come back for you," Sister Brigitte had said.

Madame Mercier meets him in the foyer with her usual tidal force, a flood of words as she straightens his collar and vest with several sharp tugs. "You know the rules: no wandering off. You're to stay in the sitting room. I have business to attend to." Head half-turned, she's already on her way, her large behind swaying. Roger looks about the house, everything the same as it always is. The porcelain bulldogs on the shelf, the vase of silk flowers at the table, preserved in time.

The house is on a fancy, tree-lined street in view of La Bonne Mère, but Roger isn't permitted outside to look at it. He crosses into the sitting room, severe with heavy upholstery and dark paintings. He scans the titles of the books cased along the wall, hoping for new ones, but they are the same dreary texts, many with religious titles. He thinks he knows their ordering by heart. Eventually he seats himself at the window, smoothing a crumpled piece of paper he's taken from his satchel, wondering what stories he could possibly invent while here. Maybe one about a dark queen or a dragon? Or about children knowing things adults don't, like the fact that there can't be miracles in a world where mothers and fathers take wrong roads and children end up orphans.

Roger can hear Madame Mercier banging about in the kitchen, speaking sharply to the maid. He finds a strange reassurance in the thought that she's like this with everyone: store clerks, the fishmonger, even the brothers and sisters at Sainte Marie.

He looks up when the doorbell sounds. Madame Mercier sails past and opens the door.

"Madame," comes a man's voice. "The solicitor has sent me here with the petitioner's latest response."

"Why didn't he bring it himself? Let me see that—"

"I—I'm his new clerk. It seems the relatives have appealed to the Rabbinical council."

"Get down from my step," she says, following him outside and shutting the front door behind her.

Roger can't hear their conversation now. He peers out the side window to see a man with a high-collared coat and a case of papers clutched beneath his arm. The man's feet are angled, as if trying to step away, but Madame Mercier has him pinned to the gate with her big bosom and she's doing all the talking. Now and then she throws a look in the direction of the house and the man's eyes warily follow. Every so often he gives a slight nod of his head, noncommittal. Catching sight of Roger at the window,

Madame stomps toward the flower boxes, waving her arms. "Get away from there," she shouts. When she comes back inside, red-faced, Roger quickly looks down at his paper. "Shut the curtains and go to your bedroom," she says, reaching for her coat and hat. "I have to speak to my solicitor."

At the supper table, Madame Mercier's words are a torrent of complaints. Roger sits quietly, eating his soup—more than he gets at Sainte Marie's and tastier. He wishes he could say something to please her, but he can't think what. Her expression is vexed even as she ferries a large spoon from her bowl to her mouth. He ventures to thank her for dinner, hoping to be excused. She starts up again. "Of course *you* show proper gratitude, *I've* brought you up right. The affrontery, when *I'm* the one entrusted with saving you. Well, let me tell you, it's astonishing how *un*gracious other people are, after all I've done and continue doing. . . ." She sweeps her thick arm across the table. Roger squirms in his chair.

Over the course of the week, each time Madame Mercier pulls her hat over her head, feather bobbing, and bustles away toward town, Roger imagines official-looking people pinned to gates, blinking and captive, wishing to escape. He stays in the small bedroom most of the time, reading his schoolbooks and writing stories. She doesn't seek him out there.

Now he writes about a boy who finds a lost wolf pup in a blustery snowstorm. The boy carries the pup in his arms, uphill and down, following the sound of wolf howls until, finally, he comes across the pup's pack and (carefully) returns him. But on the way home, the boy falls into deep snow. The wolf pack surrounds him, and at first, he fears they will hurt him. Instead, they keep him warm and howl, *Owooo,* until the boy's parents, trudging through the snow, find him and take him home.

Mealtimes, Roger has no choice but to face her. At his final

Sunday lunch, she drones on about her role in his salvation: "Thank goodness I arranged for your proper instruction and conversion. Don't worry, you were a small child when I took you in, too young to be tainted by Jewish parents. I just thank Jesus that I could do this for you. Not every child has been so lucky."

Roger wonders about his luck. And Jesus'.

He sits on the foyer's slate floor, his packed satchel slung over his shoulder, waiting to be returned to the convent. Before the recess, he'd watched as other boys' parents came for them. Now, they'll be bringing them back.

When Roger enters the Sainte Marie courtyard with other returning boys, Sister Brigitte gives him a welcoming embrace.

"How was your holiday?" she asks.

"Why do I have to go there?" He sinks into her, fighting the urge to cry.

There's a halt in her words. "I know it's hard to understand—"

Roger looks up at her, waiting.

"Madame Mercier brought you to us," she says, finally.

When he nods, holding back tears, she says, "Come with me." She has him wait in the garden.

She reappears carrying a notebook, crisp and pale blue, with delicate vines in black ink traveling the cover. "Over the recess, I made a start on sewing your papers together so that your stories will be collected and won't get lost. But I think you'll be happy to have this real notebook to write in."

He doesn't know what to say. It's better than croquembouche.

Back in the dormitory, Roger finds Henri lying on his bed, legs kicking the covers, a thick textbook on his pillow, the page turned to a full-color picture of an eye, red veins running this way and that. In place of any greeting, Henri says, "Look, it's blood-shot!" And Roger knows, Henri has been eager for his return.

Roger stows his notebook in the cabinet beneath his folded clothes—in case Albert goes poking—and climbs beside Henri on the thin, pointy-coiled mattress. Henri flips the pages to pictures of cells, with sidebars printed in narrow columns, explanations about cell structures and how they divide.

Henri stayed at Sainte Marie's during the break. He found this book about cells and another one about sea life—thick, sticky-paged, and dog-eared—buried at the back of a storage closet. He reaches under his bed for the sea life book and finds a picture of a squid, a detailed box-drawing of suctioning arms. "Like Madame Mercier," he says, and they both laugh.

After they look at that one for a while, Henri asks, "Want to see if we can find other books?"

Roger nods. Henri means the monks' library. They've talked of it but have never ventured inside. They creep toward the doorway and wait. Footsteps. Father Louis emerges from a hallway in front of them, and feigning innocence, they trail him toward the chapel, then break off at the library door. They look down the corridor in both directions before sneaking in.

It is disappointing. The faded tomes, all religious in nature, fit on a few shelved cupboards:

Bibles (a lot of them)
The writings of Saint Augustine, Saint Ambrose, and Saint Jerome
Assorted sermons and meditations in paper piles, not even bound

"Hmm" is all Henri says.

Roger thinks the books look boring, but he tries to stop thinking it before God might notice.

They walk to the garden and sit together on the rock bench. Roger tells a joke:

"Why couldn't Noah catch many fish?"

Henri looks up. "Why?"

"He had only two worms."

Henri laughs. "That's a good one."

Roger is happy to be back, even when Albert walks past, smug, wearing a wristwatch he got from his father over the recess. Roger noticed through their car window that Albert's father's face was splashed with freckles, too.

On the morning of his first Communion, along with the other boys from Catechism, Roger is brought into the chapel and seated in alphabetical order, to be taken one by one to confession. He is nervous and in a hurry to get to the Mass, especially to its end, when he will swallow the sacrament, the body and blood of Christ, and be sure of belonging in God's kingdom.

Inside the dark-paneled booth, it smells of rosewood and polish. A scalloped metal screen conceals Father Louis, yet his words ring startlingly close.

Roger recites as he's been taught, "Bless me, Father, for I have sinned."

"How have you sinned?" Father Louis asks.

Roger holds himself back from scratching the scabbed-over cut he got peeling potatoes. "I was born wrong . . . I mean, I was born to the wrong parents."

"That's not something you've done."

"I've also had bad thoughts."

"What kind of bad thoughts?"

"I've thought: I'd like it if Madame Mercier never came here again, though she is saving me."

"*Jesus* saves you, perhaps through the works of others."

Roger sits back, dizzied by the screen's grated pattern, wishing he could see Father Louis's face.

"Madame Mercier is always telling me that my parents were . . ." Roger stops, then tries again. "That got me thinking: I don't have my first teeth, and my hair is cut all the time. Maybe I don't even have the same cells! Maybe I'm not the same—not my parents' child anymore—and she can stop saying that."

6

ANA
1944

Anastazja wakes to hear Józef stomping snow off his boots, his and Agata's voices carrying from the other room.

"What are you doing? Where did you get those pelts?"

"It's fine. I traded butter and a few linens."

"But, Agata, it will look like we're spoiling—"

Is Hanukkah coming? Anastazja cracks open the door of her and Oskar's room, slowly, not wanting to ruin a surprise. She sees Agata at the kitchen table, sewing.

"It's to keep them safe," Agata is saying as she spreads Oskar's woolen coat on the table.

"Sewing fur on their collars?"

"Yes. It's forbidden for Jews to wear fur."

Anastazja closes the door and slumps on their mattress, kneeing Oskar to make room. Reaching for paper and pencil, blocking out squares.

On a late spring afternoon, a basket appears among the poppies near to where Bluma's truck stopped. Two stones inside, each the size of a small flower bulb. Anastazja kneels down and reaches in. She touches the stones, cool and smooth at her fingers. A shiver at her arm.

"Is that a nest?" Oskar asks, when she walks inside carrying the basket.

"It has two stones," she says. Handing it to Agata, searching her face.

Agata's face looks pale and when she speaks next, it's as if stones have caught in her throat. "Why don't we bake something nice, the three of us?" In a quick motion, she perches the basket on a shelf and pulls out rationed sugar from a bin. "I'll show you how to make jam cookies."

They're shaping the cookies, round, and adding dollops of cherry preserve at the center when Józef walks in. "What's going on? It's not Christmas."

"No," Agata says, her voice still craggy. "I just thought . . ."—a pause, both Anastazja and Oskar looking at her—"something sweet would be nice for the children."

A few weeks later, a man, Agata and Jadzia's friend since childhood, arrives at the door. "Zygmunt!" Agata rushes to greet him, then steps back when she registers his haggard expression.

"Agata—"

She cuts him off. "Are you hungry? We have barley soup on the stove and cheese in the cellar."

He shakes his head.

"Go to the chicken coop," she orders the children. "You may have missed some eggs."

While Oskar runs to the coop, Anastazja lingers outside, unseen, behind the open farmhouse door.

Zygmunt looks around, confused, then takes a heaving breath. "I'm so sorry, Agata. I have terrible news. There was a bombing. Jadzia and the children . . ." His voice trails off.

Agata gasps, *No*, then breaks into sobs.

"I don't know where Emil is," Zygmunt continues. "They never received word that he joined his second unit."

"It's my fault," Agata says in a choked whisper.

"What?"

Józef's voice breaks in. "Agata, come, come lie down." The door to their bedroom opens and closes. Anastazja can hear her keening.

Józef feeds Zygmunt a small meal before his journey back. From her crouching place, Anastazja watches the man leave, shoulders slumped, walking toward the road.

Ciocia Agata continues to weep. Józef returns to the bedroom. As quietly as she can, Anastazja comes inside and carries the plates from the table to the sink.

"Agata, you had nothing to do with it."

"I told lies. I told the neighbors Jadzia was ill."

"She was caught in a bombing," Józef says.

"I gave away her children's names, their birth dates, as if trading their lives in that commandant's office."

Anastazja stands frozen, still holding the plates.

"That's nonsense. This was an act of war."

"And those stones. The poor Kowalskis. It's like I cursed them *all*."

Anastazja struggles to put the parts together. Her eyes go to the basket on the shelf.

"And what if Emil makes his way here? He'll find an Anastazja and an Oskar—not his own."

"Agata—" Józef soothes.

"How can I call them by those names?"

"We do what we must."

Agata doesn't appear at dinnertime. Cries slip out from beneath her closed bedroom door.

At the table, after a stretch of quiet, Józef says, "Ciocia Agata received very sad news." He doesn't say more. He eats Anastazja's simple cucumber soup, then excuses himself to sit with Agata.

"What news?" Oskar asks Anastazja, reaching for a piece of buttered bread.

Anastazja looks at her brother. "Some in her family were harmed. Killed."

"Who?"

"We never met them. The important thing is that we take care of everything for Ciocia Agata."

The following morning, Agata is still closed off in her room. Józef leads Anastazja and Oskar through the morning chores, then to the fields to harvest whatever they can. Their haul is short of the allotment due at the collection center, but there is other work to tend to: mucking out the chicken coop, chopping soup vegetables, setting a dough to rise. Each time they come inside the house, they hear Agata's whimpers from behind the bedroom door. At supper, Oskar reaches out his hands to Anastazja and Józef. He recites "Hail Mary, full of grace" as Anastazja has taught him.

That night, just before falling asleep, Anastazja holds the photograph of her parents in its tarnished frame, wishing she knew how long they've been apart. She wants to imagine them all *home*, Mama and Aunt Freida bustling in and out, tending soup pots of steaming *kneydel*. Jars of plum marmalade lining the kitchen counter; herbs tied fresh and drying off the beam above. Just outside, Mama's garden bursting with mint and rosemary and lavender. If Anastazja sat still on the narrow bench, the perfect spot to smell the lilac blooms, Bolek the cat would climb onto her lap and purr. No secrets needing to be kept. No hiding. She'd be Mira again.

Oskar wasn't even two when they were forced into the ghetto, crammed in with the Rapoports and Kohns in that tight, dank room. In winter, the frigid air pressing through the cracks in the windowpane. Lapsed garbage collection causing it always to smell. Papa became sick and Mama got so thin her cheeks sunk. *You are my girl, and I will always, always love you.*

"Do you remember anything at all from before we came here?" Anastazja asks Oskar.

Oskar yawns, turns on his side.

"I remember rats," he says.

In the morning, Agata is in the kitchen fixing breakfast. Her face is white and puffy, her eyes downturned. She puts eggs and toast onto their plates, more than usual. Her plate stays empty.

"Ciocia Agata, aren't you going to eat?" Oskar asks.

"I'm not hungry, Os—" She takes a shuddering breath. "I'll eat later."

Later, she leads them on a walk through the woods. "Why don't you collect some nice soft things?"

"Like feathers?" Oskar asks.

"Feathers would be lovely." Agata's cheeks have regained a bit of color, but she has dark circles under her eyes.

"I'll pick moss," Anastazja says. Agata puts a hand on her shoulder and gives a squeeze.

They carry home their soft forest things. In the kitchen, Agata takes down the basket with the two stones.

"We're making a nest?" Oskar asks.

"I thought that might be nice," Agata says.

Anastazja lines the basket with the moss, and Oskar sets his found feathers in sideways. They add other things: a bit of curled birch bark, a small lavender sprig.

Agata nods and gently places the stones back inside.

Oskar runs to the windowsill, returning with one of his carved birds. He tries to put it in the nest.

"No, Oskar," Anastazja says, blocking him.

"What about the bird I made for you?"

"No. No birds."

At the Sunday sewing circle, Pani Lis, whose chin is as sharp as her needles, asks Anastazja, "Any word from your mother?"

Ciocia Agata's fingers tremor. She puts down her embroidery and rushes from the room. Everyone's eyes follow her.

Anastazja speaks, her voice shaky. "My mother has died."

7

OSKAR
1945–1946

A change in the air. German troops straggle past the farmhouse, not in their usual tight units, smug and polished, but in disorganized, disheveled groups. Talk swirls among the villagers.

"The Russians must be advancing."

"Could the war be near its end?"

Next come the sounds of distant bombs. Józef corrals Oskar and his sister into the house.

"The root cellar will be safer," Agata says, holding tight to them.

They gather candles and blankets and squeeze into the small dark space, freezing cold. The ground shakes with explosions and Oskar reaches his hand to a shelf lined with jars, asparagus with their tips pointing up. He wonders about the stork's nest that sits above them like an abandoned straw hat. He feels the helplessness of all the creatures in the forest.

When it is calm again, they leave the cellar, poised to return at first signal. One afternoon, Oskar runs out of the barn when he hears a loud rumbling from the road. Russian tanks driving past. He hears shouts from all directions as people rush from their houses and fields. He turns to see Agata's face, streaming with tears. Józef walks over and puts an arm around her, then reaches out his other to Oskar, and to Anastazja, who has emerged from the kitchen.

"What does it mean?" Oskar asks.

"The Germans have been beat," Józef says, "and they can't—"

Agata cuts in. "It means you're safe." Looking down the lane at the other villagers, Agata leans in to Józef. "We'll carry on as we have. But now I'd like to talk to Father Laska."

Anastazja walks to the road's edge and kneels, near to where the poppies grow, near to the place where she found the basket of stones.

"Stazja?"

His sister lifts her head, turns slowly toward him. "It means . . . we won't have to give over the harvest, Oskar. You'll have more to eat."

They do have more to eat, and though there are still soldiers, Russian instead of German, they're mostly left alone on the farm. In the warmer weather, Wujek Józef and Oskar walk through the woods behind the fields.

Józef points out a cherry tree with two trunks leading from the center, branches sprawling from both. "I'll need to cut one side away, probably that one." He points to the slighter trunk, with its thinner branches.

"Why?"

"Its branches will eventually grow heavy, weakening the tree at the middle. Then it could split."

"But it's healthy now. And birds like it." Oskar points to a sparrow flitting among the narrow branches.

"Yes, well, sometimes we sacrifice a part in order to strengthen the whole and secure a longer life."

Oskar puts his hand at the place where the thinner trunk diverges from the thicker one. He's seen trees weep sap when they are cut. "It doesn't seem right," he says.

Spring, a year later, the knock comes shortly after dawn. Oskar is hunched by the warm tiled oven, pulling on his boots, getting ready to help Józef in the far field with spring planting. Ciocia Agata stops kneading the bread dough, wipes her hands on her apron, and opens the door.

A slip of a woman with moss-green eyes peers into the house.

"Agata Dąbrowska?"

"Yes?"

"My name is Eva Daub. I work with the Coordination Committee."

"I don't know what that is. What do you want?"

"I hear the Germans took your cow."

Oskar stands up. He sees the woman cross her arms over the torn seam of her coat.

"I can give you money to buy a new cow," she says. Her eyes, roaming, meet Oskar's. He recognizes the forest in them.

"Why would you do that?" Agata asks.

"It must be very hard to feed, not just yourselves, but—"

"We manage." Agata steps wider in the doorway, blocking the view inside, causing the yellow squares of sunlight reflected on the floor to lengthen and thin. Oskar can't see the woman anymore.

"And it will be better for you, Pani Dąbrowska." She lowers her voice. "We can take the children."

"What?" Agata whispers.

"I know they were brought here for safekeeping four years ago—from the Brzeziny ghetto. Their names were Mira and Daniel Kowalski, eleven and seven by now."

Oskar crouches down, panic tightening his chest. *We can take the children,* the woman said. But he does not want to be *taken.*

This is where he is safe. He can see two pairs of legs, Agata's in clogs, the woman's in battered boots.

Agata glances over at him, then turns back. "We have raised them here—and in the church. Every Sunday."

"It must have cost you greatly, Pani Dąbrowska. We have funds to pay you. And we can place them with their people—"

"They don't have . . ." Agata's voice is now a low hiss. "We received a message, after the children arrived."

Eva Daub lowers her voice to match. "Surely the parents would have wanted them to be with others of their faith. Somewhere safer than here in Poland. We can move them—"

"No!" Agata tries to shut the door, but the woman thrusts her boot in to block it. She's small but strong. The sole gaps from the boot like a horseshoe.

"So many have been lost, Pani Dąbrowska. I can compensate you." Oskar hears rustling.

"Put that away, I don't want it. I said *No*. They are mine. Ours."

Agata shoves the door hard, forcing the boot from the threshold. She bolts the lock and walks to the kitchen counter without looking at Oskar now. She wipes her hands on a dish towel and returns them to the dough. Oskar stares at his *ciocia*'s tensed shoulders. He wants to go to her, wants her to repeat what she's said, that he and Anastazja belong here with her and Wujek Józef, that this is their home and she won't let them be taken away. But he's frightened.

A few days later, Józef is in the far field and Agata is outside with the children when the woman with the forest eyes and torn coat returns.

"Quick, get inside," Agata tells them. They scramble in, and

Agata moves to shut the door, but the woman is there already, her boot stuck in the jamb.

"Pani Dąbrowska—"

"I told you, *No*. Please don't come back here."

"A court will rule on this, and I believe they will come down on the side of redeeming the children."

"*Redeeming* them?" Ciocia Agata asks.

"*Returning* them, I should say. To their people."

"I told you, their parents are gone. This is their home. We *raised* them."

"In the church, as you said."

"Did you want neighbors asking questions? Are you aware of the dangers we faced?"

"You were brave and righteous, Pani Dąbrowska. But now. Now that they can be returned, I—"

"I said *No*."

"We have avenues to pursue this," the woman says before she turns and walks away.

Agata keeps them inside after that. She has them canning potatoes, even though that's a fall chore, and mending socks. She gives Stazja red and green floss to embroider a tablecloth, and she permits Oskar to whittle inside, even though she used to insist that he do it outdoors. They don't go into the village. Józef runs the errands now.

"Who was that woman at the door?" Anastazja asks.

"We're just going to stay inside a little longer," Agata says.

"What about our chores?" Oskar asks.

Agata looks out the window. It's nearing dusk. "I guess you can go to the coop."

"Can I thin the seedlings?" Anastazja asks.

Agata checks the window again and gives a quick nod. "I'll

carry these jars to the cellar, and I'll join you as soon as the bread is out of the oven."

Oskar is sprinkling feed, the chickens swarming his feet, when he hears a shriek. He rushes out and scans the property, purpled by the falling light.

Another shriek.

He runs toward the sound. In the back garden, he sees Anastazja being hoisted over a strange man's shoulders. She's grasping on to the bean poles, the whole trellis of sticks and strings ripping from the ground.

Oskar tramples the sticks, rushing toward the man. He aims to kick him in the shins.

"You can't take her!" he shouts. "Our aunt said no!" He calls out, "*Ciocia Agata!*"

Someone grabs him from behind. He turns back to see that it's the woman with green eyes locking his arms, lifting him up. He tries to twist away from her. She's barely taller than his sister, but her grip on his wrists is tight. He shouts again, as loudly as he can, hoping someone working the Nowaks' farm will hear. Paweł or Tomasz.

He and his sister are heaved into a truck bed tented with a tarpaulin. The woman climbs up to sit with them. Oskar keeps yelling as the truck clips down the road.

"Let us out!" He pulls at the tarp's sides, hoping to find a gap that he can widen enough for them to fit through. It's secured all around with thick, ungiving rope. When the truck hits a bump, he is thrown sideways.

Anastazja reaches for him, clasps tight to his hand. She addresses the woman. "Where are you taking us?"

"Everything will be all right, you'll see. We're taking you somewhere better."

"Where?" Anastazja asks.

"If it's better, then bring our aunt and uncle, too!" Oskar says.

"You'll be with your own people." After a fretful silence she says in a small voice, "I'm Eva." Rummaging through a bag. "Would either of you like a candy?"

"I want my *ciocia* and *wujek*," Oskar howls.

They can't see where they are or where they are going. The truck bed is hard, and the night's air riffles in through the gaps. Eva gives them each a blanket, scratchy and smelling of sweat and camphor, but warm.

Anastazja whispers in Oskar's ear, "We'll be okay; we'll get out of here. I'll think of something." She's not rough the way she can sometimes be, calling him names when the Dąbrowskis can't hear. *Did you remember to close the gate,* ty gnojku? *Why aren't you sleeping,* ty gnojku? Not now.

Yet she makes no move to escape as the truck drives on and on, rattling and shaking. Oskar is knocked on his side, the hardwood handle of his whittling knife, low in his pants pocket, grinding against his hip. The next moment he is bounced in the opposite direction, pressed flat against his sister. The wind whistles in his ears.

Anastazja speaks close, in a gentle voice, of when he was a baby, of when they were together with their mama and papa, before the Dąbrowskis. "Mama used to put you inside a soft blanket and swing you, back and forth. You were so light, her slightest move had you flying." Then Anastazja starts to cry. "They're gone, Oskar."

Oskar starts to cry, too. Lost. His tears are for the Dąbrowskis.

Later, Oskar would wonder why he didn't wield his whittling knife. He could have pierced the tarp or cut the rope. He could have threatened the man who grabbed his sister. He could have forced Eva to stop the truck. The knife-edge was sharp. Wujek Józef saw to sharpening it so that Oskar's birds could have beaks like spears, feathers ruffled as if by the wind.

Later, he'd wonder why Anastazja held so tight to his hand.

One inside the other inside the other, we are gifted to a little girl. She chooses me, the smallest of our set, to take with her wherever she goes. Round-framed eyes, a polka dot behind her ear; it is her lost history that I alone will remember.

Together, the girl and I skip and swing on playgrounds and weave through the holiday markets. We marvel at the decorated eggs, bright and intricate. I am painted simply, but the girl doesn't mind. At home, while my family nests, we sit at the table as her mama spoons plum dumplings into bowls, and her papa says grace.

We are in the park one morning when we spot the toy soldiers. They speak strange words, sharp and halting, their eyes cold like wolves'. They are not *toys. The girl screams when they grab her, she calls out, "Mama! Mama!" I call out, too, thrust inside the girl's pocket, my shouts trapped in the folds of lining and wool. We are jostled and bounced to the steady clatter of a train.*

Though the girl is measured head to toe and given a different name, she is still the same inside. She reaches for me when we enter a house with the mingled smells of pretzels, burned sugar, and chestnuts. She cries for home, for her mama, but she lets the lady with velvet-brown eyes lead her to a table to drink cups of milk. Squeezing me tight, my red-flowered coat peeling off in her hot padded grip.

In time the girl will settle here, abandoning me for a toy broken into a hundred pieces. She'll spend hours fitting it back together. She will eat the lady's frosted cakes and listen to the man's fanciful stories. Just before sleep, she will play with me. Sugar on my braids.

8

RENATA
1968

It's best not to mention we're from Germany, her mum repeatedly schooled, but Renata wouldn't have, anyway. She was just six when they left Tübingen for Zurich—the same year Papa died—and began their intensive English tutoring. Renata's German accent quickly fell away, while Mum insisted that her own unyielding accent was Swiss. By the time they moved to Oxford three years later, they spoke English exclusively, and Renata's sense of a German childhood had faded. She and her mum embraced life as Brits.

Mum sewed their clothes from patterns in *Home Notes* magazine and learned to make fish sticks, toad-in-the-hole, Scotch eggs, and Yorkshire pudding. She could pass as English, with her wispy hair circling her brown eyes like an upside-down nest. Renata's blue eyes and blond hair weren't as typical, and Mum sometimes made her wear a kerchief to keep her hair from lightening more. It was a surprise when, in her last dying months, Mum's Germanness came out, a directness that often startled the nurses.

Now, in Jerusalem, Renata feels keenly conscious of her features and roots. Memories of her mother's warnings to hide her Germanness, evidence of bloodlines that led to so much Jewish destruction. At the dig, though, the focus is on destruction at the hands of the Romans. The team unearths a layer revealing ash and charcoal, charred seeds, and carbonized grain.

The daily 5:00 A.M. start allows them to beat the heat.

Midmorning, Robert brings back lunch from one of the nearby stands and Ian coaxes Renata to join them. "C'mon, I won't make it through the falafel deconstruction without you."

She sits beside him, the foil wrapper a napkin on her lap, the filled-and-folded pita too big for civilized bites. Robert, Linda, and Margaret get down to business, trying to figure out what the Israelis had been talking about.

"This one has a looser batter," Margaret says.

"And doughier pita. You have to eat it quickly or it will get soggy." Linda takes a healthy bite.

"It's the right amount of coriander, I think," says Robert.

"But is there too much lemon?" Margaret wonders.

Ian nudges Renata, shoulder to shoulder. When she looks over, he smiles, amused. There's a boyish roundness at his cheeks.

They resume eating, but their shoulders are still touching and she can feel his warmth. She grows more and more conscious of him, aware whenever he turns his head to look at her. She wraps the remainder of her falafel and scrambles to stand.

Afternoon in the lab, they clean and catalog the finds of the morning, working to establish contexts and chronologies. The hours spool out with light group conversation at times, deep concentration at others. More than once, Renata catches Ian's eyes on her. They both smile.

The workdays are intense; the Israelis, boldly direct in their communication. Oxford could be another lifetime ago, a different world.

On their first day off, Ian finds Renata in the breakfast room. "Hey, let's go be tourists." They walk the quarters of the Old City, people rushing past in opposite directions: dark and leathery; pale with bushy beards; hooded, hatted, collared, turbaned. Her own fair hair and light skin, pink from the sun, stand out.

They view the Jewish quarter in its postwar reconstruction, walk the stations of the Via Dolorosa leading to the Church of the Holy Sepulchre, and explore the market stalls. Their conversation flows nonstop, each equally excited about the history, all there is to see.

"In an art history class, we talked about those tiny crosses on the walls leading to the Chapel of Saint Helena."

"Have you ever seen so many different kinds of fruit? I don't even know what some of this is."

Just outside the Old City, an antiquities museum. Rock-cut ossuaries with circle-inscribed florets. Glass-topped cases with vessels and vases and bright mosaic tile fragments. There's a display of eighteenth-century silver Hanukkah lamps, each wrought in the shape of a Torah ark, with intricate engravings and piercings. The metalwork reminds Renata of the Pair of Gates, silver gilt and molded iron, on display in Oxford from the same time period. Christian rather than Jewish. *Why can't people recognize their commonalities, so much greater than their differences?* It's what she loves about archaeology: it links people together, across geography, time, and culture.

She turns to Ian, thinking to ask if he saw the Oxford exhibit. She takes in his warm copper eyes, his faint scent of wet earth and citrus. They've hardly spent any time together outside academic settings and now she's seeing: he's fun to be with. And *quite* attractive.

"Want to get a coffee?" he is asking. His eyes locking with hers.

A wing of butterflies in her belly.

At a bakery, they order coffee and pick out several varieties of halvah and rugelach. Renata reaches into one of her pockets for cash but instead pulls out her magnifying glass.

"How much will that get us?" Ian asks.

They sit at a small round table in the corner. Ian's legs brush hers, sending her insides further aquiver. She shifts to give him room in the tight space. To pull herself together. But his legs find hers again. She swigs her coffee and eats two rugelach in succession, an apricot, then a chocolate one. Ian is smiling, relaxed, asking what first got her interested in archaeology, what her favorite field assignments have been. He is looking at her, intent and fond. She doesn't know what to do with it.

Before leaving, she orders a bag of pistachio cookies, rounded and rolled in powdered sugar, the kind that coat your lips white. As she waits at the counter, a sudden memory: her mum, not sick and dying, but from earlier days, laughing as Papa took a fingerful of frosting and dotted first Mum's nose, then Renata's.

Out on the street, Ian says, "Do you remember, in second year, I asked if you wanted to get dinner with me but you needed to get home to your mum?"

Heat rushes to her cheeks. That was before he met Olivia.

"I know she was ill," he adds quickly.

In fact, her mum wasn't ill, yet.

Another stretch of workdays. Between the lodging house and the dig site is a cave of interest, its lore featuring a lion believed to protect and guard the bones of those killed in a siege.

"There are differing accounts," Professor Shomron told them, "with a lion figuring in each."

The Christians believed that a lion, accompanied by God, carried the bodies of twelve thousand martyrs killed by Persians into the cave. According to Jewish tradition, those killed were not Christians but Jews, in a fight between the Maccabees and the Greeks, and a lion miraculously appeared to protect the bones of the dead. Muslim oral tradition has it that thousands of Muslims were killed in the siege of Jerusalem during the First Crusade, but by Allah's providence, the bones were moved into the cave and a lion was stationed at the entrance to protect them forever.

"So you see, it's another spot where several religions converge—and clash. In this case, they all claim the lion as protector." Professor Shomron, a bit like a lion herself. *She'd* know what to do when a man looked at her.

Renata and her fellows pass the cave each early morning on their way to the dig site, where they unearth fragments of a clay lamp, broken jars, and stone stamp seals. A bent earring. Scattered beads in a linear distribution, likely evidence of a rapid retreat. No trace of a protective lion.

On the next free day, Renata decides to go into Tel Aviv by herself. She needs time away from everyone, from Ian, time to think. She boards a Central Station bus and, once in the city, finds her way to a neighborhood she likes with textile shops and carpentry studios. She decides she'll just wander, browse the shops, or walk in this sweet little park on a path lined with ficus trees.

She steps around a wiry terrier chasing a band of pigeons and continues circling the park. On a wooden bench ahead, a little boy holds on to a gray knit owl, its black-stitch eyes angled down, giving it a sleepy look. The boy, not sleepy, asks his mother a question. His mother whispers something in his ear to make him smile. He, in turn, whispers to his owl. Renata watches as the mother carries the boy off, owl dangling from his hand.

Renata stands still for a few moments after they've gone. She begins to walk but finds herself sinking, instead, onto the now-empty bench. It is staggering the way her grief ambushes her in different ways, turning her fragile, like she could break into a hundred pieces.

Before this trip, alone in their shared flat, Renata would find herself crying and laughing in a single gulp remembering a playful moment with her mum. She'd missed her on a level that was cellular. She'd missed her in the air she breathed.

It's felt more complicated since being here, separated by distance and time. To hear Margaret and Linda, it's as if they talk to their mums like they're girlfriends. It was never that way between Renata and her mum. Renata feels estranged, questioning if they actually shared the connection she'd always thought they had. She'd counted on that connection and never really made others. Finally, now, she's making up for lost time with people she's been in school with for ages. If only she'd been open to Ian when they'd had a real chance— Even so, he seems to really want to know her. Did her mum want to know her, to be known?

Her mum kept to herself, kept secrets—and not just with her petit fours. She hid away in her room, and when she came out, she would look like she'd been crying yet would never say why. Sometimes she powdered her face to cover her reddened cheeks. When Renata was younger, she thought it was her mum missing her dad. She didn't ask because she didn't want her mother to be sad. Later, she just knew not to ask.

And then her mum was dying. Caring for her was all Renata could manage, overwhelmed and heartbroken, struggling to keep up with the postdoc while shuttling to and from hospital. She nestled each night beside her mum's withering frame, woke early the next morning to shower at the flat before heading into university. Her mother closed up, closed off, so that Renata couldn't ask what she was feeling.

Lifting herself from the park bench, she buys orange juice at a stand and sucks down the sweet tang. It steadies her. She moves toward a line of market tables, all variety of nuts and dried fruit and bright jelly candies. Her mum would've liked to decorate her gingerbreads with these, she thinks, walking past.

On a side street, she enters a shop gleaming with silver jewelry, *hamsas* with turquoise centers. When the shopkeeper approaches with a too-wide smile, she leaves.

Maybe she's not in the right mindset for shopping.

But there's a hand-chiseled chessboard on display at that carpentry shop. Peering in farther: a set of nesting boxes, large to small, fitting one inside the other.

Through the entry door, a loud whir, woodworkers crafting side tables and hoop-backed chairs. Close up, each piece of the chess set looks to be carved with its own personality, except for the pawns. One knight has a tousled mane. Another has its ears back. Every face unique. She's never seen a set like this.

"May I help you?" one of the woodworkers asks, a bit shyly in stilted English as he brushes wood dust from his broad shoulders. Wood shavings speckle the dark curls of his hair and the tips of his eyelashes, golden in the sunlight.

"This chess set is brilliant," she says.

A genuine smile. "Thank you. I made it."

She moves to examine the nesting boxes. The flower design carved on the top of each box, in descending size order, is warm and cheery, and it's painted red.

"Did you make these, too?"

"Yes."

"How do you get them to fit so perfectly?"

"They are a set, they must fit just right to belong together."

Unlike her single matryoshka, here is a whole family of boxes. No orphans.

"I'd love to buy this," she says, pointing to the set of nesting boxes. "It may not be the easiest to fly home with, but . . ."

"I can wrap it, safe."

"Yes, that would be great."

Back in Jerusalem at dusk—streaked orange sky, silver crescent moon—Renata could walk straight to her lodging, but instead she makes her way into the Old City to visit the Western Wall. Dated to the first century BCE, it is the most sacred of the retaining walls surrounding the Temple Mount, closest to the inner sanctuary of the Tabernacle. Yet it's not as an archaeologist that she stands here, heart hanging on its hinges. She feels the coolness emanate from the ancient stones and sees the hundreds of tiny papers stuffed into the cracks. Wishes. Prayers. Pleas. *What would her own folded note say?*

People move in groups, in families. Individuals bow at the wall. She feels an ache, not just for herself. For all of them. It gathers in her throat. Not grief, exactly; not the way she's been feeling it. It's something else: the sense that, despite the presence of others, each of us is profoundly alone.

She turns and walks, feet throbbing, toward the blue-shuttered lodging house. A mother aswirl with five children brushes past her. She pictures Ian's wife, drawing a bath for their son in their flat, on her own.

Arriving at the house, she winds up the stairs with her bundle. Her room is a mess: the swaybacked bed unmade, the bureau littered with wax bags from various bakeries. Shedding her scarf, slinging her satchel over a chair in the corner, she settles on the floor, legs splayed with the package between them. The nesting boxes have been wrapped for travel but she unpacks them, lifting them out, one by one. She considers that what is held in the earth's ground—ashes and tools, cups once brought to lips, bones filled with marrow—entwines with what lives still, the roots of plants, the wending stems of trees. She lines the boxes up, smallest to largest, touching her finger to the red-painted flowers on top of each—*poppies,* she thinks, symbolic of regeneration—then nests them back, one inside the other. She's glad to have something made of wood.

9

ROGER
1946–1948

Roger notices adults huddling and whispering, stealing glances in his direction, and he worries he must be in trouble. Was it because, just yesterday, he asked Brother Jacques, "If God is my father, but my father died, does that mean God is dead?" Or was it because of the game he'd begun with Henri, in which they took turns telling jokes—faces serious, no laughing—just as they walked past Sister Chantal into the classroom?

Yet no one has come to scold him or twist his ear.

For a week, nuns encircle themselves in private conversation, and monks cluster and speak in low tones, jittery like before the war's end. Roger goes searching for Sister Brigitte but doesn't find her. She's not in her usual places, waiting by the classroom door before morning studies, or walking in the garden after lunch.

Then, on Sunday, Father Louis isn't in the chapel leading Mass.

He overhears one of the older boys saying he saw gendarmes take Father Louis away.

"Why?" he asks.

"No one knows."

Roger can't sleep that night, thinking about Sister Brigitte and Father Louis, wondering what happened to them and worrying that it's his fault.

Next day, Brother Jacques is corralling the boys for a walk in the fields when Madame Mercier bursts on the scene. Brother Jacques stands, stiff and tall, as Madame Mercier does all the talking. Brother Jacques ordinarily brightens in conversation like there's a lantern inside him. But today he looks wan, as if doused by water, and it's Madame Mercier who has gone pink-faced, her arms bouncing from her middle.

"After all we've done, where is their gratitude? I don't know why Judge Alarie isn't defending us. His son was at the Saint Vincent nursery."

Brother Jacques casts a quick glance at the crowd of boys. His eyes linger a long moment on Roger.

It *is* his fault. He never should have asked if God is dead!

Roger wants to rush over to Brother Jacques, ask after Sister Brigitte and Father Louis, and beg to make amends. But Madame Mercier is still talking, her eyes darting over, her voice rising and falling now, in and out of earshot, fragments about "court rulings" and "the aunt."

When finally she leaves, it is time for chores and Roger is afraid to be late. He hurries to the rear of the refectory, pulls open the rickety service door. He peels more potatoes than he's ever peeled before, and afterward he lugs firewood and stacks it in neat piles by the fire grate.

In the dormitory at night, the older boys are talking. One says that something happened in court and that the Church lost.

"Lost what?" another asks.

"I don't know but Father Louis has been jailed."

Jailed!

"Maybe he's paying for the misdeeds of others," Albert says. His eyes roam the faces of different boys. Henri. Roger.

The following morning before lauds, Madame Mercier, stiffly dressed and powdery, finds Roger in his room and orders him to pack his satchel.

"Please, no," he starts, but her face is set like flint.

He fights back tears as he gathers his clothes and his notebook and pencil. *What do you bring to jail?*

Madame Mercier escorts him downstairs. He holds himself in, trying not to cry in front of her or any of the boys who might see him, especially Albert.

Brother Jacques is standing in the courtyard outside, his own bag slung over a shoulder. The gate is open and a truck is stopped in front of them. Brother Jacques stumbles over his long robes to climb in. He holds his hand out for Roger, but Roger steps back now.

"Hurry, Roger," Madame Mercier hisses.

"I want to see Sister Brigitte."

"You must get in, right away." Her squid arms surround him, prodding him into the truck.

"But I haven't had a chance to say goodbye to Henri!"

"I told you, there's no time!" Before he's even seated properly, the truck begins moving.

Sainte Marie de Sion disappears from view as the truck lurches out of the gates and away, along narrow curving roads, past stone houses and fields. Roger watches out the window, confused when the truck doesn't turn toward the center of Marseille but instead moves deeper into the countryside. There are meadows carpeted in wildflowers. If he could get to them, he could run.

"Why couldn't I see Sister Brigitte one last time?" he asks, fighting tears.

"I'm sorry you didn't get a chance to say goodbye to her, or to Henri, before you left," Brother Jacques says. "Sister Brigitte made me take all this, though it's going to weigh down my pack."

Roger sees now, the pile of papers sewn together into books, stacked by Brother Jacques's feet. Everything Roger ever wrote, even when his handwriting was giant and messy and his stories were two sentences long. She saved it all.

"They're going to let me have all of that in jail?"

Brother Jacques looks surprised. "You're not going to jail." He sighs. "I don't know why this hasn't been explained to you. If you're of the age of reason, you might as well know why you're being moved about. You have relatives who survived the war."

"Is that why Father Louis is in jail?" Roger asks. "Because my real father is alive?"

"No, not your father. Your father's sister. Your aunt."

Roger feels confused—he has an aunt?—but the jostling movement of the truck, and the fact that Brother Jacques hands him a biscuit, the vitamin kind, calms him. He chews and tries to make sense of what Brother Jacques told him. He has an aunt. He's being taken to her.

He wonders what she's like. Maybe she has a wild imagination. Maybe she enjoys jokes? He ventures to tell one to Brother Jacques.

"What did the green grape say to the purple grape?"

"What?"

"'Breathe, my friend. Breathe.'"

All this morning, Brother Jacques's face has looked shadowed and dark. Now, there's a hint of a smile. Roger tries out another:

"A teacher scolds his student: 'I told you to draw your favorite animal, and you've done nothing.' The student answers: 'But I have, Teacher. I have drawn my black cat on a dark night!'"

Brother Jacques laughs, a high chirp that sounds like a hiccup. Roger is grateful to Henri for this game. He offers one more:

"A clown says to his doctor: 'Doctor, I feel funny. . . .'"

Brother Jacques smirks, then says:

"A mother warns her little girl, 'If you behave yourself, you'll go to Heaven, but if you don't behave, you'll go to Hell.' The daughter asks, 'So, what should I do to go to the circus?'"

A joke about Heaven and Hell! Roger laughs uncertainly.

"I was going to make a joke about Latin nouns, but I declined," he says.

Brother Jacques's eyes fold into tiny lines when he laughs.

The sun is high, it must be near noon. Still the truck drives longer than Roger has ever driven anywhere.

"Will my aunt let me come back to see Henri?" He'll *definitely* want to hear the Heaven/Hell joke. "And Sister Brigitte?"

Brother Jacques says, "Why don't you rest now. We have a long way to go."

When the truck finally stops, Brother Jacques confers with the driver. He comes around to Roger, tells him to gather his things.

"We'll be traveling the rest of the way by foot. I should warn you, it won't be easy."

"Why? Where are we going?"

"To Spain."

"That's where my aunt is? In Spain?"

"No."

"I don't understand."

Brother Jacques's mouth tightens. But his eyes are still gentle. "Your relatives want to take you back, they want to raise you. But they are Jewish and you . . . Well, you've been baptized. You've taken your first Communion."

"So?"

"So, you are Catholic, and if your relatives raise you, they'll want you to be brought up in Judaism."

"But maybe they'd let—"

"The Church fears for your soul."

Roger doesn't understand. He tries again. "What's in Spain?"

"A different parish. We're just going to spend a bit of time there, until—" He pauses.

"Until what?"

"We get word. Madame Mercier—and not just her, she has advisers in high-up places—think it's best if you're not easily found for a while. There is a court order, requiring you to be delivered to the petitioning relatives."

"My family." Isn't it what he'd stared out the gates for, hardly venturing to hope?

"We can't cross the border by truck," Brother Jacques continues, "so we will be walking over the mountains."

"You're hiding me?" Roger wants to ask if this is Godly, but he doesn't.

"Yes. Well. Protecting you."

Brother Jacques hoists the heavy pack onto his shoulder as the truck drives away. Roger stands, shivering.

"We'll warm up as we go," Brother Jacques says, walking with an awkward, shifting gait.

Roger follows him along the narrow, winding path, edged with thyme. Both of them are ill dressed: Roger, in cotton pants and his uniform shirt and vest; Brother Jacques, in vestment robes that reach the ground. His hem has grown dirty with his first steps.

Roger blurts, "I don't understand. Why was Father Louis jailed?"

Brother Jacques sighs again. "It was the Church's decision to keep you against court dictates."

"So he *did* go to jail because of me!" Roger starts to panic, truly. What of Sister Brigitte? He hasn't seen her in days. He stops walking.

"Roger." Brother Jacques inserts himself into Roger's cascading thoughts. "You mustn't feel responsible for this. The Church has a commitment to protect your—"

Soul, Roger thinks, but now he's no longer listening. He's burning up, despite the cold.

He doesn't even believe in Jesus' miracles! When he prays, uncertainty creeps through him.

He must be swaying because Brother Jacques takes his arm. "Why don't we sit for a minute?"

Brother Jacques finds a cluster of flat rocks. Roger leans against them, a damp cold seeping through his clothes.

Brother Jacques describes the route they'll take, how they'll stop along the way to eat and sleep. "The Church is helping us on the journey, and when we get to the monastery, you'll see. There will be lots of other boys there."

Roger is shaking his head, but Brother Jacques continues. "We have a walk ahead of us today, and you'll get cold if we stay still much longer."

Brother Jacques rummages through his pack, pulling out coats for each of them. Roger's coat doesn't help much against the cold. Still, the collar carries the scent of Sainte Marie's, wood polish and wax and must. He tucks his nose in to smell it.

While they are in the foothills, the path is wide with the tracks of horses and carts. But as they continue higher, it narrows. The ground here is wet and Roger's leather shoes soak through. Soon his socks chafe against the tops of his feet and his toes begin to ache and throb with cold. Brother Jacques's brow furrows, and his eyes shift between Roger and the mountain ahead.

As they climb higher, snow begins to fall fast and steady, obscuring the footpath. Brother Jacques mutters, "I didn't think the snow would start so soon."

The wind picks up, and they angle themselves like commas

against it. Cold air presses in through the seams of their clothes. Roger feels chilled to his core, yet his feet burn with each step. Brother Jacques takes a map from his pocket, unfolding it, trying to straighten it in the wind.

Roger thinks of the roads to good and evil. He doesn't know where he is going.

After what feels like hours of walking, a man in shirtsleeves steps out of the tree line. Roger startles, but Brother Jacques greets the man, who ushers them into a rough wooden cabin, firelit and warm. The man doesn't *look* to be part of a church network. His cheeks are ruddy and his muscles bulge—and he doesn't seem to realize it's cold.

Inside, Roger can't stop shivering. The man inspects Roger's toes, swollen, shiny, and pinkish blue. He prepares warm water, snow in a kettle over the fire, and warns Roger to keep his feet far from the flames.

"You won't feel the heat, and next you know, they'll be burning."

He brings them both dry socks, stew, and bread. Brother Jacques rushes to say grace as Roger brings a shaking spoon to his mouth.

"You two going to be all right?" the man asks, standing by the door, looking uncertainly between them. Brother Jacques gives his bright assurances and thanks. The man gives a reverent nod to Brother Jacques before taking his leave.

Brother Jacques falls asleep quickly, lying on his back, stick-straight, his feet hanging over the edge of the straw pad. Roger is too agitated to sleep.

A Jewish aunt, trying to claim him.

Maybe she wouldn't mind if he was Catholic, since they are related, since he's her nephew.

He hears a noise, high and creaky, outside the window. It sounds like the wind whipping in the trees. Or maybe it's dogs, wolves even. A whole inseparable pack, howling together.

Roger's feet are in continuous revolt. With every step he takes, it feels as if the skin around his toes is ripping. He shifts his stride, only to bring on a biting pain at his heel.

"Why can't we just go back?" he whines.

"Here, let me carry your things."

"You haven't told me about Sister Brigitte."

Brother Jacques lets out a breath. "She was also summoned for questioning. But you needn't worry, Roger. She hasn't been involved, in fact . . ."

"What?"

"Nothing. I'm sure she'll be back at Sainte Marie's soon, if she's not already."

When they get to the next safe house, Brother Jacques inspects Roger's feet. Raw, torn skin, and multiple blisters. Brother Jacques washes them and gently pats them dry. "We're going to wait a day, let things heal."

The next day is bright and not too cold. They sit outside in a patch of sunshine watching two goats gambol amid scrubby trees.

Jacques says, "I want you to understand, I don't know if it has been explained to you: during the war, Jewish people were in grave danger. The Church took you in and kept you safe."

"But now my aunt wants me—"

"We all want what's best for you, Roger."

From the mountain slope, clouds drift in the sky, obscuring the view of the other peaks. It is midday, yet the moon is visible. Roger doesn't know where one thing ends and another begins.

The man who let them into yesterday's safe house returns with a pair of well-worn boots that, stuffed with socks, fit Roger. Also: news of a wild boar sighting. "You'll want to be extra mindful of sows."

When Roger and Brother Jacques resume walking, Roger is in less agony, and his socks stay dry inside the boots. He keeps his eyes out for boars. New questions swirl in his head.

How long will they stay in Spain?

What will the monastery be like?

Will they have to walk all the way back when this is over?

Why can't he just *meet* his aunt?

Brother Jacques breaks into his thoughts. "How are the boots?"

Roger wriggles his toes and gives a nod.

"Why don't I start us off with a joke?" Brother Jacques's expression is playful. "A teacher asks his student: 'If you have ten francs in one pocket and twenty francs in your other pocket, what do you have?' 'Definitely somebody else's pants, sir.'"

Roger replies with a joke he learned from Henri:

"Why are fish so intelligent?"

"Because they're always in schools."

Brother Jacques counters:

"A student returns home from his exams. 'How did you do?' asks his father. 'We'll have to wait for the results,' says the student. 'But you must have a sense of your oral examination, at least. What kind of person was your examiner?' 'Very religious. Each time I answered a question, he looked up to the sky, crossed himself, and said: 'Holy Jesus and Virgin Mary!'"

Roger can't believe that Brother Jacques tells jokes like this. He wishes Henri were here, too.

"Do you know any riddles?" he asks.

"One," Brother Jacques says. "I'll try to say it correctly. 'I have something in my pocket but my pocket is empty. What is it?'"

Roger thinks awhile, then gives up.

"A hole."

In the afternoon, snow turns to rain, weighing down their coats and packs, and causing the shale beneath their boots to grow slick. *What if a boar charges them, and they can't get away in time?* Roger imagines a large sow, red-eyed, growling and squealing. The thought moves him to stumble, but he rights himself before he falls. The sky darkens to a stormy gray, and it feels as if the mountains are drawing in around them. Roger shivers as he walks on. Brother Jacques reaches for Roger's hand and leads him, step by slow step along the slippery stones, to a spot beneath tree cover. They sit against the trunk of a pine, the ground carpeted with wet, soggy needles. Wind still whips at their faces, but there are no boars. The hem of Brother Jacques's robe is fully crusted with dirt and his hands are red and raw. He rummages through his pack for more biscuits and Roger takes one, grateful, before they continue in the open pelting rain to the night's sleeping hut.

The next morning breaks clear, blue and bright. They have gained significant elevation and Roger looks about, wondering how the trees grow out of the rocky cliffs. How do they take hold here rather than lose their grip in the gusting wind and slide rootless down the slopes? Even on the flat ground at Sainte Marie's, the roots of the stooped oak tree tangled and poked through the buckled cobblestones.

They continue on. The weather cooperates and their boots hold. When Roger's energy sputters, Brother Jacques produces a potato or a hunk of bread, saved from last night's dinner, and if there are border patrols out there, none bother with a religious brother and a boy. One late afternoon, Roger looks out over the mountain's crest and sees, in the distance below, a church spire nestled in a hillside, glinting in the sunlight, edged by the sea.

The descent is steep and difficult to manage but Roger is mesmerized by the view of the water, sparkling silver in the sun. At Sainte Marie's he could smell the sea, feel it in the air, but not see it. Now it's in his constant view. They walk through the day and reach the night's hut just when the sun dangles over the horizon, as if suspended, bathing the whole world in golden light. The mountains, the treetops, the water, Brother Jacques's face. *Perhaps this is a miracle,* Roger thinks.

Finally, they're closer in, traversing sloped hills, then cobbled streets. Roger sights the stone arches that encircle the monastery, grand and beautiful. A thick smell of sweetness and wax permeates the air. Brother Jacques smiles and puts a steady arm on Roger before calling at the gate. They've made it.

Roger's relief at the journey's end evaporates as Brother Jacques is whisked into another huddle of adults, and Roger is swarmed by boys speaking in Spanish, words he doesn't understand. One boy, with a constellation of small brown spots in the whites of his eyes, stares at him intently and won't look away. Another takes Roger's hand and leads him around as the other boys trail them. The grounds. The refectory. The chapel. In the corridors, the paintings are scary, far scarier than at Sainte Marie's: Jesus' crucifixion, gory with blood. Roger wonders, *Is there any religion that is safe?*

He is sitting on a bench in the courtyard, his arms wrapped around himself, when he sees Brother Jacques walking toward him. He's accompanied by a monk who takes them to a bathhouse, handing them a bowl of honey cream meant to soothe their chafed feet, and a folded pile of clean clothes for each. The

uniform at this monastery is a white collar and black smock, no
gray vest. After his bath, Roger dresses himself the same as the
other boys, and he pats down his cowlick, so that no one will call
him hedgehog, though he wouldn't know the word in Spanish.

At dinnertime, they sit at long tables like the ones at Sainte
Marie's, and things start off with Latin prayers that Roger knows.
There is honey here to eat with bread—the sweetest thing he's
tasted since the doughy ball of croquembouche when he was baptized. Delicious. He perks up, happier. But then the remainder of
the meal is strange: a garlicky fish stew with brown beans.

Brother Jacques is across the room. There are lots of boys, yet
Roger can't follow their conversation, and they're not talking to
him. Suddenly his eyes prick, wishing for Henri, for Sister Brigitte. The only moments of calm that night come at vespers, because of the Latin, and because the priest, Father Vicente, smiles
Roger's way.

The boys' dormitory room is the one place that doesn't smell
of honey; instead, it smells of stale sweat and feet. Roger is assigned to a bed in the center row, boys on every side. Brother
Jacques hovers while Roger changes into nightclothes, as if he
might forget his modesty. Roger notices the other boys exchang-
ing glances, eyes darting to Brother Jacques, but Roger is thankful when he learns that Brother Jacques will sleep on a cot in the
small makeshift room nearby, rather than in the monks' quarters
several corridors away.

The next day Father Vicente takes them to see the apiary on
the grounds, a honey business run out of the monastery. What
luck to have *this,* rather than a measly vegetable patch! Roger
watches as two monks—with gloves to their elbows and net-
ting over their hats—lift the frames from their boxes, hexagonal
sheets like the gridded pages in his writing notebook, great combs

swarmed by hundreds of bees weaving in and out. He stands a distance away at first, then inches closer. He used to watch single bees nestled in the flowers at Sainte Marie's, wondering if they returned to the same hive each time, like a home, a family.

The monastery produces beeswax candles, honey-based soaps, and balms, which they sell along with other products in a small shop. Roger's chore assignment is to help with the baking of biscuits, packaged with ribbon-tied pots of honey for sale. Brother Ignacio, in charge of the kitchen, teaches Roger how to prepare and shape the dough on large sheet pans, headed for the hot ovens. As the biscuits cool, they make a game of inspecting the trays to remove—and eat—the broken bits. When no biscuits have broken, Brother Ignacio "accidentally" drops one on the clean counter.

"*Cielos!*" he exclaims, looking upward, or "*Dios Mio!*" which makes Roger laugh.

A pattern of days takes shape: Roger visits the bees between early morning prayers and his lessons with Brother Jacques. After lunch he bakes biscuits with Brother Ignacio. Two other boys join on a rotating basis to help with the baking; one with a jagged scar beneath his chin, the other with the thickest eyebrows that Roger has ever seen. They measure out the flour on a baking scale, adding scoops somewhat carelessly at first, then growing more precise as they approach the target amount. If they go over, they'll have to take some out with a spoon. Brother Ignacio shows Roger how to use the flat edge of a knife to level off the added cups of ground almonds.

Later, when the boys see Roger in the refectory, they greet him and he greets them back. He knows their names, Ander and Iker, and they know his.

After baking with Brother Ignacio, it's outside time, during which Roger often returns to the bees. The monk who originally led him and Brother Jacques to the bathhouse hangs an extra netted hat on a hook in the supply shed for Roger to wear. Roger gets daringly close to the hive boxes, listening to the bees' deep and steady drone. Several times, the speckle-eyed boy approaches, standing a bit behind, watching, too. In the late afternoon, more studies with Brother Jacques, supper (during which Roger eagerly slathers honey on his bread), vespers, and bed.

Time passes this way, the bees clustered in their hives, autumn's sun casting the sea a silvery white. Until a day dawns once again full of huddles and whispers: Brother Jacques with Father Vicente and several others.

"Is something wrong?" Roger asks.

"The courts are pursuing you, even here in Spain."

"What is going to happen?"

"We are discussing it. I don't want Father Vicente to get in trouble."

"Me neither."

They are taken by truck along dirt roads to a small house hidden by grape vineyards. There are apple orchards, too, and a steep path down rocky cliffs to the water. Maria Dolores, a woman not much taller than Roger, sees to their meals. Roger walks in and out of the unfamiliar rooms. He thinks of the fun he had in the baking kitchen, Brother Ignacio gently teasing, "Time to work, bakers; we must rise up." He thinks of the bees clinging to their frames; the boys walking past: "*Hola,* Roger."

He'd like to bake here, but Maria Dolores shakes her head and shoos him away, so he settles at the table with his books. He can hear her singing in the kitchen while she cleans. When she brushes by with flower stalks from the garden, he wonders what

Sister Brigitte would look like if she dressed like Maria Dolores, in a brightly embroidered red dress, her hair down.

Brother Jacques keeps Roger on a schedule of prayer and instruction. Even with the jobs of carrying wood from the shed so that there's kindling for the fire, and collecting the fire ashes to mulch the vineyards, there is still plenty of empty time. Roger asks if he can write letters to Sister Brigitte and Henri, and he is told: no, he can't, because it would allow the authorities to trace his location here, and he must remain in hiding. He fills his notebook with questions he'd like to ask them, saving up for when the hiding is over.

On New Year's Eve, Roger and Brother Jacques sit together with Maria Dolores, each with a goblet of twelve grapes. They listen for the church bells and eat the grapes quickly, one by one, in keeping with the chimes. For luck.

Every night they bank the fire to keep it going while they sleep; every morning they add fresh wood to the glowing red coals. Roger makes frequent trips to the woodshed, shuttling heavy logs in the bows of his arms to feed the fire throughout the day.

He sits at the table with his notebook, thick socks on his feet and a warm blanket over his legs. He writes the story of a tree that grows in the mountains, high above the sea. One day, a bird perches in its branches. The bird thinks she might build a nest here, make it home, but soon, she is scared off by a cat. The cat is just settling in between the tree's largest boughs when he is chased away by a fox. The fox is driven out by a bear; and the bear is frightened by a tiger (who, incidentally, has stripes beneath his fur). The tree stands steady through it all, though it clenches its roots with fear when the scent of burning wood fills the air.

In early spring, an actual bird's nest appears, tucked beneath the eaves of the house beside the patio. A pair of warblers join the residence, chirping a call-and-response each morning at dawn. A natural wake-up, rousting Roger for lauds.

Roger and Brother Jacques take to walking along the beach at sunrise. Roger's toes press into the coarse sand and his feet shock anew at the cold with each frothy wave. As they walk he wonders why everyone is making this fuss over him, just one boy. Are there other boys like him, whose relatives want them back?

He thinks of his baptism, the priest's one magnified eye, Madame Mercier's words, "Thank goodness I was able to do this for you." Over the water, plovers dunk and fish, fluff their wings and fly away. The sky striates pink. Roger wonders, *Who does a soul belong to?*

Eventually, Maria Dolores relents on the use of the kitchen, and Brother Jacques—having obtained a bundle of ingredients from Brother Ignacio "for Roger's edification"—teaches Roger how to bake cookies that are decidedly French: *navettes* and *palmiers*. Maria Dolores even assists, pulling out mixing bowls and whisks. For the *navettes*, she suggests the substitution of orange zest for the orange flower water.

They make, and devour, what they bake. Roger exclaims "Oops!" when a cookie breaks and he saves the leftover crumbs for the birds.

Father Vicente comes to pray with them some evenings, driving up through the vineyard in the battered truck, old bee boxes rattling in the back. After dinner, he retreats to the patio with Brother Jacques over a glass of wine. When Roger carries out a plate of freshly baked macarons, Father Vicente smiles his wide-open smile and puts his hands together like a prayer asked and answered.

One morning Roger walks onto the patio to find bits of cracked blue shell on the slate pathway, remnants of nest, twigs, and leaves scattered in the grass beyond. Brother Jacques comes out and, seeing the evidence of the raided, ravaged nest, puts a gentle hand to Roger's shoulder. He leans in, stooping, head-to-head, as if wishing to pull the scene from Roger's mind and carry it on his own.

A warm day, Father Vicente's truck pulls up and Roger sees him wipe his brow with a cloth. Another priest is with him, someone Roger hasn't seen before. The two men huddle with Brother Jacques, outside. From his study table, Roger can see them through the window, talking. Brother Jacques shakes his head, takes slow steps, back, back. When he opens the door to the house, his face has fallen. "Roger, come with me."

The new priest has orders from the cardinal: The Church can no longer resist the French Court of Appeals, which awarded custody of Roger to an aunt who lives in Israel. An agreement has been reached between the Church and the petitioning rabbinate: the hiding must cease. Roger is to be taken to Paris and travel to Israel from there.

It is over.

Roger looks up at Brother Jacques, standing close beside him. Just the other day, he told Roger a new riddle:

If you don't keep me, I'll break. What am I?

A promise.

Brother Jacques gets into the truck with the others to collect what Roger will need for his travels. As the truck disappears at the end of the long drive, Roger walks into the vineyard, lit gold by the afternoon sun. Against the purple hills, the new vines in their tight rows grow entwined, their coiled tendrils wrapping around woody supports. He has been harbored and hidden, sanctified and saved. Now, he has been claimed. He is going to Israel. He is going to be with family.

Roger kneels in the dirt and, at last, he cries.

10

OSKAR

1946–1947

I t is dawn when the truck lurches to a stop. Eva's hand is tight on Oskar's arm as she steers him and Stazja from the back of the truck toward a large house, white and imposing, with arched windows and dormered roofs. Oskar squirms out of her grip and reaches for his sister's hand. Inside, Eva ushers them to a room with a faded, sunken sofa the color of the washed-out sky. Pine logs burn in the wide brick fireplace, but it's still cold.

Eva wraps her arms around herself and drops into an oversize chair. Oskar thinks she looks like a small forest animal, watchful in her burrow. "Are you hungry? Would you like a snack?" she asks.

They shake their heads. Oskar's eyes sting from the night's crying.

A young man pops his head in and offers to take Oskar to the boys' quarters. Oskar clings tighter to Anastazja.

"He can stay with his sister for now," Eva says.

They are led to the girls' quarters. It is stuffy and dark, the room warm with so many sleeping bodies pressed together in narrow beds. Tentatively, Oskar sits next to his sister on a lumpy mattress that squeaks with their movements. After the man leaves, Oskar hears the squeaks of other mattresses as some of the girls begin to rouse. Two come to kneel and fuss over Oskar's thick curls and long eyelashes. He wriggles away and runs back the way

they came, through the common room to the front door. He tries
the knob. It is locked.

Eva finds him at the door and leads him to the dining room as
others troop in for breakfast. He's seated beside his sister. "Children," she says to the group, "this is Oskar, and this is Ana."

Ana leans over to him and whispers, "It's better, more like
Chana, for our mother."

Oskar blinks away the children's stares, his sister's new name.
She will always be Stazja to him.

In the center of the table is a full basket of bread. Eva points
to it and to various other things on the table, naming them in
Hebrew. The words sound gravelly in her throat. Oskar mouths
grace as Wujek Józef would say it, his thoughts chasing after the
Dąbrowskis, the golden fields, the forest at dawn.

Despite Eva's repeat attempts to get him involved in circle
games and lessons, Oskar spends his first week by the locked
front door. Rain spatters the pane. There is a maple tree in the
yard, no birds in its branches. He cranes to see past the curve in
the road.

Oskar is taking up his position at the door early one morning
when several boys approach him as a group. Not an exultation.

"Why are you standing there?" a tall boy asks. His cheeks are
marked with pocks.

When Oskar doesn't answer, the boy leans closer. "There's no
one coming for you."

Oskar tries to angle away, but the others encircle him.

"You think your family is out there? They've forgotten all
about you—if they're even alive."

Oskar looks at the boy who's said this, tiny blue lines veining
his nose.

He ducks between them and runs to find his sister in the girls' room. Other girls, getting dressed, hold their clothes up against themselves.

"Are *ciocia* and *wujek* alive?"

"Yes, of course, Oskar. Now leave, we're getting dressed in here."

"Do you think they've forgotten about us already?"

"No." She softens. "They're never going to forget."

The following afternoon, he sees through the pane that the sky is clear, no rain. He goes searching for Ana and eventually finds her in the sewing room. She is chewing gum and talking with another girl while she adds a white zigzag border to a skirt.

"Stazja, when can we leave here? You said you'd get us back to the Dąbrowskis, that we could run."

"That was before."

"Before what?" He stares at her.

"There's a dance lesson starting soon. We can learn the steps and the words to the songs. I think Mama and Aunt Freida knew them."

"Why should we learn that?" Oskar asks.

She rolls her eyes. She never did that at the Dąbrowskis' and he dislikes it. She must have learned it from that girl. Ida.

"You said we're going back to the farm, and—"

"Oskar, I'm not in charge."

Eva teaches them Hebrew songs and reads them stories. She speaks endlessly of the colors, flavors, and smells of Palestine—the sea and sand dunes, camels and palm trees and orange groves. The children slip into reverie—what would a juicy orange taste like right now?

"Mama and Papa spoke of Eretz Yisrael," Ana tells Oskar one night after dinner. "I guess you don't remember."

Oskar looks out the window at the blue-black sky. The glass rattles in its casing as a train hurtles past without stopping.

Many, especially the littlest children, smile by day but cry by night. Sometimes Oskar even sees Eva pacing the hall at dawn, whispering to herself, words that sound like names. She enters the breakfast room, hair messy, eyes red-rimmed. He understands, now, that they've all lost loved ones—but *his* are alive. He could be with them this minute, sitting at the table Wujek Józef built from a felled pine. He can't help hating Eva for not understanding this.

Still, he begs her to take him to a Mass nearby, and one Sunday morning she does. The church isn't like the one he is used to. No hatted spires. No carved crosses, painted gold and white. Here, dark beams line the arched plaster ceiling and small stained-glass windows dot the walls. Oskar feels awkward in a pew without the Dąbrowskis beside him, without Father Laska at the pulpit. All the people are strangers. Several crook their heads to get a look at him. Eva shifts and fidgets, then buries her hands in her lap and sits still.

As the service progresses, Oskar finds his place. He sings the hymns and prays in earnest. He prays for the Dąbrowskis, and for the hen whose bent feet Józef taped so they would straighten and the others wouldn't peck at her. Over and over Oskar prays that he and Stazja will find their way back to the farm.

When the service ends, Eva ushers him quickly from the church. The sky is a cloudless blue. Oskar lingers in the courtyard, watching the congregants greet one another.

"We should get back," Eva says.

"Why did you steal us?" he asks.

Eva stops walking. "I didn't steal— Oskar, I saved you."

"You took us from our home."

Oskar had arranged his carved birds on the windowsill, each pointing toward the woods behind the Dąbrowskis' fields. Finches. Sparrows. Skylarks. *Were they there still?*

"Oskar, every Jewish child—"

"I'm not Jewish."

"Your first family, your real parents—"

"The Dąbrowskis are my parents. You took us away and I didn't get to say goodbye."

Eva grips tight to Oskar's arm as they walk back to the children's home. He refuses to look at her. Their shoes scuffle along the cobblestones. Leaves rustle in the wind. His eyes move to the trees, searching, branch by branch, for birds.

Ana dotes on the littler children, particularly a four-year-old girl who arrives with the name Nieznana, "*Unknown,*" renamed Zissa. Fair-haired, with round cheeks that splotch red when she's about to cry. Ana pulls the little girl onto her lap and hugs her to chase away tears. She shapes her hand into a butterfly, landing it with a flutter, a tickle, and a kiss upon Zissa's nose. *Flutter tickle kiss. Flutter tickle kiss.* She turns *away* from Oskar, rolls her eyes when he sulks. And she's rude about the drawings he makes at art time. ("What's that even supposed to be?")

He seeks her out anyway.

"Why can't we go back to the Dąbrowskis?"

Ana bounces Zissa until the giggles start. Oskar looks back and forth between the two, then plants his stare on Ana. "They wanted to keep us," he says.

"They weren't our family."

Oskar leans against the wall, watching as his sister links hands with others to dance—arms outstretched, weaving around the room, first one way, then the other—and afterward sashays to the refreshments table to guzzle water in big, greedy gulps.

Oskar sees Eva walking toward him and turns away.

"What's the matter?" he hears Eva ask him.

"I don't want to be here, and I don't want to go to Eretz Yisrael."

"Does Ana feel as you do?"

"No." He rotates farther so that he can't see Ana either.

"Don't you think your parents would have wanted you to live among Jews?"

"They sent us to the Dąbrowskis!"

"Yes, but now that the war is over—"

"I want to stay with the people who love me."

One evening, Eva gathers the children in the common room. Some sit on the floor, some in chairs; the older kids lounge on the sofa arms. Eva stands in front of the fire. Though her back is close to the flame, she wraps her arms around herself again.

"We're going to be leaving here in the morning."

"Where are we going?" several ask.

"We're going to cross into Germany—it's safe now, safer than Poland," she says.

There's a murmur at Germany. One of the older children begins arguing, "I thought we were going to Palestine."

"It's just temporary. We're going to stay at a children's home in Bavaria until we can make our way to Palestine. We will be one step closer."

Oskar stands up. He runs to his bed, burrows under the covers.

A bit later, Eva finds him there.

"I told you, I don't want to go," he says.

Eva sits beside his bed, stroking his curls. He writhes away, out of her reach.

"I know it's hard, Oskar, but if we trust in God—"

Oskar rolls over, face toward the wall. The paper crucifix he made is taped there. He drew small poppies on it, just like the flowers on the nesting boxes at the Dąbrowskis'.

The children don't have much to pack. A few clothes. A photograph. A pine cone or a treasured rock from an outing in the woods. When it is clear that the preparations are going forward, that they are really leaving, Oskar asks Eva, "You're coming, too?"

Despite everything, he hopes she is.

"Yes, Oskar, I am going with you."

In the morning, Oskar stands beside the maple tree in the yard. He wonders, *Do its roots entwine with the roots of other trees? Do its branches? Might a message be carried, root by root, leaf by leaf, all the way back to the farm?*

Under gray skies, they board a train at Lodz, the children paired, holding each other's hands. Eva grips tight to her satchel, in which she carries a list of the children's names. Also: vodka, cigarettes, a few watches, and money. They disembark at Szczecin and wait. Oskar snugs close to Ana, and she lets him.

Eva talks to the *Brichah* operative in charge of their crossing into Germany. The story they've prepared for the border patrol, if they are questioned, is that they are families, Germans repatriating to Germany. Of the guards here, the operative knows who will examine the group closely, and who will look away; who will be drunk by midnight, and who, with a pack of cigarettes in his pockets or zloty in his fist, will coax the other guards inside for a game of cards.

A group of adults, also seeking transit to Palestine, are here, and Eva creates the "families." Some children hesitate to take the hands of strangers; others clasp tightly. Zissa stares up at the tall, kerchiefed woman she's paired with, her eyes wide, cheeks splotched red, a hand in her mouth. Eva attempts to place Ana apart from Oskar, matching her with a single dusty-haired man who could be her older cousin. But then Oskar refuses to let go of his sister's arm, and it's decided that Ana will cross with Oskar, together with the couple Eva has chosen for him. Oskar looks back and forth between the faces of the man and woman: bedraggled and dirty, with nervous but kindly eyes. He lets the woman take hold of his other hand.

It is after midnight, the moon a rib in the sky, when the signal is given. They run from the tree line, toward the border, the ground stretching out before them. Oskar doesn't dare look back but keeps running, through the gap, crossing into Germany, moving with the others toward an area of woods. Once there, signaled to stop, they stand, breath heaving. Both the woman and Ana let go of him. The woman gives him a sad smile before turning away.

Eva collects all the children, then hurries them along. Another train. A debarking. A wait, sitting on the floor of a local synagogue where someone passes out dry biscuits. Then, boarding a train once again, the final leg of the journey to their next "home."

Oskar sits apart from his sister now, choking back tears as they hurtle yet farther away from the Dąbrowskis. Somehow they will find a way back, he tells himself.

A flock of chickens, a swarm of bees, a quiver of cobras, a crash of rhinoceroses, a shrewdness of apes.

At the children's home in Dornstadt, as in Lodz, lessons and songs are taught in Hebrew. Oskar begins to learn the language despite himself. Eva calls the house *bayit,* "home," and all of them together *mishpacha,* "family," and every story she tells is about

Eretz Yisrael, which she *also* calls home—but how can it be? Oskar doesn't want to hear stories of a land that will always be foreign to him. He wants to hear of stringed music boxes and of birds who brighten the forest with colorful feathers and songs.

Eva has a list of jobs, and they can sign up in groups, which she calls "committees," one in charge of decorating the house, another in charge of organizing parties, a third producing a newspaper of events. Each day begins with roll call, calisthenics, and breakfast. When Eva asks for an orange, calling it *tapuz,* a skinny six-year-old boy, a new arrival named Hershel, begins to cry.

"What's going to happen to us if someone hears?" he asks Oskar, his face full of fear.

Hershel tells Oskar that he hid in an attic with other orphaned children. Once, gunshots came through the floor. "There was a chink in the wall, the only light from the outside."

Oskar thinks, *Even a shade tree needs more light than that.*

Oskar finds Eva while she's slicing bread for breakfast. "I want to go to church again. Will you take me?"

"Let's get settled here first."

He can feel the Christian prayers receding from his mind. He wants to remember the psalms, the hymns.

A different day. "Please, Eva, will you take me to church?"

"Oskar, you're doing so well with your Hebrew."

The older kids get to learn sewing and gardening and carpentry, but Oskar has to stay with the little kids. It makes him mad because there's so much he can do. He can collect eggs without disturbing the hens and getting pecked. He can pull weeds and spread hay. He can carve a spoon.

Ana spends hours in a dressmaking shop, sewing clothes. One afternoon she arrives for lunch wearing a skirt layered in ruffles of

every bright color. Oskar wonders at all the birds that might have
flown to them, if only they were still on the farm.

"Are you the Sister of the Birds?" he asks her excitedly.

"No, *ty gnojku*, I'm just your sister."

Oskar can't turn away from watching Ana as she links arms with
her friend Ida. They are always walking around, their chests puffed,
noses in the air, talking endlessly of Palestine and kibbutz life—as if
they know. They act like Eva's special helpers, lining up the younger
children for dances and feeding them the words to songs.

"Here they come," Hershel says, but he's talking about the
boys who tease Oskar.

"Your only friend is a baby," the boys sneer, walking past.

At mealtime, a table away from his sister, Oskar overhears Ida
confide that she was beaten at her prior home. He is studying
Ida's eyes, which for once are dark and downturned, when he
hears Ana say, "When Eva came for us, the Dąbrowskis didn't
want to give us back."

"We would never have become friends!" Ida says and reaches
for her hand.

Pushing his plate away, Oskar rises from his seat, and leaves
the room.

Oskar discovers the woodworking shop where a man, Yuri,
teaches joinery to the older children. Yuri doesn't mind Oskar
hanging around and trying out the hand tools. He even takes
time to show Oskar how to make complementary rectangular
cuts into pieces of wood, then join them together with glue for
a close fit.

Oskar visits the woodshop every chance he gets. Amid the
smell of cedar and the whir of saws, he drops into concentration
as he tries over and over to cut and join the wood the way Yuri
showed him. At first his cuts are jagged and the pieces jut out,

uneven. But with consistent practice, he learns to cut more accurately, and eventually he is able to align the parts perfectly. Like they belong.

A new boy, around his age, is there in the woodshop when Oskar arrives one afternoon. He's settled in a corner, drawing on the pages of a pad. Oskar says hello, but the boy doesn't look up. Oskar waves, and the motion catches his attention; he looks over and gives Oskar a tentative smile. He has a wide jaw and keen hazel-colored eyes.

Later Oskar will learn that his name is Szymon, and that he stopped hearing—and speaking—after a bomb killed his mother. He came to the Jewish children's home by way of a priest who found him sitting on the pavement beside her body.

In the moment, Szymon's golden hair picks up flecks of sawdust as he bends his head toward his pad, and Oskar can see that he is sketching a woman's face, page after page. Oskar understands: it's the same as him, carving and recarving the joints of a box.

One day Oskar taps Szymon on the shoulder and gestures walking together. Szymon tucks his drawing pad under his arm and they follow a narrow trail to a stream, taking turns to hold the brambles at bay. They see the silver flash of a fish just below the water's surface, the flutter of golden leaves above. Oskar wonders if Szymon remembers sounds, the lapping of water at the bank's edge, the drill of woodpeckers overhead.

Oskar checks for his whittling knife in his pants pocket and begins foraging for branches. Szymon looks to see what he's gathering, the lengths and thicknesses of the wood, and helps to collect more into a pile. Stazja never did this when she walked with him in the woods; she was crabby and impatient, hurrying him along.

Still, as he reaches for a piece of river birch, Oskar considers carving his sister a spinning top like the one she left behind at the Dąbrowskis'. She already has another, kept from a Hanukkah party, so he begins carving a skylark instead. He hasn't wanted to whittle much until now. Forging cut after cut, finding the bird's form in the wood's core and setting it free, he loses himself in thoughts of the farm, the nearby forests. A gusting wind riffles the pages of Szymon's pad and tosses his shaggy hair. A stork, spindly-legged atop her nest, turns this way and that, not settling. Józef could always tell when a stork had eggs in her nest, and when she didn't.

Oskar hears the children up the path, gathering for afternoon lessons. He reluctantly pockets his knife and carving, and Szymon follows suit, folding his sketch pad under his arm. They head back and join the line, a step apart.

Now that Szymon is here, he's the new target of the bullies. They push and shove him and call him a dummy for not talking. "What's wrong with you?" "Did an elephant stomp on your ear?" Though Oskar, not yet eight, is younger and smaller than most of the boys, he steps between them. Ezra, with eyes like a frog's, makes an odd swipe, his hand moving into Oskar's pocket. Ezra yelps and pulls his hand out, cut and bleeding from the whittling knife. He, and the others who circled Szymon, run off. Oskar pulls the knife from his pocket and wipes the blade off in the grass.

Eva collects the children in another circle. "You mustn't bully one another," she begins.

Oskar wonders if the bullies are going to get in trouble, or if he is.

"We're here together; we need to help one another. That's why it's important we learn new ways to communicate with each other."

A few days later, she introduces them to a woman with books

and pamphlets from an office that, before the war, supported Jewish German Deaf-Mutes. Eva wants them to learn a sign language for Szymon. She does her best to form the signs for foods, for the days of the week, for colors, for animals. Palms together: *please*. A hand circling the stomach: *hungry*.

On walks, Oskar likes how Szymon notices the same things he does: bright green moss that's springy to the touch; tree roots that stick out like claws; a dark blue feather nearly concealed by leaves on the path. He wishes he could bring Szymon to the farm. He'd be quick, quicker even than Wujek Józef, at spotting birds in the trees.

In the woodshop, Oskar ventures to shape joined boxes in sizes, larger and smaller, for nesting. Szymon draws his mother's face, but also takes to sketching furniture designs, measured and precise, inspired by draftsmen's drawings that Yuri shows him. When they head to the stream, as they do most mild afternoons, Szymon continues with his drawing while Oskar whittles, wood shavings falling away like apple peels, figures coming into view.

They find an old, dusty checkerboard in the shop and scavenge for wood scraps, to which they assign pieces for a chess game. Szymon knows how to play—and win. While Oskar is easily distracted, turning the wood shapes over in his hands, daydreaming about how a *real* horse would jump, square by square, over a bishop, Szymon keeps his focus. Oskar comes to know, without signs but by the slight rise in Szymon's left eyebrow, when Szymon questions Oskar's strategy. He is usually correct to question it, as Oskar contorts his game to keep his knights on the board—he likes it when they're both there, a pair—rather than sacrifice one to protect another more "valuable" piece. Oskar wonders why Szymon always begins with the Queen's Pawn opening. Yet it's the way of their friendship to understand that there are complexities beyond a straightforward win of the game.

Late one evening, Eva announces that they are again moving homes, first thing in the morning.

"It's exciting, as we're getting closer still to Eretz Yisrael!"

This time Oskar doesn't run for the cover of his bed but stands, unmoving. He remembers Wujek Józef speaking of foresters who drove bison to new woods if it meant a stronger herd. "But the old forest was their home," Oskar had objected. Didn't it matter that some were settled there?

"I want to go to *my* home," he now says to Eva. *Szymon could come with me.*

"Oskar, I wish I could help you understand—"

They're delivered by trucks, then train, to an old château in Marseille with stone terraces and winding garden paths. It is clammy and damp despite the sunny day. Oskar looks around, bitter, but cheers a bit when Szymon reveals the chess set, smuggled in his knapsack.

When they are called inside, Eva announces that they're going to live "kibbutz-style" here and enlists the older kids' help with the younger ones. Several times over their first week, Oskar looks for Ana, but she is always bouncing Zissa in her lap.

The routine is the same: morning exercises, story circles and songs, preparations for upcoming holidays. The next festival is Shavuot, for which they will prepare cheese blintzes for dinner. Hebrew lessons continue here, and Oskar finds a favorite word: עץ, which means "tree" and also looks like one.

He and Szymon discover a small woodshed with tools. Dov, a teenage boy whose father was a tinsmith, shows Oskar how to connect metal plates to wood pieces to create a box that hinges open on one side. Outside, Oskar gathers branches, beech and chestnut and pine, and sets to work whittling new, better chess pieces. In time he will trade them into the collection, one by one, making each piece unique while still of a set. Of the four knights, one will have a scruffy mane; one, a flicking tail; one will hold its ears back; one will stand mid-whinny.

Two weeks into their stay, a frail, worn-out woman comes to the château saying she is Zissa's mother.

"Her name is really Luba," she says, "but the records list her as Zissa. I traced her here, with the help of the Jewish Committee. Thank God."

Eva enters the foyer with the little girl clinging to her legs. When she tries to bring her forward, Zissa ducks behind Eva's knees.

"Zissa—" Eva twists to address the child with choked cheer. "What wonderful news. Your mother has returned, she's come for you."

Zissa, wide-eyed, looks at the woman and shakes her head, *No*. She reaches up for Eva to hold her.

The hurt is plain in the woman's furrowed face, her liquid eyes.

"Come," Eva tries again, "why don't you greet her? She's had a very difficult journey."

When the woman reaches out her arms, Zissa cries, burrowing tighter into Eva, who caresses Zissa's hot, teary cheeks.

"What, Zissa? She's your mother, she wants to take you home." Eva's voice shakes.

"I don't want to."

Oskar wants to step in, say she should stay with whomever she feels closest to.

He looks over at Ana, and sees her eyes are red and puffy. He feels a flash of gladness for his sister's sorrow. But then the boy next to her, Yehoshua, extends an arm to comfort her.

Eva turns back to the woman. "It's best if you come in for a while, let the news settle. Sit beside Zissa—*Luba*—and have a bit of lunch, beets and onion. How old was she when you parted?"

"Ten months."

The mother stays, Zissa refusing to go near her at first, then slowly warming. It takes three days before Zissa can be held in her arms, walked out the door.

In the wake of Zissa's departure, the air hangs in the house, heavy and close. Eva calls the children into a circle, and though she, too, is puffy-eyed, she speaks of Zissa's "wonderful outcome"—from Unknown on a convent's steps to a reunion with her mother. Oskar wonders what Eva would say if the Dąbrowskis came for him.

The children sit silent until Hershel—the boy who hid in an attic, gunshots coming through the floor—knocks down a tower of wooden blocks. Eva flinches, opens her mouth as if to say something, then closes it.

When the others disperse, Oskar and Szymon stay by Hershel. They slowly rebuild the block tower. "You can knock it down again if you want to," Oskar says.

Hershel looks at him for confirmation, then kicks at the tower, sending the blocks crashing.

Oskar and Szymon build it again, and again Hershel knocks it down.

They do this over and over.

One early summer evening, Oskar comes upon Eva sitting in a grassy patch with Miriam, a woman who was introduced to the children at lunchtime as a friend, here with news and instructions for their next move. He steps quietly closer.

"You have to stop torturing yourself," Miriam is saying to Eva.

Peering in the twilight, Oskar can see Eva's face, crumpled in anguish. "I can't," she says.

"You said yourself, Rachela wouldn't quiet. You had no milk; she was starving."

"I should have tried to get to a town, somewhere to find food."

"You would have both been killed."

"How could I have let . . . I can't stop seeing . . ."

"Eva. Listen to me. You'll start anew. You're doing this important work now, and—"

Eva's choked tears loosen to sobs. "But how can I leave her? How can I move away and leave my baby buried here, alone?"

Eva isn't at dinner. The next morning, after breakfast, she gathers the children around her and announces news of their boat passage. Her face is composed, the shattered bits sanded away; the Eva of last night is gone.

At dusk, Oskar is stuffed once again into the back of a truck, and hours pass in bitter, rolling darkness. The truck lurches and shakes, as if also in resistance to the journey, then takes its place inside a huge freight shed by the pier, where Oskar and the other children are made to disembark and line up. It is dark, wet, and cold, and the scent of sea, of salt and fish, is unlike any forest.

Each child is given a slip of paper with a letter and a number: the letter notating the assigned section, the number the assigned bunk, for sleeping on board the boat. Also, a rolled blanket with a tin cup tied to it. The other children excitedly compare their lodging numbers. Oskar stands beside Szymon, his eyes fixed on Eva, who confers in the shadows with the same man who led them into Germany.

She may not be crying now, but Oskar knows that Eva carries her sorrow as he carries a wooden bird in his pocket. Why won't she see that he can still get back to the only parents he knows? He twists around in the dimness. Szymon, sensing his agitation, presses a shoulder to his. Oskar takes hold of his friend's hand and pulls him, running, toward the rear of the shed.

Eva sprints after them, catching hold of their arms.

"What are you doing? Oskar, we're about to leave."

Ana pulls out of her place in line and runs over. "Oskar!"

"I don't want to go!" he yells at Eva. Turning to his sister, "You said you'd get us back. You didn't even try!" Tears run down his face, but it's fury he feels.

"It's too late, Oskar. We're going. *I'm* going," Ana says.

"Please. Get back in line," Eva coaxes. "Oskar, don't cry."

"But *you* cry!" he yells.

Oskar is shuttled onto the boat. He glimpses polished railings, sailors bustling about, shimmery water below, but once on deck, he is shunted quickly down a narrow staircase to a cramped quarter, the fresh air lost to the stench of sweat, urine, and fish. Ana keeps her arm on his until he's in his assigned bunk, a splintery, unfinished platform, no mattress. He lies down. Shuts his eyes. He can feel her standing over him, waiting. Someone begins singing a Hebrew song and others join in. He keeps his eyes shut from his sister and presses the blanket against his ears to block out the song. When he opens his eyes, she's gone.

They're not permitted on deck during daylight. Only in darkness can they come up and gulp the fresh air. For the first several days, the seasickness is near constant. Ana's bunk is down the long, narrow hallway with the other teenagers. She doesn't come to check on him.

"Being on a boat is different from being on a train or in a truck," Eva explains when everyone is a bit acclimated. "The way for us to be safe on our journey is to stay below deck. We can sing and play cards and tell stories during the day. And then, at dusk, we can take turns going up."

Szymon has again smuggled the chessboard, along with Oskar's carved pieces, and so they sit cross-legged and play. When, finally, they are permitted on deck, Oskar and Szymon stand at the rail and watch the hammered silver of the sea, the swoop of birds in the plunging dark.

Approaching Haifa port, the boat engine cuts out and a racket ensues above deck.

Children begin shouting, "We're here! We're here!" Eva silences them. She mounts the stairs, then returns in strides shaky and uneven.

"Children, we won't be able to land in Palestine. The British forces aren't letting us in. We're being transferred to a British ship and brought to Cyprus, where we'll have to wait until we can gain entry."

Some children begin to cry.

"It's just one more stop. We'll get there, I promise," Eva says, though her face doesn't match her hopeful words.

Disembarking in Cyprus, they straggle out, dejected, as they are led to an encampment of metal buildings baking in the sun. The fenced-off ocean out of reach, no trees in sight.

ANA
1947–1948

Not a single flower grows here. Barracks in long rows squat upon the barren earth, and tall, spiky fencing blocks off the sea. They're led inside a tin-roofed shed that pulses with heat. Ana stands clustered with Ida and the boys, Yehoshua and Dov, with whom she grew close on the boat, talking and singing long into the night, their shoulders pressed together, their limbs tangling. She surveys the new, bleak surroundings.

"Children, listen," Eva says. Her voice is strained, her face pale. "Many boats have been rerouted to Cyprus on their way to Palestine. Ours is not the only one. I'd hoped we'd sail straight through. But"—she hesitates—"but this . . . diversion . . . will give us a chance to really prepare ourselves. We'll get accustomed to the heat and the sand . . ."

Herman, a boy with a scraggle of hairs at his chin and pimples on his forehead, talks over Eva. "Get ready, I think there's just one shower for all of us to use together."

The immature kids laugh. Eva waves a hand to signal quiet.

Ana feels her lower lip quiver, her eyes grow teary. She'd expected everything to be different.

Moments later, a detention official comes in carrying a ledger and a basket of name tags. "I'll need everyone to be registered." *Like when they had to be registered with the commandant.*

He examines the list retrieved from Eva's satchel and begins entering names, one by one, into his ledger while Eva writes the children's names on tags. As the tags pile up, she hands them in batches to the teenagers to pin to the shirts of the younger children. Ana tries to stay composed as she walks around the room, matching tags to children. When most of the names have been called, but not hers, she comes to stand by Eva.

"Mira Kowalski," the man then says, and he begins writing it in his book.

Eva's pen is poised above a blank name tag. Ana gives a swift shake of her head.

Mira Kowalski. *That* girl believed in fairy tales, believed she herself was a fairy with glistening hair flowing down to her waist. *That* girl believed she'd find her home; her mother and father waiting here, somehow, to fold her in their arms.

Eva's hand begins forming the letters. *M-I-R-A.*

"I'm Ana," Ana says.

"We need to list your documented name."

"I am Ana."

Ana runs off to the farthest-away wall and slumps to the floor. Yehoshua walks over and, with a concerned look, kneels beside her. Ana spots Oskar, watching. She flops an arm across her face so he can't see her. So she can't see him. Yet she pictures him anyway, anguish on his face. From the moment they were loaded into Eva's truck and hurtled away from the Dąbrowskis, *he* knew what they'd lost. He has known each step of the way.

She moves her arm, her eyes momentarily flooding with light. Out the open door, the fence walls are topped with barbed wire. Soldiers stand guard in watchtowers.

Eva keeps them to the routines and rituals they've always followed: calisthenics, songs, story time. She draws attention away

from the lousy food in tins and the filthy latrines, and she re-
institutes their committees in charge of decorating and events.
She scavenges for extra pillows to create a "clubhouse" with sofas
and books, and helps the children cut out paper flowers to tape
onto the tables. She allows them to ignore the unfamiliar names
pinned to their clothes. There's no time frame for their leaving
here, for entry into Palestine.

There is a sewing tent, at least. Ana seeks refuge in pressing
a needle through thick wool, trying to mend a seam. She has to
angle the needle and push with her nail, rather than with the tip
of her finger. As she finally manages a rhythm, pulling the thread
through, and through again, she doesn't want to think of Agata
teaching her how to embroider. She doesn't want to remember her
father telling her she inherited his steady hands, or to think of him
bedridden, eyes milky and unfocused, his narrow shoulders shivering. Her mother giving the sleeping potion to Oskar but not to her.

Eva comes to find her. "Are you all right?"

Ana twists her name tag, bending the pin. "The Dąbrowskis
were raising us. Maybe—"

"Yes, but now—soon—you'll live in the land of Israel with
other Jews, you'll build a new home." Eva touches her arm. "Why
don't we take a little walk?"

Ana is reluctant, but Eva's hand is still there. As they begin
circling the camp's perimeter, Eva says, "You know, *my* papers
say I'm Eva, but that's not my true name. Sometimes we have to
conceal, in order to protect who we really are."

Ana isn't sure what to say.

"Remember the garden patch you started in Marseille? You
can plant another one in Palestine. There's fertile land."

Ana looks out at the sun-scorched earth. She'd planted the

Marseille garden from stalks she found on scouting walks across hillsides and past the wrought-iron gates of a convent. Wild sage, lavender, yellow cowslip, yarrow, black cohosh—plants she knew from walks with her mother, dug up, and placed in soil they'd root into. Rich cool dirt. Not like this.

One evening, the teens still awake, sprawled on pillows, Ana sees: Ida flirting with Yehoshua and Yehoshua flirting back. Jealousy flames inside her. She stands up to leave.

"What is it?" Ida asks, rushing to follow her.

Ana can barely look at her friend, can only utter, "Leave me alone."

She avoids both Ida and Yehoshua for days after that, busying herself with tasks, helping the littlest children. Her anger swells, unrelenting, even as she recognizes that it's outsize. It won't recede.

"Ana? Please, tell me what's bothering you," Ida asks again.

"You only think about boys!" she snaps.

She begins a routine of walking with Eva each morning. Before calisthenics, when the others are still in their beds, they latch arms and weave around the barracks, skirting early-rising refugees, peeking into tent rooms demarcated by hanging blankets. Ana admits to her crush on Yehoshua. As they walk, Eva's eyes flick among the other women who are also stuck here. Ana steers a path away from those rounded with pregnancy or with new babies cradled in their arms. She thinks of Zissa's solid little legs wrapped around her hips.

Eva continues with her talk of Eretz Yisrael, describing not just the beauty of the land but also how they will work it and enjoy the fruits of their labor; how they will be happy and live in peace.

Ana wants to believe it. It is a lifeline, the only lifeline.

Days in Cyprus turn into weeks, then months. They endure a frigid winter. Fires in barrels sending ash into the air; Eva visibly struggling to buoy their spirits. In spring, news comes of the war for Israeli independence. The children beg Eva to share every detail she learns. They wish they were there, playing a part in establishing the State where they will finally belong.

But wishing aside, there's nothing to be done from across the sea. Afternoons stretch long. In the clubhouse, Ana reaches into her pocket for the dreidel she's kept hold of since Hanukkah at the children's home in Germany. Other kids hoarded tart-sweet candies, but Ana held on to the simple wood dreidel because it reminded her of her old spinning top, a gift from an older girl at the Brze-ziny market. The girl had darted forward—as if seeing Ana and wanting to give her something special. Ana used to imagine the top contained magic in every turn. Could it still be tucked in the topmost drawer of the bureau at the Dąbrowskis'?

Before she gives the dreidel a twist, sending it spinning in the air then touching down to the floor, rotating a full minute before tipping, she looks over at Oskar. Stretched out, long, on the floor, his head propped on a cushion. A *boy* now. No longer a toddler, or a small child.

Ana looks back at her dreidel and thinks, she can't fully re-member her parents or the nights around the table with their aunts, uncles, and cousins. The image that always surfaces is Os-kar in their mother's arms, turning to listen to the neighbor's violin, eyes wide, then sinking into sleep, just before they were sent away.

She pinches the dreidel's thin wood stem, torques it between thumb and forefinger. She can remember spinning her top while listening to Agata's stories, Agata inviting her to snuggle close like Oskar. She remembers, too, the softness of the fur at her coat collar;

the smooth plaiting of her hair, now a tangled mess; cookies with jam; the fruity scent of tea to chase away her cramps—

She blinks it away.

As she sends the dreidel spinning, Ana tells herself: the Dąbrowskis were repaying a debt for their mother saving Agata after miscarrying. It was only to be for a short time. Their parents were to come get them. She tells herself: it's better that she and Oskar are no longer hiding, Jews among Christians, passing for what they're not. She tells herself: they are inching home.

12

ROGER
1948

Keyed up and fidgety, Roger stands with Brother Jacques beneath a twinkling hotel chandelier in Paris. A woman rushes in, curls springing from her head, tan arms splaying wide. It's her, his aunt Sarah. She's seen him and is heading toward him. She wraps him in an embrace, not the way Sister Brigitte did, gently, as if he might break, but tightly. Her words come in a torrent, first in French, then in a confusing combination of French and Hebrew, of which he can understand only the gist: her dear brother's last wish has finally been honored. *Roger, Roger, Roger*—she says his name, over and over, with tears and more hugging—her beautiful nephew will be with his family!

At the airport—alongside Aunt Sarah, still talking and hugging, hugging and talking—Roger watches other planes take off, their engines blowing white smoke, same as the bellows the monks used to get the bees moving. He's still confused. He'd tried asking Brother Jacques: Why does his aunt's family live in Israel? ("A lot of Jewish people have moved to Israel, and it has just won its independence.") Will I be hiding again? ("No.") So, it's a *safe* place? It was then that Brother Jacques told him they had to get him packed and ready.

Now, next he knows, they're boarding their plane. He sits, strapped into his seat, looking down at his new clothes—quick shopping with Aunt Sarah, a white buttoned shirt and gray pants, similar to what he wore at Sainte Marie's. He plucks at the pants, stiff beneath his fingers, and he thinks of Brother Jacques's downcast face, saying goodbye, his narrow, retreating figure, smaller, smaller, as he walked away.

There's a hush on board, air whirring through the vents. The plane shifts and clatters and begins moving, wheels on the ground, then ascending. Up. Up. The prospect of flying had excited Roger, but as they tilt into and above the clouds, he grows scared. *If God meant for us to fly, wouldn't He have given us wings?*

He prays silently to Jesus. Aunt Sarah doesn't say anything but takes his hand in hers.

Eventually, the plane levels out, and it's like they're suspended, not moving at all, though the stewardess tells him they're traveling more than three hundred miles per hour. Out the window, he sees only sky and ocean, no land between.

Every place Roger has known—Sainte Marie's, the monastery in Spain, the vineyard house—held an assemblage of people bound by restraint and ritual, orderliness and purpose. Even the bees followed their regimens. But coming off the plane with Aunt Sarah, Roger wades into a crowd of exuberant chaos. He meets his uncle Uri and his cousins. *Five* of them! Amid the crush, he notices that many of the people have five children, and their children have five children, so that a family is more like a drove, arguing, laughing, tugging, crying.

Headlong into the bustle of Aunt Sarah's house, Roger feels as if he's still afloat between worlds, watching. Every day the door revolves with yet more people shuffling in and out, cooking, eating, and talking. Everyone is always talking. But what are they saying?

Spanish was foreign to Roger, but Hebrew is an utter mystery. The alphabet is entirely different; the written word runs the opposite way across the page; and a spoken conversation, even when friendly, sounds like a squabble bordering on a fight. Aunt Sarah and the older cousins who know some French try to translate, but the sentences come so fast! Before Roger has figured out one topic, they're on to the next.

If there's any rhythm to life here, it is marked by the Jewish Sabbath, the family joining together to light candles, sing Hebrew prayers, eat and drink. It is warm and lively, but Roger still says *his* prayers in the garden, which is by far his favorite place, a place of solitude, set to the side of the house, scented with mint and honeysuckle.

One day, coming in from the garden, Aunt Sarah hands him a small, embossed-leather book. "The monk let me know you like to write," she says. Roger thanks her, turning it over in his hands, thinking of his blue notebook and the pages sewn together by Sister Brigitte, stowed in the closet of his new room, still in their twine. The binding of this book is set for right-to-left writing, but because the pages are blank, he could continue with left-to-right.

But writing words don't come either. Roger's mind flits to the Basque monastery, baking biscuits with Brother Ignacio and taking seaside walks with Brother Jacques; to Sainte Marie's, joking with Henri on the way to class or to the bathhouse, and to the solace always forthcoming from Sister Brigitte. He thinks, perhaps he could compose letters now, especially one to Henri. He could include the jokes and riddles he's wanted to share. But he hasn't seen Henri since he was hustled away to Spain, and then Paris, and now he's here, nine years old, and so much has changed.

He prints his own name in French: Roger. He tries the Hebrew name they're calling him: Rami.

The rest of the page, for now, remains blank.

Hebrew comes in small steps—café is קפה; *le lait* is חלב—then in leaps. In time, he can follow the simpler conversations around the dinner table, can even (timidly) offer thoughts of his own. He speaks most easily to his youngest cousins, who don't correct his grammar or pronunciation.

When they go out, the sun presses down on Roger, direct and unrelenting. The street food surprises him, with unexpected spikes of lemon and mint. The market stalls of the *shuk* carry the scents of bread dough, dried oregano, and fresh-squeezed pomegranate; the sounds of rustling and haggling punctuated by the chimes of church bells and the thunderous cries of the muezzin from minarets across the city. Some people clothe themselves head to toe, while others bare their arms and legs. Roger wears belted pants and collared shirts, out of place amid the children in jeans and T-shirts. As far as he can tell, Israeli boys are tan-skinned and they swagger when they walk. Roger is pale and knob-kneed. He'd hide here, but it's impossible, and nowhere can he find the calm orderliness of his former life.

Aunt Sarah takes him to buy proper hiking boots, "to walk in the hills with your cousins."

Roger's oldest cousin, Binyamin, whom they call Bennie, walks beside Roger, connecting French words with Hebrew words as he points out sites along the mountain trail. He moves sure-footedly and speaks so assuredly, he makes Roger feel safe.

Roger's boots match his cousins', prompting the youngest, Avi, to say, "You're like us now."

Roger shakes his head. "I think I'm different."

"One way or another, we're survivors," Bennie says.

"Not my parents."

Bennie gives a small nod. "It's only because we left France sooner that we're here."

"And why I'm here now, too," Roger says, looking out over a canyon, dusty and red.

The last time he crossed a mountain, he was a Catholic orphan.

They continue hiking and eventually stop by a spring, where the smaller cousins dip their feet and Bennie opens a backpack, taking out a seemingly endless array of food: bread and boiled eggs, peeled cucumbers, olives, nuts and dates, apricot *leder,* halvah. Roger looks at all of it, spread on a blanket atop a rock. He looks at Bennie's pack, midsize, and puzzles over how it all fit.

In Aunt Sarah's garden afterward, he cracks open his new journal. He writes about a boy who finds a bag that holds whatever he puts inside, yet never grows overly full or heavy. The boy packs it with his favorite books and a sack of marbles. Also, a writing journal and pencils. He lifts the bag to test it. No bulges and it's perfectly easy to carry, so he adds a rubber ball. Still fine. He stuffs in a folding chair. No problem! The neighbor's fluffy black dog, Pluto? He fits! (Pluto's head sticks out the top, and he pants excitedly.) Rolled-up towels, one each for the boy and dog, as well as a baguette with jam and plenty of honey biscuits, and off they go for a day at the beach, full of relaxing, snacking, and playing chase.

It is the first writing Roger has done here. Afterward, he sits, watching bees flit, flower to flower. He joins the family for dinner that night, feeling more at home than he has since arriving.

Early one Sunday morning, Roger attempts to bake biscuits by himself. He's assembled ingredients on the kitchen counter. He thinks the sack labeled קמח is flour; but perhaps that's salt? He might have to dip a finger, to be sure.

An hour later, two trays cool on the counter, the biscuits a bit misshapen but tasty, a treat for Aunt Sarah. Bennie joins him in eating the "broken" ones.

"Would you take a walk with me?" Roger asks.

"You want to walk past the churches, don't you?"

"I like the smell," Roger admits. Candles and incense. And near to Ha-Nevi'im Street, one church has a courtyard that reminds him of Sainte Marie's.

"Rami—"

Roger meets Bennie's eyes. "I'm still a bit Christian, you know."

What he is, is *mixed-up*. He wonders: Why did the Church keep him from his family? Why didn't they want him to feel he belonged? At the same time, he can't easily shake the prejudice he grew up with, and so he is conflicted about having Jewish relatives, about *being* Jewish. He's both circumcised and baptized— the first in accordance with his parents' wishes, the second, he now understands, with Madame Mercier's. But who is he?

Aunt Sarah and Uncle Uri show him long-ago photographs from albums they spread over the kitchen table. His father as a small boy, standing in front of a bakery, a long baguette balanced in the crook of his arm. On a sea dock with his sisters, including Aunt Sarah, their feet dangling in the water. Older, at graduation from medical school, the tassels of his cap in his eyes. His parents together, newly married, his mother's head tilted toward his father; and one with Roger, an infant in his mother's arms. Roger stares at their faces, nestled close and smiling. He peers at his own bundled form.

"You see? You've had that little dimple at your chin ever since you were a baby," Aunt Sarah says.

Roger touches the indent, still there. They turn the pages, rustling the filmy plastic that covers each side. In several photographs, his father has a pencil tucked behind his ear.

With all of Madame Mercier's talk, Roger had wished to disavow his connection to his parents and their Jewish heritage. Yet he can't help feeling wildly happy when his aunt says that he has his mother's eyes, the exact shade of amber, and that he got his flair for writing from his father. That he is, clearly and visibly, *of* his parents.

He doesn't have memories from before he was at Sainte Marie's. But in time, it's as if images come to him, or else he constructs them, from features in the photographs, from the stories Aunt Sarah tells. He pores over the pictures of other family—aunts, uncles, and cousins he still hopes to meet, though they are far-flung, across the world in New Zealand. He thinks of his story about the boy whose bag would hold whatever jumble he put into it.

"It's beyond me, how the Church tried to steal you away," Aunt Sarah says. "All that lost time."

"What happened?" Roger wants to know.

"I'll tell you what happened," Aunt Sarah says. "Your parents desperately wanted you to live. You were just three when they got word of a roundup." She describes how they placed Roger with the director of the local Catholic nursery school, with clear instructions to return him to family, if any survived. But Madame Mercier, the school's biggest patron, imagined that, for all the money she gave to the nursery and to Sainte Marie's, she was entitled to keep him. Aunt Sarah gives Roger's hand a possessive pat. "Well, we survived! And we searched for you. When we learned where you were, we wrote to the directors of the school and the convent. We sent pleas to the local mayor, the French foreign ministry, the Red Cross. We even located a bishop to intercede, but he told us that Madame Mercier was firm in her refusal to give you up! She said the Jews were ungrateful and she spurned our attempts to get you back, even in the face of court orders."

The fact that Madame Mercier had Roger baptized *after* Aunt Sarah petitioned to reclaim him is what rankles Sarah the most, even more than that they took him on the run.

"They were only concerned with your being Catholic. And look how difficult it's made things for you."

Uncle Uri puts his arm around her shoulder. "It's over, Sarah, we have him here with us now."

Roger remembers one of the last things he heard Madame Mercier say to Brother Jacques before they drove off in the truck, away from Sainte Marie's: "The Church is a Mother, too, and cares about the souls of the children."

Roger no longer knows what soul is inside him.

13

OSKAR
1948

To be delivered to Kibbutz Neve Ora after thirteen months' detainment in Cyprus is to be set free. While Eva registers the children in the office and helps the littlest ones get settled, Oskar and Szymon wander the grounds. They dodge the low-slung buildings and explore the wide, scrubby expanse of land. There are trees Oskar knows, pines and sycamores, and others he doesn't know, with spindly trunks and spiny leaves. He puts his hand to their trunks, looking to see which birds perch in the branches, listening for their songs.

A winding path leads to a glimpse of sea, a ribbon of sparkling cerulean. They cross a hillside to see groves of orange trees: orderly rows planted in tracts of red, rutted dirt. An intoxicating smell, honey-sweet and floral, carries on the wind and dizzies them like bees. Szymon breaks into a big smile. Before turning back, Oskar bends down where he's standing and touches the soil, dry as dust.

They are given Hebrew names, Yossi for Oskar and Shimi for Szymon, and are assigned to a room with two girls, Leah and Rut, who crowd the doorway and hand them each, by way of welcome, a bookmark made from dried red leaves. Four narrow beds line the room's corners, each with a squat night table beside it. Same as the other rooms in the house.

They report for a required medical exam, at which Oskar

explains to the doctor that Szymon cannot hear and that he doesn't speak.

"How old is he?" the doctor asks.

Oskar isn't sure. A lot of the children have made-up birthdays and ages. Maybe nine, same as him?

The doctor places a scope in Szymon's ears.

Oskar repeats what he overheard Eva say to the office lady, pointing to Szymon before he and Oskar left to go exploring: "His mother died in an explosion."

The doctor nods. "I suppose it could have been noise-induced deafness, or—"

Oskar looks at his friend.

"Or a psychological reaction," the doctor says.

"A what?" Oskar asks.

"To what he couldn't bear hearing," the doctor answers.

Their group is called the Charuvim, for the sweet carob trees, and they are given sandals and clothes that match the other children's. Then they are introduced to their teacher, Devorah. In time, Devorah will take them to look for salamanders; to view the constellations of stars; to learn about explorers and poets, cooking, and gardening. On hikes she will point out scattered almond trees and mulberry bushes, traces of past villages on the terraced rock. But first, she seats them inside a classroom, stuffy and hot. Pinned behind a small desk, Szymon tries to lip-read, or else follow Oskar's interpretive signs, but misses most of what is said. Oskar wishes to be outside, or else making things. When he is outside, Oskar longs for lush, leafy Poland and thinks he'll never get used to the hot sun here, the sand.

There is a children's farm, different from the Dąbrowskis', yet Oskar is pleased because the Charuvim are charged with caring for the rabbits and the geese, cleaning their pens and feeding them a mush of bread and water. Afterward, they play tag or dodgeball, climb up on the old tractor, or linger inside an animal pen, laughing, as Szymon imitates (with stunning precision) how the shoemaker scowled, or how Ida sauntered past. Then on to work, helping with the vegetable harvest and cleaning the classrooms.

Oskar and Szymon are assigned foster parents, whom they visit in the late afternoons while Leah and Rut visit their real parents. Oskar offers him cookies to eat and games to play, blocks to build towers with; yet he feels antsy and uncomfortable in their room, homesick for the Dąbrowskis. He hurries out as soon as the time is up, wondering which family Stazja—her name now changed again, from Ana to Chani—has been assigned to, and what her foster parents are like. He's barely seen her since arriving here. When he has, she's been with other teenagers, part of a swarm.

The Charuvim eat together in their house, their hands sticky from pine sap and oranges, their feet sore from going barefoot (after ditching the stiff sandals); then it's the shower and bedtime. When they can't sleep, they tie their sheets around themselves like togas, or else they run in circles with wet towels on their backs to cool off from the still-stifling air.

Occasionally Oskar hears a gunshot. Soldiers continuously patrol the kibbutz perimeter, and reservists leave in uniform, reporting to duty. Leah keeps track of their returns.

Though Leah and Rut are Israeli-born, they're not mean like some of the sabras, who call the new arrivals weak—"lambs, not lions"—and laugh at their European-accented Hebrew. The worst is doled out to the bullies who came with them from the children's homes, no longer smug, while Szymon and Oskar are mainly, miraculously, left alone—a bit of justice.

Oskar and Szymon play chess when they can, retrieving the board from the communal game area and setting up in the shade of a favorite bent, windswept pine. Oskar keeps his eyes on the board, noting every possible move he might make. He savors having options, the steps that can move him from where he is to where he wants to be.

Their school schedule includes twice-a-week woodshop sessions, where Oskar and Szymon enjoy the movements of plane and pencil, the scents of sawdust, varnish, and glue. They like tending the animals and sorting the harvest, yet wonder: Can they train to work here in the woodshop? Gideon, the lead carpenter, in charge of all the furniture-building at Neve Ora, walks between their worktables. Oskar eagerly shows him his carvings; Szymon, his sketches.

"You'll have strong skills to bring when you're older," he says.

Reading Oskar's disappointment, Szymon droops. Gideon smiles and puts a hand to each of their backs. "Let me see what I can do."

Devorah arranges their classroom so Szymon can see everything that's going on, and she works with him, specially, to learn signs. Oskar is nearly fluent in Hebrew by now, but he holds back, barely mouthing the words when the whole of the kibbutz gathers and breaks into their songs.

At a harvest festival, hovering near a photography display his sister has created for the occasion, he turns at the sound of her voice.

"*Ty gnojku.* It was clear even in Lodz, you were never going to adjust."

She stands behind him, imperious. Her hair tied in a kerchief.

"What about you?" he wants to say, but he doesn't need to

ask. He can see, she fits in here. She has a group of friends, including Ida. For a while they weren't speaking, but now they are together more than ever. And Ana spends hours in the darkroom with a boy, Boaz, who works there. A camera always hangs from a strap around her neck, and she develops these displays.

"You told me we'd escape and then you did nothing," he says.

"It wasn't easy for me either, you know." Her face has a scolding expression, like when he would pull her toward the Lises' fence to see their horse.

"It looked easy," he says.

"You don't remember Mama and Papa. But I remember."

"What about *Eva*? She's the one who. . . ." His voice trails off. "And then you stuck with Ida."

"Well—"

"Well, I had no one," he says.

"You have Shimi." She means Szymon.

"We're here with no parents at all, and no home."

He thinks of Hershel, who, because of his time enclosed in the attic, pleads for the windows of every room he steps into to be opened.

Ana levels her eyes. "What you don't understand is that our 'home' at the Dąbrowskis was a hiding place."

"It was home to me."

"You were always protected. It's easier not to remember. Mama gave you a sleeping potion the morning she sent us to the Dąbrowskis; I *know* you don't remember that. You didn't have to watch our parents give us away to strangers. But *I* had to. I had to watch. And I had to watch over you."

Oskar looks at his sister, her cheeks scarlet, her eyes glinting, angry and wet. He is unsure of what to say. He thinks, now, of how she'd hurried him through the lanes, avoiding the neighbors' questions, rushing into the house, her hands pressed to her stomach.

She goes on. "The only thing protecting me was my light skin and hair. My blue eyes. I could pass as Christian. But it didn't do much good, given that you couldn't."

Then she stomps away, leaving Oskar standing in front of her photographs. In each square: children bunched together, smiling, but there are shadows on their faces.

14

ANA
1948

There is a moment, liquid time, just before a photograph's image appears on the developing paper, when Ana conjures the faces of her parents. Their actual features have blurred in her memory but she fills in with her imagination, Papa's warm eyes peeking out from the soot and sparks of the smithy; the curve of Mama's cheeks when she smiled.

Other moments, looking through her lens, she finds hidden truths that break into the light in momentary, unwitting flashes. There's the recent picture of Eva, her left arm absentmindedly cradling her belly. Oskar, leaning against a sycamore tree at Neve Ora's edge, his dark eyes searching. An outsider still.

Ana struggled at first, feeling an outsider herself. The girls in her room snubbed her, rolling their eyes when she snapped photos, teasing her for keeping hold of the dreidel, carried in her pocket all the way from the German children's home. One of them even defaced a photograph of Eva that she stowed in her cubby, scribbling over it in ink. Ana snubbed them back, staying close to those she came with: Ida, whom she's forgiven; Yehoshua and Dov, both now just friends.

In time the girls softened—it didn't hurt that one of them developed a crush on Dov—and Ana found herself part of a large group, pulled along to meals, to farmwork, to the nightly fire, her ears buzzing with ideological talk: the kibbutz as a chance to build something *new*. Neve Ora, collaborative and communal, bent on equality. Avoiding the traditional traps of wealth and religion, the roles of men and women. And they, the youth, at its forefront, doing something never done before.

All the talk she'd heard before this—overheard, really—was the hushed and frantic whispers of her parents, or the strategizing of the Dąbrowskis. The focus was on safety and hiding, every utterance laced with fear. This talk is different, exciting. Israel has won its independence and at Neve Ora, the focus is on building a fair and worthy society where everyone works and shares equally in the bounty.

Only when words and voices are spent, in the wee hours, the guttering moments, does Ana perceive the loss undergirding everything: they, the survivors, are creating this future *without* their beloved parents, their brothers and sisters, their aunts, uncles, cousins, lovers, friends.

She's called Chani here. She loves the name, so close to her mother's. Her brother still calls her Stazja, which is all right with her; it's hard for her to think of him as Yossi.

In the darkroom, she arranges her photographs into groupings—solitary children matched with adults, creating families, this one, then that—before quickly shuffling them into random piles. The mute-red safety light flickers. Her stomach rumbles. She looks at her watch, wondering if Boaz will come. He's fourteen, a year older than she is, with shiny dark hair and beautiful brown eyes. He grew up with an uncle who was a photographer, and sometimes he offers her tips about composition and light.

For an entire year in the Naliboki forest, surviving in dug-out burrows and hollowed tree trunks, Boaz carried a roll of film in his sock. Pictures of his lost brother, Ari, now developed and pressed between the pages of a book beneath his bed. When Boaz is there in the darkroom, his arm brushing up against hers in the tight space, Ana flicks electric.

Ana plans out an herb garden, permission granted by the kibbutz council. She consults library books on medicinal plants as, once again, she tries to remember what her mother put into different remedies, her honeys and elixirs. She gathers starters of mint, lemon verbena, shepherd's purse, and mallow, and coaxes them to take root. Even in the Israeli heat and dry soil, the plants flourish.

Oskar helps with the garden. It's a rare way they spend time together. Oskar is often in lessons or in the fields, playing chess with Szymon, or hanging around the woodshop. Ana has school assignments and orchard work, shifts in the nursery and in the darkroom, developing photographs with Boaz. Much of their gardening time is spent wordlessly, and when Ana sees Oskar tend so gently to the new plants, she wishes the strain between them would pass. Sometimes they do speak—of the farm, the cow the Germans took, the hen with bent feet, how Ana taught Oskar math with cabbages.

One afternoon Ana says, "If we'd stayed at the Dąbrowskis' we would have grown up to be Christian farmers."

"And here, we're growing up to be Jewish farmers," Oskar says.

As they work the soil an unexpected storm blows through, a soaking downpour. They run for cover beneath the large sycamore tree. Ana sits at the base. Oskar stands, a hand on the smooth trunk, a foot on a thick, knotty root, the rain still coming down. Both of them waiting.

I stand watch, waiting for the girl to return home from school, when a woman coated in olive green steps into the room. Insignias ornament her sleeves, yet she doesn't march like a soldier, and her eyes are soft and sad, not like wolves' at all.

She walks over to my bureau and stares at me, stares at pictures of the girl. I hear her say, "She belongs to another mother."

"No. She is ours. Mine." The velvet-eyed lady waves away the woman's papers, ushers her out the door. Later, she packs up the girl, who grips me tight, and we are, once again, clattering across landscapes.

The girl cries, "Please, I don't want to go!"

I cry, too, lost outside my mother, outside her mother, outside her mother, shuttling farther and farther from home.

15

RENATA
1968

Renata sits outside the lab and takes apart a pomegranate, round and jewel-red with a pointy crown at the top. The fruit seller scored it into quarters and demonstrated how she should peel back the skin to get to the seeds. A more involved process than she imagined, one that won't yield the calories to justify itself, but delicious.

Elbows propped on her thighs, legs spread like a man's—she's low on clean clothes and doesn't want red dots on her outfit—she extracts the seeds one by one from the fruit's peel and pops them into her mouth, the perfect balance between sweet and tart.

Her mum would've been horrified to see her like this. But her father would've laughed. He was far more relaxed—and funny—with his wacky inventions (her favorite, a makeshift bird feeder that funneled crumbs from the bread slicer to the kitchen window) and his silly language games.

"It *a*ppears our *a*partment is *a*bsent *a*n *a*lligator," he'd say, making an exaggerated show of looking, first in the bathtub, then in the kitchen sink.

"Yes, Papa, but my *b*rown *b*ear is in my *b*ed," Renata would reply.

"And our *c*lever *c*at is *c*lawing the *c*abinet."

She looks up to see Ian walking toward her. She tries to tamp down her excitement, to stop wanting what's impossible.

"Ah, a pomegranate—the geologist's favorite fruit," Ian says.

"Funny, I was just thinking about word games my father played to teach me English when I was little." There's a pleasure in telling him this. She rarely speaks of her father.

"Teach you English?" he asks.

"I'm from Germany, originally."

She knows her mother meant for her to keep it a secret always. But here, with him, in the blazing sun, far from Oxford, she feels released from the walls her mother built up around them.

"I'm amazed," Ian says. "I haven't noticed any hint of German in your speech, and your sentences aren't thirty words long."

"Want some?" she asks, the pomegranate splayed open in her palm.

He sits down and she places a few seeds into his cupped hand. As he eats them, one by one, he says, "I feel like Persephone."

"What?" *Is this a way of flirting?*

"You know, the myth. Persephone was stolen away by Hades and her mother, Demeter, was so distraught that she let all the earth's plants wither and die. Before returning to earth, Persephone ate six pomegranate seeds that Hades offered her, and it bound her to live in the underworld for six months of every year."

"So, if you're Persephone, I'm keeping you in Hell?" *She really shouldn't be playing into this.*

He laughs, his lips pink from the juice. Their faces are so close they could kiss.

In the lab, while the team is processing pottery—as well as three arrowheads, two iron and one bronze—Professor Shomron asks to see the catalog of the last few days. In addition to finds coming from a Second Temple destruction layer, they've collected baskets of First Temple pottery as well. A discussion ensues about the archaeological map, the topography and elevation of the dig site, and where they would expect the First Temple walls to be built. Talk continues through the afternoon and into the evening, as they drink beer and wine, overlooking the city.

The following afternoon, after the morning's dig, Renata meets Professor Shomron standing outside the lab building. The professor's face is tilted upward like a sunflower, her hair loose, spilling this way and that. Renata wishes for a fraction of her confidence, to feel rooted *and* free. Renata puts a hand to her tight braid.

"I was hoping for a word with you," Professor Shomron says.

"Oh?" A flood of self-doubt. Renata has been preoccupied; grieving her mum, distracted by Ian. *I've been found out, an impostor. I'm not up to par.*

She braces herself as Professor Shomron tells her that she's secured permission and funding to dig a bit farther up on the slope, immediately after they complete their current work.

"Congratulations, that's wonderful," Renata says.

"So, can you stay on a couple weeks?" Professor Shomron asks.

It takes a moment to catch up: this is an invitation, not a sacking. "You want me to join you for the new project?"

"Yes, that's what I'm asking."

"Of course, I'd love to," Renata says, flooding now with relief. What's there for her in Oxford? Her mum's boxes can wait.

Two days pass before she finds herself alone again with Ian, the final two straggling to finish up in the lab.

"Do you want to grab a pint? You can tell me what Shomron has planned for you."

"Ian," she blurts, "I need to ask, what are we doing?"

Ian takes a small step back from the lab table. "Renata—"

She struggles to continue. "It's just, it feels like—"

"I'm really sorry," Ian says in a quiet voice. "Mortified, actually." He looks away.

"You don't have to be mortified," she says.

"I do. I am."

"Well, should *I* be?"

He looks back at her then. "No, it's my fault. Everything's been so intense here; it's felt like we've stepped out of our regular lives."

He looks away again, down at his hands, considering his words. "But I don't want to hurt you."

"And I'm sure you don't want to hurt Olivia. Or Mark."

"No, I don't."

The large table is between them. She forces a smile. "Well, you probably haven't slept much the last couple of years."

"I'm not letting myself off that easily—though it is true, I haven't slept much."

He looks stricken, and she doesn't want to lose his friendship. They were both flirty. The notion of a relationship with someone like Ian—so intelligent and engaging, with those copper eyes—was thrilling. A welcome respite from her grief, even if it was impossible.

"You can make it up to me," she says with mustered cheer, "by accompanying me to the museum again. I want to look more carefully at the carved wooden panels. We can ask the others if they want to go with us."

He nods. "Yes. But no falafel deconstructions, please."

The following week, a letter arrives from Renata's landlady in Oxford. Condolences, again, and the news that there's a buyer for the building. Renata will need to find a new flat. This letter marks her notice of three months.

Three months! The current dig is set to last four more weeks, and she's just agreed to join Professor Shomron on the next one. She'll arrive in Oxford with barely time enough to sort through her mum's things and find a new flat to move into.

She's lived in that flat since she and her mum arrived in Oxford. The idea of having to move out, and with hardly any time to manage it, hits hard.

She must look as she feels because, late afternoon at the lab, Linda asks, "Are you all right?"

Ian looks up from his work.

Renata sighs. "It seems I have to move flats."

"What a ruddy nuisance," Linda says. "Do you have any idea where you'll move to?"

"Not really." In recent years, other than attending university and visiting the Ashmolean nearby to campus, she'd circled between the flat, the pharmacist, the grocery, and the hospital.

"I'm sorry to hear that," Ian says. Since their talk, there have been no more outings together, no trip to the museum. They've practiced mutual, polite avoidance.

She meets his eyes. "Thanks."

"There's not much you can do from here," Margaret says. "Do you want to grab a bite to eat? Linda and I have some shopping after."

As they walk down Jaffa Street, Linda says, "On the bright side, you have a chance to decide where you want to live."

"Maybe you can find a flat near the botanic gardens, or near a bakery you like," Margaret says.

"I'd do well with a livelier place," Renata admits.

"You should look in our neighborhood," Linda says.

They eat at an outdoor café, their table in the sun. Renata's mind flits to her stolen glances into the apartments here in Jerusalem and in Tel Aviv. Lemon trees in pots on terraces, colorful hand-painted tiles, doorframes marked by mezuzahs. She can't even conjure Oxford's neighborhoods.

Afterward, they part ways. Renata enters the Old City. She wishes she could slip a prayer—or else a hope—between the stones of the Western Wall. *Is it too trivial to pray to find a nice flat?*

Through the narrow, rubbled walkways of the Jewish quarter, boys with curled sidelocks and black yarmulkes slalom past. Renata remembers, once, when she and her mum first arrived in England, her mum had intimated a Jewish heritage in a conversation with someone. Renata instantly gave her away, saying something about Christmas. Back at their flat, her mother chided, "I don't want you contradicting me."

"But we're not Jewish, we go to church," Renata said.

Her mum darkened, muttering about anti-German sentiment and her own lingering accent, finally insisting that what was most important was sticking together.

Is that what her mum had been doing, sticking together, or had she been going it alone? So many questions play over in Renata's mind. Mysteries, really.

Why didn't they get mail at their flat? After collecting the mail from the post office, Mum would sometimes close herself in her bedroom, emerging red-eyed and muttering a vague "I'm sorry" as she walked past to begin cooking the night's supper. Later, Renata would come across letters, Tübingen-stamped and forwarded by their old neighbor, Gisela. They were in German, so she couldn't read them. She wouldn't have, anyway, wouldn't have invaded her mum's well-defended privacy.

Why did her mum always keep such close tabs on her when she said she wanted Renata to have a bigger social life? And why didn't they ever visit their friends in Tübingen, with whom her mum clearly kept up? They could have visited Papa's grave. They used to go, she remembers, just after he died, to place fresh flowers there. The cold dirt at her knees, the solid stone beneath her palms, a comfort after his sudden, shocking death, a clot that stopped his brain while he sipped his morning coffee.

In the final moments of her mum's long, drawn-out illness, shrunken and pale in the hospital bed, she had pulled Renata close, whispering as if no one else should hear, "I'm sorry if keeping you was wrong of me."

At the time, Renata thought maybe her mum felt guilty for not allowing them to return to Tübingen after they moved away. Now she's not sure what she meant.

In her purse she carries a photograph of her mum, one to blot out images from those last, grim hospital days. Mum is young and laughing in the picture, standing by the Neckar River, arms wrapped around her. Renata is holding up her small wooden doll, its red and black paint mostly peeled off. The littlest of a set of nesting dolls, without the others to nest in.

16

ROGER
1949–1952

Roger revels in leading his little cousins in pranks to play on Aunt Sarah and Uncle Uri:

"Shh, quietly, and without them noticing, tape this drawing of a fish on the back of their shirts, and we'll see how long before each of them takes notice."

"While they're still in bed Sunday morning, sneak down here and flip all of the framed photographs upside down."

"It's Uncle Uri's birthday tomorrow. Replace his pillow with this balloon and wait for the pop!"

And he challenges them with riddles:

What disappears as soon as you say its name?

Silence.

What can travel around the world without ever leaving its corner?

A stamp.

What is always in front of you but cannot be seen?

The future.

In the evenings, after dinner, they sprawl out on the floor together and build with the wooden blocks that Aunt Sarah bought in Paris. Roger likes to build the places he knew—Sainte Marie's chapel, an assemblage of bee boxes, the Basque house hidden amid vineyards. He likes to remember their structures, put them together from parts, fitting the shapes together. His cousins build new places every time, and they always end by building a bridge from his to theirs, connecting them.

At school, though, he's lonely. He feels awkward around his classmates; no one to joke with, share his stories, flip through the pages of a book. Luckily, Aunt Sarah has the wisdom to realize he needs something different. She arranges for Roger to take classes at the nearby house of a teacher named Eitan. Eitan has a bushy gray beard that he tugs on while he thinks, and eyebrows that form an unruly canopy over his dusky eyes. His study room smells of paper and cloves, and he offers snacks: cookies one day, raw-cut radishes the next. No matter what he serves, he pours a spicy sauce on his own portion before eating it, even the cookies. Music floats in from another room, and books crowd the shelves, some upright, some stuffed in sideways.

There are eight other students, all boys, serious and thoughtful, including Itzhak, who slips his snack to Eitan's cat, and Noam, who twists a strand of his hair while he thinks, a coil that *boings* when he finally lets go. They sit together around a large scuffed table, and Eitan raises questions.

What does it mean to be *lucky*? What does it mean to be *wise*? They try out answers; they argue and debate. Roger loves it.

Sometimes when Roger enters Eitan's house in the morning, there are lit yahrzeit candles in the kitchen sink, same as at Aunt Sarah's. White paraffin in glass, no smell of beeswax. It seems everyone has lost family, in the war for Israel's independence or before, in the Holocaust. Aunt Sarah's albums of photographs show Roger's parents in the bloom of life; his father as a boy, his parents married, his mother cradling him in her arms. Yet Roger can't help conjuring other images: emaciated, laboring, gasping for air.

He thinks about the questions Eitan recently raised about

forgiveness. Can we forgive on behalf of others? Does forgiving lead to forgetting?

Roger settles himself at the dining table, where he can see into the kitchen, the white porcelain walls of the sink glowing golden from the candle flames. He sits between Itzhak and a slightly younger boy named Avrami, who is a math wizard with a quake in his right hand. He avoids Nahum, who is always trying to outwit everyone, to be cleverest and impress Eitan.

Eitan offers Roger an endless supply of books on loan, so long as he promises to meet and discuss what he reads. Roger scans the shelves, excited, and finally pulls out the Midrash.

"Ah, you like puzzles."

"Yes."

"Then you're in luck, because the ancient texts are filled with them."

Roger reads the Proverbs containing questions that the Queen of Sheba posed to Solomon.

How would he distinguish, when disguised, males from females, a real flower from a fake one, the circumcised from the uncircumcised?

On his walks home, he stops to stare at the lions of Judah carved on the gate of the Ethiopian church. He thinks of his own concealment, his sense of self tangled up.

In time, he prepares for a bar mitzvah. His parashah is about Moses' grief over the death of his sister, Miriam; the mistakes he made in the wake of his loss, his trouble listening to God. The study roots Roger further to his aunt and family, no matter his ongoing religious confusion.

All the while, he continues writing in his notebook:

When Truth appears naked, the villagers won't let her into their houses. Parable finds her huddled in a corner, shivering and hungry, and taking pity, gathers her up and brings her home. Parable dresses Truth in Story, warming her before sending her out again. Clothed now, Truth knocks at the doors and is welcomed. The villagers invite her to eat at their tables and warm herself by their fires.

At home after the temple service, the family milling about, cousin Bennie flops down on the sofa beside Roger and presents him with a book. "For the Jewish boy who was baptized then moved to Israel and became a bar mitzvah!" he says, handing it over. Roger looks eagerly at the title: Maimonides' *Guide for the Perplexed.* "It was Eitan's suggestion," Bennie confesses.

There's a lot in the book that Roger doesn't understand, but he feels an affinity to it anyway. Maimonides argues against literal readings of the Bible! He doubts miracles and embraces parable! The thought that God's essence is unknowable and indescribable—not like the accounts given by either Christians *or* Jews—is comforting to Roger. And there's something else: the idea that righteous people facing evil and suffering might be buffered by their closeness to God. Maybe his parents were shielded somehow? Roger wonders about righteousness; why it is so often mixed with hate, and why the righteous don't seem to grow *wiser,* which, according to Maimonides, would remove hate.

He takes to carrying the heavy book around with him. It feels like a hundred puzzles in one, Maimonides' thoughts on different topics cut like a jigsaw and scattered throughout its pages. Somehow, it pulls him closer to his lost parents.

And then Roger turns to the puzzles of his own life.

Is he the same person as the French boy who peppered Sister Brigitte with questions, who exchanged jokes with Henri before walking into class, who hid in a Spanish monastery with Brother Jacques? What if he doesn't remember the details of their faces or their conversations? What if he believes in an entirely different God? Or if he doesn't believe in any God at all?

Brother Jacques said the Church was trying to save his Christian soul. Roger is pretty sure the rabbis who appealed to the French courts on his aunt's behalf sought his return to Judaism, in addition to connecting him with relatives.

He feels close to his family, especially to Aunt Sarah and Uncle Uri and Bennie. He feels happy here, circling Eitan's study table, ambling in the garden, writing stories. In photographs of his parents, he sees his own resemblance in his mother's eyes, his father's cheeks and the tip of his nose. But will he ever feel grounded in this life, will he ever feel he truly belongs?

17

OSKAR
1952

Gideon, true to his word, has arranged for Oskar and Szymon to be trained in the carpentry shop. Now, Szymon learns to draft and Oskar to build the beds, bureaus, tables, and chairs that furnish the kibbutz. In spare moments, and using leftover scraps, Oskar works on pet projects. A set of boxes that can nest, one inside the other, with smooth joints. A chessboard made of squares that alternate dark and light woods, with uniquely carved playing pieces, the knights still his favorite. So long as the new chess set is for communal use, Oskar and Szymon can take it for their ongoing tournament, which they play outside beneath the bent pine.

A girl named Adina, with apple cheeks and a lion's mane of hair, takes an interest in their chess games, but more so, Oskar thinks, an interest in Szymon. She is nearly as quiet as he is, and she watches unobtrusively—unlike those who like to coach from the sidelines, or who carelessly let their ball game drift over, distracting Oskar far more than Szymon. Adina learns many of the signs that Szymon and Oskar use to communicate. Oskar observes her watching Szymon, head cocked, curls in a halo around her face, while Szymon—usually a far more careful observer than he—doesn't notice her attentions. Oskar isn't sure Szymon notices girls at all.

Oskar has his own eye on an older girl, Tzofia, who plays the violin so beautifully that his heart threatens to burst open. He doesn't speak to her. (Not yet.) He takes note of how she spends her free time in the music room, practicing, except for afternoon family time, which she spends with a girl named Rivka and her parents. Nightly, she plays at the campfire, her dark hair glossy in the firelight. Standing across from her, watching the quick movements of her nimble fingers, as fine-boned as her face, Oskar listens to her music, hauntingly delicate and full of wanting.

When, one day, Tzofia shows up at the woodshop to deliver a package for Gideon, Oskar hastily brushes the dust from his shoulders and straightens his station, a mess of paper-and-pencil drawings, whittled birds, assorted boxes, varnishes, and glues.

"This smell," she says, taking a deep breath.

Most people dislike the pungent, resiny scent of the shop. "I'm sorry," Oskar says.

"No, I like it."

She looks for a long time at Oskar's birds, but when she extends her hand, she reaches for one of the boxes.

"They're meant to fit, one inside the other?" she asks.

"Yes. We had a set . . . when I was a child. I liked to play with it."

She turns the box around in her hand, places it back on the table among the others.

"I've wished I could make you a violin," he blurts, the words unexpected even to himself.

She smiles tentatively. "Why is that?"

"The one you play looks small for you."

"It is, but it is special to me."

Oskar dares to talk to Tzofia again, when they're standing by the campfire another night.

"I really liked what you played," he says.

"I've been thinking about what you told me, that you wanted to make me a violin," she says. "My grandfather made violins."

"Did you see how he made them?"

"I was too young, but I know it's intricate." She holds out her violin so he can look at it. The striated maple gleams in the firelight. He leads them to a sitting log.

Tzofia tells Oskar how she was hidden during the war, first in a farmer's barn with her mother, then in a convent, apart. A rabbi and his wife came to the convent to collect her out of hiding, taking her to a Displaced Persons camp, where she became close with Rivka Levy and eventually voyaged here with the Levy family.

"I didn't want to leave the convent. I had a dear friend there, and two nuns who specially cared for me. But I longed to find my mother and they told me I was going *home*. I thought they meant—"

Oskar nods.

"I believed that my mother would come. Well." She looks toward the fire. "At the DP camp, the Levys took me in."

Oskar thinks of Eva, how for other kids, she gave them a family.

"At the convent, Sister Nadzieja arranged for me to have violin lessons and plenty of time to practice—unlike here, where I work at the dairy and play mostly at the campfire. She gave me my . . . the . . . violin to take with me."

"It has to stay in the common music room?"

"Yes, but I wish I could keep it beneath my bed."

Oskar's next project is a box that he crafts from heartwood. Each side, beautifully burled; each joint, a perfect fit. He attaches delicate strings across the box's opening.

Night after night, Oskar stands in his usual place, eyes closed, listening to Tzofia's music while others around him dance. Tonight she is playing something fast, boisterous. A folk dance. When Adina jostles him, he opens his eyes. She's got Szymon by one hand, and she takes Oskar by the other, pulling them into the circle of dancers, exuberant, weaving around and around. As the music builds, Adina lets go and begins clapping, motioning for others to join; then, when the rhythm is strong, she moves to pull Tzofia in. Oskar sees Tzofia hesitate: she tilts her head down, shakes it. Oskar steps forward and reaches out his hand.

Tzofia looks at him for a long moment. She sets the violin and bow on her chair and lets him lead her into the dance. They circle and whirl, her hand warm and strong in his, her hair the scent of pine. Without her playing, the dance founders, then picks up, faster and faster. Oskar and Tzofia move with the crowd, first in one direction, then the other, their legs rock-horsing, backward and forward, their hands now squeezed tight. When finally, the dancing stops, neither lets go.

They walk, still hand in hand. *It's a dovetail fit,* Oskar thinks. He leads her to his workshop.

"Will you wait? I'll just be a second."

He comes out with the music box. "This is for you," he says.

Tzofia takes it with both hands.

Oskar tells her the story of Bachtalo and his beechwood box, how the Spirit, Matuja, pressed her laughter and her tears into it so that the music would gladden and sadden people, both.

"It is my favorite violin yet," she tells him.

"And you can keep it under your bed. I doubt anyone will object."

Oskar watches Ana and Boaz, a couple now, and he wants to be like that with Tzofia. He grows restless when he's apart from her and presses her to walk with him along Neve Ora's paths, fallen

palm fronds rustling at their feet. Tzofia smells of the bonfire and
pine sap and of the olive oil soap she washes with after her work
in the dairy. Her eyes are flecked with yellow-gold, the tops of
her hands softer than the lamb's ear in Ana's garden. Her laugh is
like birdsong. And her playing is a gift she creates with wrought
wood. When they link arms beneath the trees, Oskar feels shot
through with joy and thinks, finally, this could be his home.

Yet she is elusive. There are frequent nights after she plays at
the campfire that she declines Oskar's invitation to walk.

"I need to go to the music room and work on my bowing. It
wasn't right."

"It sounded perfect."

"But it wasn't. It was bouncy, weak."

"Just a short walk, and then you'll practice?"

"No, I'm sorry. Maybe tomorrow."

He tries to understand: her violin playing matters deeply to
her. It is her connection to lost family—both her parents and her
grandfather. And she is extraordinary. But sometimes, he can't
help feeling jealous, as music pulses through her veins—her
lifeblood, her home—and he stands on the outside, wishing he
could come nearer.

18

ANA
1952

The high schoolers board away from Neve Ora, but they return each day for work and meals in the kibbutz dining room, embracing the collectivist ideology even as they debate everything: Israel's recent military actions, the individual's place in society, what it means to be a Jew. Ana is swept up by the spirited commitment all around her, awed by Boaz's political passion. She is equally dismayed by Oskar's apathy. His attention is turned to playing chess, studying the figurines of some master wood-carver named Hans Teppich, and chasing after Tzofia like a lost puppy. What *is* it about him and the violin?

When Ana and Boaz spend time in the darkroom—and afterward, when they take long walks and talk—he shares his ideas for how Neve Ora can become truly egalitarian and achieve Zionist self-sufficiency. He asks for her thoughts, listening to what she has to say; he pays attention.

She could swim in the dark pools of his eyes. His features are angular, yet the overall effect is soft. The tips of his fingers hold the lingering scent of vinegar, reminding Ana of her mother's herbal tinctures. After developing a roll of photographs, her fingers carry the same scent, and she brings them to her nose, breathes it in.

The photographs Boaz keeps of his brother Ari, pressed within the pages of a book and stowed beneath his bed, had startled Ana when he first showed them to her. Ari was younger than she'd imagined, frail but smiling, his face like Boaz's, only mushier. In one picture, he clung to a tree trunk, just as Oskar might have done.

"He died a week after I took this one. I couldn't protect him—" Boaz had said.

Ana had taken his hand, thinking of how she'd promised her mother that she would protect Oskar; knowing then, it was only by luck that they were here.

She looks over at Boaz in the shadowy, red-tinged light as her newest photographs emerge in the chemical bath. Even the youngest of the children born at the end of the war are nearly eight, growing up. Unlike Ari, who will never grow up, who will always be that little boy.

"These are good, Chani," Boaz says.

He leans in to kiss her, his lips thick and soft, a gentle pull that reaches to her depths. She wraps her arms around him, heady and hot. Bereft and alive.

When Eva visits Neve Ora, she is swarmed by "her children," who gather to encircle her, to give and receive greetings and hugs. Ana waits, apart, noticing that Eva looks somehow smaller than on their journey, thinner and paler despite the desert sun. When the children recede, Ana and Eva walk together, up and around the curving paths, to a spot where the view opens out to the sea.

The water glitters, and they stand, silent, looking at it. Ana raises her fear of Boaz leaving soon for military service.

"I'm worried about what will happen to us."

"You're both so young, just seventeen and eighteen. A lot can change," Eva says.

Ana doesn't want anything to change. She stares out at the water, vexed, but she makes herself ask, "How are you?"

Eva sighs. "I don't know. Everything that once seemed right, I'm questioning now. Tell me, how's Oskar? *Yossi.*"

"He's fine."

"He hates me, I know he does," Eva says.

Ana looks at her, surprised to find pain etched in her face. "He doesn't hate people. Don't mind that he didn't come to greet you. He's always in the woodshop; no one can pull him out of there."

"I was so sure it was the right thing," Eva says. "Reclaiming every possible child. 'Redeeming' them. 'Ransoming' them. There were debates over what to call it. At the time, I didn't consider that there might be exceptions, that some children might be better off staying put."

Ana thinks of the early morning her mother led them up and into Bluma's truck, away. Her wish that her mother had kept them, that they'd stayed with her and Papa, no matter their fate. Doesn't it live, always, alongside her other wishes?

Over the next few weeks, Ana takes more shifts in the infant and children's rooms, as there is always a great need for caretakers. When she isn't bouncing a child, she's sewing stuffed teddy bears to place around the rooms, or weaving flower crowns for the young "Queen Esthers."

"You know what's *not* egalitarian?" Ana asks Boaz one day. "That only women caretake the children."

"You're right," he says.

"Then why don't you sign up?" She isn't asking for the principle of it; she wants to spend every minute she can with him before he leaves.

Boaz nods, but his name doesn't appear on the sign-up sheet. She asks again, and again he agrees, but nothing follows. At first

she thinks he's avoiding it because, as a man, he doesn't see himself as needing to do it. But over time, she wonders if perhaps it's
too difficult for him, given memories of Ari.

She decides not to push the subject. She is content in the
work, feeling swells of pleasure when a baby reaches out his arms
for her, or when a little girl rushes to her with a lavender stalk and
then burrows into the folds of her skirt.

19

ROGER
1954–1960

In the move to high school, Roger misses everything about Eitan's, especially the lively debates around the table. With Aunt
Sarah's encouragement—and after several afternoons circling the
university campus, then the philosophy department, rallying his
nerve—Roger asks two professors for permission to sit in on their
courses. They both hesitate, but Roger's curious and thoughtful
manner wins them over, and in time, Roger is shuttling to the
university several afternoons a week, feeding his passion for meta-
physics and epistemology.

He finds himself utterly in his element:

If you rebuild a ship over time, replacing each plank as it de-
cays with a new, stronger plank, is it the same ship? What if you
take each of the discarded planks and build a second ship; would
that be the same as the original one?

What of *persons*: Can they be the selfsame if they change over
time?

What of *him*?

It seems that, no matter how long Roger lives in Israel, he will
always be French. He dreams in French, and when he's distracted,
oui slips out, rather than כן. He has a certain unshakable aesthetic
sensibility—not in how he grooms himself, hence the common
occurrence of finding himself in mismatched shoes—but in how
he keeps a tiny potted plant in his high window and takes the
time to lean out with a watering can to water it. And in how,

when he bakes madeleines or *navettes,* he refuses to let them be
served until he has sprinkled powdered sugar on them, despite
Bennie saying, "They're ready and they'll be delicious as they are."

"*Non.*"

René Descartes writes in French! He writes in Latin, too,
which comes easily for Roger, given his study of liturgical texts.
Roger reads the *Meditations,* on what may be known and what
must be doubted:

One must doubt if one's *body* exists but not one's *thinking self*
because thinking is itself a precondition of doubting. To persist
over time is to persist as a thinking being. Yet one must doubt
what one perceives through the senses because, behold this wax
which, when melted, changes in color and smell and shape. . . .

Roger sometimes feels himself to be as changeable as wax—
but French wax! He wonders what became of the person he once
was. Did he ever simply *believe,* or has he been questioning always? And what of his friend Henri, who locked eyes with him
over the refectory table, another lost child masking the confusion
of his life with riddles and jokes, casting about for home?

After Descartes, Roger reads Locke. Locke says that a person's identity over time requires a persisting consciousness, but
his theory raises questions about what consciousness is, and how
it must persist in order to connect a person from one life stage to
another. What happens in the absence of memories, moments of
forgetting, when a person is asleep, and so, not thinking?

Can we persist through our *regrets*? Roger thinks back to
the time he confessed to Father Louis his wish to be a different
boy, no longer of his parents. He shakes the memory off, even as
he delves into the arguments for how a person's remembrances
might link the self over time.

He wishes he could shake away considerations of faith, too; yet he can't help questioning: What connects a person whose soul was, in the past, devoted to Jesus, to one who now prays to the God of the Jews—or else to no One at all?

Roger reflects on the one truly dangerous moment on his journey with Brother Jacques. For all he'd feared it, the wild boar had never appeared. Instead the danger had come in silence. They'd been walking for hours, and dusk's light began casting long shadows, obscuring their view of the path. They were on a decline, and fresh sleeting rain brought slush to their feet. Roger skidded, his boots on black ice; Brother Jacques reached out to steady him and lost his balance, too. They toppled, but Brother Jacques held Roger aloft, even as his own head hit an icy rock and he went sliding. A large jutting tree root eventually stopped their descent.

From the start, there was a prayer on Brother Jacques's lips, a prayer for *Roger* to be safe, to be unhurt, which he uttered over and over. At that night's lodging, a man cleaned Brother Jacques's scrapes, packed snow on his bruises. Roger didn't have a single cut.

Sometimes Roger wonders what had motivated Brother Jacques. Was it religious conviction, or a commitment to the Church's mission to keep Roger for its own? Was it a sense of moral obligation, to save a child before himself? Was it love?

Classmates invite Roger to join them after seminar, on the grassy lawn or at the campus café, talking for hours. No one seems to mind that he's younger than they are. If he wants to, he can read in the small philosophy library, smelling faintly of vanilla, filled with books and periodicals and overstuffed chairs. His professors encourage him to attend the weekly colloquia and the departmental receptions. One arranges with the registrar for his class-by-class matriculation, so that he accrues credit for his coursework.

When, at eighteen, Roger is drafted, he serves in an intelligence office in Tel Aviv, deciphering codes and listening to the French news coming over the wires from Lebanon and Syria. He convinces Bennie to send him philosophy books to study by flashlight while others in his barrack stare at pictures of their sweethearts or compose letters to family and friends. But with everyone bunked together, he can't keep his head in the texts. He reaches for stationery and pen, and a full eleven years after Madame Mercier hustled him into a truck headed for Spain, Roger writes to Henri, c/o Sainte Marie de Sion.

He receives a reply in a month's time. Henri is still there, having taken vows. He is a monk now.

Roger writes back: "Me, too. Only without the praying."

And he includes a joke:

A new monk arrives at the monastery and is assigned to help the other monks in copying the old texts by hand. He notices that they are copying copies, not the original books. He goes to the head monk to ask him about this, pointing out that, if there was an error in the first copy, that error would be continued in all of the other copies. The head monk says, "We have been copying from the copies for centuries, but you make a good point, my son," and he goes down into the cellar with one of the copies to check it against the original.

Hours later, nobody has seen him. One of the monks goes downstairs to look for him. He hears sobbing at the back of the cellar and finds the old monk leaning over one of the original books, crying. He asks what's wrong.

"The word is celebrate, *not* celibate," *says the old monk with tears in his eyes.*

After his military service, Roger returns to his philosophy studies, and in time, he is hired to assistant-teach. Students flock around him. They crowd his tiny office, trail him in the hallways, even show up at his rented room, which is largely unfurnished and lacks most comforts except for an oversize, paper-strewn desk and a back-friendly swivel chair. He always has coffee close at hand, at least. Most students who stop by casually reveal a box of takeout: "I picked up extra, in case you haven't eaten." (Usually he hasn't.)

Bennie jokes that he is like Socrates with his disciples. When they meet on campus for lunch (Bennie, too, likes to ensure that Roger eats), his students find them, even tucked away at a back table of the café. Apologetically, the students interrupt to ask their questions about reason and will and personhood. Roger listens, nodding, and answers their questions with subtler, more complicated questions. They go off wide-eyed.

When he isn't teaching, he is reading or writing or thinking. He continues penning stories, markedly philosophical in bent, with characters grappling over memory and faith. Only on Fridays does he stop, to join Aunt Sarah and Uncle Uri and whichever of the cousins are home from military service or work, for Shabbat.

This Friday, as is typical, he arrives to his family's house distracted, his head still in his thought experiments, a pencil tucked behind his ear.

"You're going to poke my eye out," Aunt Sarah says, hugging him especially tight. And Roger knows, they're both thinking of his father.

By the time they're sitting around the table, he settles in, reminded of his time in the house and garden, writing about expanding backpacks and the travails of naked Truth.

During dinner, Aunt Sarah stuffs him with food, as if it's all she can be sure he'll eat for the week, and afterward she pulls him out for a walk. They take Ethiopia Street to the rounded Kidane

Mehret Church, marked by the lion of Judah, symbolic of the meeting between the Queen of Sheba and King Solomon.

His aunt says, "I worry about you, Rami. You are alone with your studies, your writing. Why don't you find a nice girl and start a family?"

"The only people I can think of bringing into the world are fictional," Roger says.

She looks at him askance.

He takes her hand. "I'm fine. I'd like to meet someone, I would. But for now, I'm busy with my students."

"I may not know the fancy lingo you use, but I do understand some things. What happened to you, so little, being taken on the run and into hiding. Raised Catholic, then brought here. You had a terribly confusing childhood, but now— well. *I* believe you have the power to determine your life."

He knows the smile he gives her is limp. He's not going to argue with her about the conditions of autonomous agency.

"Sometimes I feel as if I'm still floating somewhere over the Pyrenees," he admits.

"It would be hard to feel grounded after so much tumult," Aunt Sarah says thoughtfully. Then she turns on him. "But all that questioning you do . . . is that really helpful?"

"*Doda*—"

"Well. All I'm saying is, you're a brilliant and bighearted boy. Try to let yourself get close to someone."

"I still don't know who I am," he says.

In the darkness, the mournful cries of the city's muezzin.

20

ANA
1955

Even through separations owing to Boaz's army service and then Ana's, they remain committed to each other. They could marry, but Boaz says that marriage perpetuates social conventions that fuel inequality. So they move in together, falling asleep side by side each night and waking in a contented, sweaty tangle each morning.

They both want children, yet when Ana becomes pregnant, she is beset by troubled dreams.

She's walking, room to room, through the Marseille children's home, carrying little Zissa, who slips out of her arms, falling to the floor. . . .

She is at market, piling goods into her basket, unaware of holes in the corners, and everything drops out behind her as she walks. . . .

She tries to calm herself with memories of feeling safe. Before the ghetto, times with her mother by the river, collecting herbs, or in their garden, Bolek's purring in rhythm with her father's hammering in the smithy. Later, listening to one of Ciocia Agata's stories, the neighbors off in their houses, lanterns winking out.

She drifts to sleep but wakes to other memories that set her heart pounding.

German soldiers tugging their cow down the street . . .

Zygmunt, delivering news of the bombing . . .

A basket with stones where the poppies grew . . .

When will she be free of terror? She tells Boaz of the

burned-down barn by the Dąbrowskis' farm, certain now that there were Jews inside.

"Ahuvati, try to keep calm," he says.

She puts her hand to her stomach. "I don't know that I can do this," she says.

"Of course you can! You're wonderful with children."

"I don't feel whole."

Boaz looks at her, stricken. When he remains quiet she asks, "What? What do you want to say?"

"You at least have your brother."

Ana wakes one morning with cramping, low and tight. She sits up, aware of wetness, the scent of rust. The bleeding is spotty, not severe. She hasn't lost the baby. Still, Ana is wrecked.

"You just need to rest," Boaz says.

But it isn't that, she thinks. She pictures her childhood drawings—all those squares, crammed with people, parents and children; in truth, emptied out.

When Oskar comes to check on her, Ana says, "You'll be gratified to know, I'm missing something from your dear Poland."

"What?" Oskar asks.

"Raspberry leaf," she says with a sigh. "It would really help me just now, but it doesn't grow here."

"Is there something else that could help?"

"Well, nettle. But the plant has terrible stingers—"

"I'll get it for you, Stazja."

For the next several weeks, Oskar collects herbs and roots, per Ana's instructions, that Boaz boils into soothing, strength-giving teas. They draw condemnation from the hardline kibbutzniks because it's special treatment: the teas aren't on offer to the entire

community. Her friends, Ida and Yehoshua and Dov, stop by
at different times to check on her. Ana grows steadier, rounder,
less spooked by the prospect of motherhood. She sips the tea at
bedtime, the flavors of grass and pepper warming her. Her fear-
dreams drop away, replaced by maternal memories: Chana, in the
kitchen, swirling Oskar to and fro, the shift of her skirts releasing
the scent of lilac. Agata, a bowl of turnips on her hip, arranging
soft fur at Ana's chin. Eva, holding up a homemade newspaper,
cross-legged in the children's circle, teaching them the words to
"Hatikva."

When, during labor, the pain turns bone-splitting, Ana calls
out for Oskar. The women tending to her with clean towels and
boiled water exchange looks. Ida takes her hand and says, "Your
brother is right outside, pacing alongside Boaz."

Ana delivers a boy, rosy and plump, his fingernails the trans-
lucent pink of pomegranate seeds. She and Boaz have discussed
names beginning with the letter *A*. Asher or Amos for a boy;
Avital or Aviva for a girl. But with the baby bundled in her arms,
Ana says, "Boaz, let's call him Ari."

Ari is a smiler from the very start, spreading happiness with
the wonder of his huge slate eyes. Boaz and Ana soak up the
precious minutes of their allotted parental visits, bouncing him
and singing to him, watching for every new expression before his
required return to the communal baby room. Oskar whittles a
lion from olive wood, a gift for Ari when he gets older. Ana places
it on her bureau, to wait.

When Eva comes to meet Ari, she is skinnier even than last
time. There's a tremor at her lips as her eyes rove Ari's round cheeks
and thighs.

"Why don't you stay and we can have lunch?" Ana asks. "It's

nearly time for me to return him to the infant room. I'll just nurse, quickly." She's awkward, nursing in front of Eva. Thinking of what happened to *her* baby.

Eva's eyes flit around the room, landing on anything and everything except her and Ari. "I thought your brother might be here," she says.

"Oskar is *fine*," Ana says, a little exasperated. "He has a great friend in Shimi. He is a star at the woodshop." Ana wishes Eva could set her torments aside just once and acknowledge this joyful moment in Ana's life.

But how could she?

Ari's tiny fist clasps around Ana's finger. She breathes in his doughy scent. "You know, I think Oskar may be in love," she offers.

Eva's smile is pursed. "Do you think he'll ever feel this is his home?"

"He's settled here. And he has told me more than once how much your teaching hand signs, so that children could communicate with Shimi, meant to both of them."

Ana lifts Ari to her shoulder, patting his back.

Eva looks away. "It's very hard, when Rachela—"

Ana nods, repositioning the baby. With her spare arm she reaches out to Eva. "I'm sorry."

"What if she'd survived without me?" Eva asks, her eyes welling. "Would I have wanted her to be taken from a family who loved her?"

"I believe you would have wanted her to be raised Jewish. To know her roots."

"I used to feel so certain," Eva says. "I'd lost everyone I loved. And I didn't trust the Poles to care for Jewish children. Some took them in for farm labor, extra hands. Anyway, there were so few children left. It felt crucial to save every one. But maybe, in certain instances—"

Ari begins to fuss, and Ana gives him a gentle bounce. "Won't you stay? Maybe we can swing by the woodshop."

Eva stands, unsteadily. "No. It's better if I go. You have a beautiful baby. A beautiful, healthy son, born in Eretz Yisrael."

21

OSKAR
1956–1960

Tzofia is "discovered" the night a violoncellist from Tel Aviv, a player with the Philharmonic Orchestra, visits Neve Ora and hears her play at the campfire. The next night the orchestra director comes, too, and Tzofia is swept up by their eager questioning: "When did you begin playing?" "How much training have you had?" "Have you ever performed?"

Oskar is by her side as she answers their questions—"I was six; a teacher came to the convent and gave me secret lessons; I played for an *Oberleutnant,* and at campfires"—and explains that, though Neve Ora has arranged for some instruction, most of her days here are spent in the fields and in the dairy, with little time left over to practice, save late at night.

"No one is exceptional here," she tells them.

"*You* could be, Tzofia." The director raises the possibility of advanced training.

"But I have no money for a teacher, and I have to work."

"I know someone, a patron of our orchestra, who would sponsor you. You'd come to Tel Aviv, live very modestly, with other musicians. You'd train and practice exclusively. If you make the right progress, you could have a chance to audition." He speaks of live concerts, recordings. Her chance to be heard far and wide.

Oskar knows this is Tzofia's dream, cracking open like the window she lifts each time she practices, her pent-up notes floating out on the reverberating air.

She turns to him. Buoyant, yet with sorrow at the edges of her eyes. She's found love here, and family. But her music—

"I need to go," she says.

Oskar nods. "I know," he says.

He fights the tightness that seizes his chest as he helps move Tzofia, by bus, from the kibbutz to the dormitory-style building near Heichal HaTarbut. Her room is just large enough to walk around the bed that occupies the center. A shared bathroom is down the hall. They've spoken of visiting each other; how he'll come to see her, how she'll come to Neve Ora. But this is a world unto itself, and a busy one. Already, Tzofia has received her lesson schedule and the key to a practice room that can be used anytime day or night. The trills of a flute float in from a nearby room. A boy carrying a bass shuffles down the hall. Oskar sees the mix of excitement and trepidation in Tzofia's face. He takes her hand.

"You'll be great," he says, his breath jagged.

Back at Neve Ora, Tzofia gone, Oskar hardly eats. He avoids the campfire, the music taken over by a ragtag group of men in their forties playing accordions. He tosses through the nights, then trips through the days, bleary and sad. He spends most of his time in the woodshop, Szymon quiet beside him at his drawing table. He declines games of chess. Several times he tries writing to Tzofia, but he's never written a letter like this, or received one; he's only seen letters in literature books, and he can't manage any of their eloquence. He crumples each attempt.

One night at his desk, trying again, his Hebrew stalls and gives way to new words he's learning in English, then to old words, Polish words. He takes a fresh piece of paper and begins a letter to Agata and Józef. He's never written to them, either; too afraid, perhaps, to be overwhelmed by his yearnings. Yet now his pen moves across the page. His words are simple, his grammar elementary, and at times he's forced to revert to Hebrew when his Polish utterly fails him, but he doesn't let that stop him; in the morning, he'll sit with old Aharon, who will help him fix it, and he'll write it out clean. He tells Agata and Józef how miserable he was to be taken from them. He describes the various "homes" that he and Stazja were shuffled between, how he wished to go to church but was taken only once. He tells them of the boat passage, the endless months in Cyprus, and his friendship with Szymon; how he still whittles and also makes real furniture. He's homesick for them, even now, and he's certain that his one chance for happiness here has been dashed because Tzofia is gone—

He blinks at the page, his eyes stinging. He strikes out the last part, again and again, the pen digging into the paper. He crumples the whole letter in a ball and shoves it to the bottom of a desk drawer. He wanders out among the trees.

In the woodshop—unshowered, unshaven—Oskar slouches over a tabletop, readying himself to begin sanding, when Gideon says, "If you have to follow her . . ."

Oskar looks up.

"I can get you an apprenticeship with a furniture maker I know. His name is Shmuel. He can't pay you much and he's no Hans Teppich, but you'll learn a lot from him, and he may want your chess sets for his shop."

Ana's reaction to Oskar's plan for departure isn't surprising. She treats him as a defector, turns huffy when he lifts Ari to perch on his shoulders, cantering him toward the children's farm to visit the rabbits. It stings and complicates his regret over leaving.

With Szymon it's simpler. He's going to miss time with his best friend. He worries Szymon will be alone save for a few: Leah and Rut, both apprenticing to be teachers; Gideon, always in the woodshop; and Adina, who long ago gave up on Szymon as a romantic possibility. Yet Szymon signs, over and over, that he's happy for Oskar, happy he will be closer to Tzofia. The way Szymon signs "happy"—his two hands brushing close to his chest—cheers Oskar. His friend has grown so tall, and his shaggy hair hangs over his eyes, but his warm smile is the same. As they embrace goodbye, Oskar proposes a weekly chess game. They arrange it for Sundays. Oskar will come by bus to Neve Ora for now; later, Szymon will meet him in Tel Aviv. They will have this standing game for the rest of their lives.

Shmuel's shop is located in the Florentin neighborhood of Tel Aviv, white buildings with red roofs lining the narrow streets. Oskar occupies a room in the corner apartment above the woodshop. A shared kitchen and bathroom, and the scents of wood glue and varnish following him up the rickety back staircase. He doesn't care. He likes Shmuel. Strong as an ox, yet gentle. Part poet. Shmuel appreciates Oskar's hard work, his chess sets and nesting boxes (already in the shop window), and his newest project: a carved rosewood music stand, designed like a lyre with scrolled arms and a fluted leaf base.

The trees and animals of Neve Ora show up in Oskar's dreams. Also, the sweet, honey-floral scent of orange blossoms. He's not used to the bustle and grit of the city. But having a place of his own, arranging it the way he wants, crowding the narrow white windowsill with his carvings (not worrying about "possessing" them), and working beside Shmuel to create new, original furniture, brings him pride. A sense of himself in his own right.

Best of all, he sees Tzofia. When her schedule allows, they stroll along the streets, pick up groceries, come back to his place. He holds her close, breathing in pine at her fingertips and honey in her hair, her warm body nestled against his.

Mandatory military service interrupts this rhythm. Oskar is sent to the Negev. The stark landscape stirs anew his longing for the lush forests of his youth, and the nights stir his longing for Tzofia. It is grueling, running the hills with rock-heavy packs, long sets of push-ups, and hauling gear this way and that. He develops close friendships with a few in his unit (not the arrogant ones who bully the newcomers, same as at the kibbutz), and he finds within himself a commitment to the land of Israel, this singular trunk onto which they have all been grafted, their root system deepening, together.

Now he writes letters to Tzofia, and he sends his next chess moves to Szymon, who is employed drawing maps in an office in Tel Aviv. He writes, at last, to the Dąbrowskis. He is sturdier in body and spirit than when he balled up that first letter, and his message is straightforward: he misses them deeply and, as soon as he can manage it, he wants to travel to see them.

When his service is over, Oskar returns to work at Shmuel's, and to eagerly anticipated dates with Tzofia, their connection more solid, he thinks, than before he left. He delves into the building of wood-carved cabinets and bureaus, and he resumes his careful crafting of the music stand. He takes walks through the neighborhood, stopping to chat with the carpenters in other shops, peering in the open doors of textile warehouses and ceramic studios, nodding to fellow craftsmen. He lives on practically nothing, saving most of what he earns for a future with Tzofia. He also saves for his trip to see the Dąbrowskis, which he plans carefully over the course of many months, figuring time off from the shop with Shmuel and diligently filing the necessary requests and reasons-for-travel—including a letter from the Dąbrowskis, pleading their need of his visit—in order to obtain an embassy-issued visa to enter Poland.

He's been back to Neve Ora to spend time with Szymon, and to see Ana and her family, but he's hesitated to tell his sister of his impending trip to visit the Dąbrowskis. Now he dials the office phone despite the kibbutz rule against using the common line for personal communications.

"If you'd want to come, Stazja, we could make the requests for you, too," he offers.

"I can't go, Oskar. Our community doesn't work when people leave for their own pursuits." He is reminded of how she and Ida used to walk around the children's homes, arms hooked, heads raised loftily.

Just before hanging up, she says, "Be safe, *gnojku*."

22

RENATA

1968

Professor Shomron has arranged for the Oxford students to view Masada, an ancient fortress of great archaeological and historical significance, the site of Herod's winter palaces as well as that of a Roman siege in which the last survivors of the Jewish revolt committed suicide rather than be captured.

They gather at the waiting bus. Renata scales the steep stairs to find Margaret and Linda waving her over. Linda holds out a bag of pistachios as Renata settles into the seat beside them. Immediately, Margaret turns to face her. "Do you remember how Yonatan asked both Linda and me for dates that first night?"

Renata nods.

"Well, obviously Linda declined because of Nigel, but I've been going out with him this whole time. Now I learn that he's also been on dates with Irit. He's invited *her* to Tel Aviv today! How could I not have seen it?"

Linda throws her a look.

Even Renata has noticed Yonatan's ever-wandering eyes, but heaven knows she's no authority on relationships, so she just listens, sneaking glances out the window.

"He told me he'd like *us* to go to Tel Aviv," Margaret says.

Ian is in the seat ahead, likely listening. Renata might have been flustered by this a couple of weeks ago, but the two of them have found their way back to their old friendship, with a bit more knowledge of each other now.

"What a prat," Linda says.

"I wish people would just be *honest*!" Margaret says.

From where the bus lets them off, it's a steep hike, dusty and hot, to the top of a rock plateau overlooking the Dead Sea. Within the fortress, ancient defense walls delineate storehouses, porticos, baths, and cisterns. Castle rooms. Ruins. The team examines the trenches and balks of recent digs. Professor Shomron tells of Yigael Yadin's major excavations here, the unearthing of Herod's retreat, including wall paintings and scrolls and a fragment of the Bible, chapters four to six of the Book of Genesis. She leads them to a mosaic floor in the western palace. "Notice the choice of motifs. Figs and vine leaves. Rosettes. Nothing in the patterns to religiously offend."

They view the synagogue and the ritual bath, one of the earliest found in Palestine, and Professor Shomron speaks of the sherds and whole jars found here, some inscribed with names, possibly of the last defenders casting lots to determine who should die first. Renata walks out toward the plateau's edge to look at the scalloped water, the sun's prism light. She turns back, shivering despite the heat, as she takes in the site, the acts of desperate self-determination: parents choosing to kill themselves and their children rather than let them be taken.

On the bus ride back, Margaret and Linda are quiet, and Renata closes her eyes.

"I'm sorry," her mother had said, over and over in the hospital one night, her lips cracked and dry. "I'm sorry."

"It's all right, Mum, you have nothing to be sorry for," Renata had repeated back. But her mum couldn't be appeased. She had a reservoir of unspoken regret.

The other day, Ian had asked her, "Why are you so shy to put your ideas forward in conference? You're as smart—smarter—

than any of us." With a mother so determined to conceal her, cover over their past, she wonders if she'll ever feel secure in who she is.

Is *that* what her mum was sorry for? Always trying to remake her, never encouraging her in her work. Would she have been proud to know Renata was here?

Why not cover your hair? I've sewn a pile of new kerchief-squares.

I don't want you mentioning old German storybooks. Look at the English classics I found for you at the library.

No, I'm not going make you spätzle. I didn't bring the press.

If anyone asks, you can say you're of Swiss descent.

Years of it. By now, Renata can't remember a time she felt confident asserting herself. She's always wavering, unable to break from the spectator line. Unsure of where she belongs.

She opens her eyes to the passing scenery, grove after grove of newly planted trees, trunks thin and stalky, swaying in the wind. Saplings taking to the soil, staking a *homeland*—a notion, a word, as complicated as it is elusive.

The girl doesn't remember her given name or the lullaby, Oj lulaj, lulaj, *that soothed her to sleep; the smell of beets and frying onion; the flutter of embroidered curtains, bright as her mother's smile.*

She doesn't remember the park, the soldiers with their cold wolf eyes, her mama's frantic screams, "No, no! Please! Not my little girl, not my Renia!"

She has other toys to play with, and new songs to learn; she has the baking and eating of tiny wrapped cakes. Beneath her feet, a whole world to discover.

In time, I grow dingy and coated in dust. The girl hardly notices me amid the thick books that crowd my bureau perch. Outside the window, fog and rain, and inside, still the scents of sugar and vanilla.

One day, when spring sunlight streams in, the velvet-eyed lady reaches for me and puts me inside a square. High walls, a closed top. It is dark and the air wafting in smells of mothballs and cedar.

I don't see the girl anymore.

23

ROGER
1960

Roger's older cousins get married, one after another. Bennie's wedding is held at Kibbutz Neve Ora, where Chasia, his wife-to-be, has grown up, and where Aunt Sarah and Uncle Uri walk Bennie, arm in arm, beneath the chuppah. Roger holds the marriage rings, unbroken circles of gold, and after the ceremony, he listens as one of the guests, a virtuoso violinist who apparently lived here but is now training in Tel Aviv, plays music so breathtaking that, at first, the guests forget to dance.

At twenty-one, Roger wishes for companionship of his own, someone to share his life with. He's been boxed away with his thoughts, but there's something about the day's waning light, the violinist's notes, the young women in their pretty dresses, and the looks passing between couples as they dance, that pushes him past the *Cogito*.

His parents gave him up to *live*. Roger has grappled with mind, not body, perhaps because the number six million was too big to contemplate. Perhaps because his parents were lost within that number, as he, too, would have been if not for their arranging his safety. They saved him. It didn't matter if he was to be Jewish or Catholic. What mattered was his life, his humanity, even if, for Madame Mercier, what mattered was his soul.

Not long ago, Henri sent Roger a joke:

What is Mind?
No Matter.

What is Body?
Never Mind.

It's time to embrace duality, Roger thinks, as unbidden grief rises: if he is ever to walk beneath a wedding chuppah, he'll walk without his parents' steadying arms on either side.

People mill about. To the side of the violinist is a girl Roger noticed earlier, curls to her shoulders, a sweet expression in her brown button eyes. He could ask her to dance, or bring her a glass of wine and start up a conversation. But his mind is swirling today, even more than usual. He turns away from the festivities and weaves through a garden of tall, spindly herbs.

Down the path, he comes upon a most striking array of photographs. Strung on lines, tied between rooted posts, a tented, sheltering canopy: *Home at Neve Ora: A Retrospective.* As he walks through, he sees *Series I—XVI.* Children, here from forest huts, orphanages, DP camps. Hidden and found.

Each picture displays a single child alone, caught in a candid moment, angles of light deeply contrasting a darkness, a pinprick hole at their center. Roger looks at the faces in squares, one after another, and he recognizes the slip-through grief, the patching effort, the fear tinged with longing.

Watching Bennie at the ceremony, his face so full of tender, hopeful love, Roger had nearly cried. Now he lets the tears well and stream down his cheeks. He has doubted divinity, yes. But he doesn't doubt this, hope amid dislocation. A moment of human communion.

Roger writes to Henri a serious letter, full of questions. Not the questions about oceans and bees he'd listed in his notebook years earlier while in the tucked-away house in Spain with Brother Jacques, but questions about Sister Brigitte, Father Louis, and

Madame Mercier. He wishes to learn whatever he can about the role they played in the battle for his soul, stealing him over the mountains, hiding him from the courts and his family.

Weeks later, a return letter arrives. Roger feels an uptick in his heartbeat, a slight tremor in his hand as he opens the envelope. He scans the pages quickly, searching Henri's orderly script for names. He comes across news of Madame Mercier first. As the organizer of Roger's flight from justice, she was jailed without release until Roger was found and delivered to his aunt Sarah in Paris. Yet she remains unchastened, as strident as ever—still seeking influence in Marseille's political circles. Henri squeezes in a joke about a squid (*"How does a squid go into battle? Well-armed."*), which makes Roger laugh.

Henri reports that Madame Mercier is almost never at Sainte Marie's nowadays. Also, the bully, Albert, is long gone. He works in a bank.

> But enough with the bad apples. Father Louis is safe and well, though quite old. The most important thing you need to know is that Sister Brigitte, who was also jailed, though only for three nights, fought most strenuously for your return to your family. She went against Madame Mercier and all who complied, arguing for you to be with the relatives closest to your mère et père.

Roger has been standing at his desk, hardly breathing. Now he drops into his chair.

Henri goes on to write how Sister Brigitte could have been excommunicated for her views, but she refused to back down. Eventually Father Louis came to her side *against the papal order*, and when Brother Jacques returned, they deposed Madame Mercier as a trustee of Sainte Marie's.

Roger pauses in his reading. He remembers Sister Brigitte sitting beside him on the garden bench, reading his stories, encouraging him always to express himself. She championed him, and the others at Sainte Marie's realized the fault of their ways and championed him, too. Except Madame Mercier . . .

> *Another thing to know is that we have your book,* La Liberté Vaut le Nom, *in our library. None of us completely understand its contents, but we're certain it's the best tome on our shelves— and our collection is far more extensive than last you were here.*
>   *So: if you were ever to visit, please know that you'd find welcome. You have family here, too.*

> *Your Friend and Brother,*
>   *Henri.*

> *Ps. There's a new bakery with croquembouche. Otherworldly.*

Roger looks over at his shelves of books, filled with questions about the nature of the universe, our capacity for knowledge and meaning, what it is to be a person. His own recent publication, a polished version of his master's thesis, is there, too.

He folds and tucks the letter into his shirt pocket, to be read over again. Even after all this time, Roger thinks he can picture Henri. Rising in the dark for matins, hair tousled. Greeting Brother Jacques in the corridor, the two of them shuffling toward the chapel. A riddle before they pray.

He gathers up his papers for seminar before Friday-night dinner at Aunt Sarah's.

24

OSKAR
1960

Oskar travels by plane, by train, then by foot, inhaling the crisp, hay-scented air, gazing out at the farms and fields as he walks eastward toward the Dąbrowskis'. The trees tell him he is nearly home. Tall and stately, canopying the lane. He puts a hand to the trunk of a thick oak, staring up at its leafy branches.

He stops at the church he attended as a child. Outside, it's just as he remembers: painted blue with three black-hatted domes, large crosses carved into the heavy white doors. He pulls one of the doors open. The ornate interior is unchanged but for an array of lit candles in a deep copper sand tray. Scents of wax, incense, and flame.

He slides into a pew, looking at the gold-painted crosses nested in blue arches, the pale and somber depictions of Christ in gilded frames. He'd felt so comfortable here, on Stazja's lap or nestled between Agata and Józef. It took a long time to find a Jewish sensibility. He only found his path to it, he realizes now, through music. Tzofia's haunting compositions unlocking a history lost to him. Violin notes from an upstairs room, flickering candles and liquid sleep, a truck stopped among poppies. All before he lost *this*.

It is silent here and Oskar shifts on the hard wood. He departs and continues walking, past a cluster of birch, the white bark peeling in curls. Closer. A pounding in the cage of his chest. Neighbors' houses with familiar, brightly painted shutters: the

Lises, the Niemcyks, the Nowaks. And then he is at the Dąbrow-skis' fields. He gathers his breath and listens for birds.

Finally, he comes to stand at the farmhouse door. He knocks and Ciocia Agata opens it. Her hair is lighter, her face lined, but her pale sea eyes are just the same, brimming with happy tears. They embrace one another, tight. She is *small*. He is taller than her by a foot.

She leads him inside, then steps out to call for Józef. On the living room wall is the embroidery with the yellow-breasted birds perched around the scripted words *Dzień Dobry*. On the floor, the narrow-striped rugs, crisscrossed to cover the room. Everything as it was. When he sees the nesting boxes on the side table, he kneels down, running his finger over the flower carved into the outer box. He opens the lid, inhaling the faded boxwood scent.

Agata steps back inside, puts a hand on his shoulder. He stands.

"Oskar," she says, "you must know, we never wanted you to be taken."

"I know."

"That woman offered me money, but I refused."

He nods, understanding Agata's Polish, even if he's slow to conjure his own. He remembers what she said back then: *They are mine. Ours.* He felt the same.

"We should have fled together. Gone to a place where no one knew," she says.

"You had the farm," he says.

"I had no idea she'd *steal* you. Both of you vanished. We saw later, a truck had driven over the far field."

"Yes."

"We had no chance of finding you. No—"

Her face is anguished. She pulls him in for an embrace.

"It was the most terrible thing. We couldn't eat or sleep. You were just *gone*."

Józef comes in from the field. He, too, looks older, smaller. Gray peppers his beard. His eyes glisten, happy, as he puts an arm around Oskar's shoulder.

"Son," he says.

Oskar hands them a gift, wrapped in paper, from his satchel. "I made something for you both."

Agata and Józef unwrap it to find a hinged box. On top and bottom, squares in alternating light and dark woods. The box opens into a chessboard, with the game's intricately carved pieces inside. Oskar looks down at it, pleased, knowing it's his best work.

"It's a treasure," Agata says.

She shows him his whittled birds, still on the windowsill in the room where he and Stazja slept. Atop the bureau, his other carvings: a small flute, a spoon, several acorn tops, a whistle. A spear, its point sharp.

"We spoke to the priest, you know. We'd hoped to adopt you." She stops. Looks at him. "But maybe leaving was better? You've had the chance to study? Your parents would have liked that you—"

"I never wanted to leave. Stazja . . ." A bitterness rises inside him that he wishes he didn't feel. "She remembered before."

Agata gives a quick shake of her head. "Even after the war, Poland was no place for Jews. Klara Niemczyk shunned us when she learned you weren't my sister's children, though others seemed to know already. No matter. Tell us, how is Anastazja doing?"

"She has a little boy, and a new baby coming. To be honest, I don't see much of her."

Agata frowns. "She protected you, you know. She came to me every few weeks, asking if your curls could be cut shorter." She looks up at his head of hair, wavy and dark, in need of a cut now. She goes on. "She learned all the church rituals and prayers so you would copy her—and I know she kept you from swimming with the Nowak boys in case they saw . . ." Agata trails off, pink rising to her cheek.

Oskar didn't remember any of this, but he thinks of what Ana said to him, that she always had to watch.

"Ciocia, do you remember 'The Magic Box'?"

"Oh, I haven't thought of that story in ages!"

"I made one," he says, miming the cutting of hair for the strings, "for Tzofia." He's written of her in his letters.

"Anastazja told us you always loved the violin."

That afternoon, Agata makes Oskar's favorite borscht and *uszka* dumplings for supper. Afterward, Józef steps out to finish his chores.

Agata goes to her room and returns with a gold ring cupped in the center of her palm.

"Your mother pinned this to your diaper. It should be with you."

Oskar stares at the band, bright and glinting. After a long moment, he says, "No, she meant it for you—"

"But you should have something of hers."

He closes Agata's hand around the ring. "You are the only mother I remember."

The next day, Oskar and Józef walk through the woods. At first, neither speaks. Oskar is hesitant to break into Józef's quiet. But then he sees a ringed plover and, out of old habit, he points to it. Józef smiles, a dimple pulling at the base of his cheek. A bit later, when both call out a corncrake at the same time, they laugh. Józef puts his hand on Oskar's back.

"Do you know—there have been foxes here, more than when you were a little boy."

"You've seen them?"

"Yes. Red and scrawny. Not getting enough to eat."

"How many?"

"I've seen four, but I have reason to believe there's more."

"A skulk's worth?" Oskar asks, smiling, his Polish really returning now.

"Yes, Oskar, a skulk's worth."

Over the course of his stay, Oskar helps Józef reinforce the coops and repair several fences. His boyhood experiences, out in the fields and inside the house, whittling, listening to Agata's stories, all of it has rushed back to him. He has such happy memories here. Unlike Stazja, who felt burdened with the responsibility for him.

As he walks through the woods, breathing in scents of sweet moss and pine, he thinks about how he's wished Szymon could come to the farm. He feels a sense of responsibility for Szymon, his best friend, mostly alone; and he knows Szymon feels responsibility for him. But it's different from what his sister felt. Stazja was charged with Oskar's safety when she was still just a child, in need of protection herself.

One afternoon Oskar shoos Agata from the kitchen and cooks them dinner, a stuffed cabbage dish Tzofia taught him to make in Shmuel's cramped apartment kitchen. They sit a long time at the table, reminiscing. After the dishes are cleared, Józef brings Oskar's chess set to the table.

"It's beautiful, Oskar. The board, and every single piece," Agata says.

"Nicer than my grandfather's set," Józef says.

"It was all the whittling," Oskar says as Józef sets them up to play.

The morning he's to depart, Agata holds up a lunch bag she's prepared for him. "I've packed a few other things in here, as well. The photograph of your parents that Anastazja kept by her pillow. She'll want to have it."

"I'll get it to her. Thank you."

"I know you don't have memories of her, but your mother cherished you. She told me, she would have named you 'miracle' if she could." Agata reaches for the basket on the high kitchen shelf. "This was left by the side of the road to let us know that your parents were gone."

He peers in at the two stones, round and smooth, nestled amid faded moss and feathers. "I remember Stazja found it. You had us make a nest for the stones."

"Yes," she says.

Oskar lifts out a small yellow feather, its barbs still downy, its shaft white. He returns it to the basket. All he knows of childhood is here. He kisses Agata on the cheek and returns the basket to the shelf.

On the train Oskar opens the bag. In addition to a lunch and the framed photograph for Stazja, he finds a small package and a note with his name on it.

Oskar, you are a son to me. I want you to have this, as a gift from both of your mothers. The smallest nesting box, and inside it, the ring.

He knows who he wishes to wear it.

Oskar proposes to Tzofia under the perfect tree in Tel Aviv, a giant sycamore on Oliphant Street that looks like two trees standing side by side but is one. As he slides the ring onto her finger, Tzofia looks at it, her expression serious.

He's fearful she is going to say no. He knows her music comes first; he can accept this, if only they can also share a life together. He lifts her face to see.

Her eyes look to be swimming, wet. Smiling.

"How did I manage to find you?" she asks and puts her soft lips on his.

He could burst.

"You'll be my husband, but you smell like my luthier grandfather," she says, nuzzling her face against his neck, laughing. "The wood varnish, I think."

"So this is why you love me? Because I smell like your grandfather?"

"This and many other reasons."

They sit at the tree's base, their heads bent together, their bodies close. Oskar presses his hand to a massive root, hoping it will convey his joy all the way back to the Dąbrowskis.

At Neve Ora, Oskar finds his sister in the darkroom even though, at this stage of her pregnancy, she can barely fit in the tight space. His nose burns with the chemical stink.

"Stazja, are you sure it's safe for you to be down here?"

"It's fine. It's mostly just vinegar in the stop bath."

"Still, it may not be—"

"How was your trip?"

"Good. I brought you something."

Ana's round face is like a child's, full of anticipation.

"Ciocia Agata saved it for you." He thinks of what Agata said, that Ana protected him. "You should have come along."

"I couldn't travel. Anyway, I wasn't sure they wanted to see me."

"Of course they wanted to! They kept asking after you. Here."

Ana lets out a small gasp when she sees the photograph.

Together they look at their parents' handsome, happy faces, not much older than they are now.

"By the way, I'm getting married," Oskar says.

The frame for the chuppah is made of cypress, and Oskar carves doves into the four posts. Tzofia wraps it with delicate fabric, tucking flowers into its folds. On the day of the wedding, Ana holds one corner, Szymon another, Adina the third, and Rivka Levy the fourth. Gathered just outside, Boaz bounces Ari and baby Iris, one in each arm, while Gideon, Shmuel, Leah, Rut, Mr. and Mrs. Levy, and several musician-friends of Tzofia's mingle and talk.

Oskar had wanted the wedding to be understated, not like the wild Neve Ora affairs. Now, standing in the courtyard of their new apartment, waiting for Tzofia, he worries that it is too subdued, that he didn't forge enough connections here for a lively wedding, that in his doubts about his own belonging he carved away the spirit of the day. But then Tzofia steps out, stunning. *Happy.* Her own longings—the absences that accompany her notes no matter how high—eclipsed by her excitement and joy.

They stand together, their rings nested in Agata's tiny box, waiting, as the rabbi joins them, his words encircling them closer and closer, so that for these moments the world feels as if it contains only them.

Just before Oskar's foot smashes glass, a pause, each person suspended in a memory of an early love. Another's breath mingled with one's own in a field, a hayloft, a garden, a square of sidewalk. And then a shattering, followed by laughter, claps, shouting. A kiss.

The musicians have brought their instruments. At the reception, they play and everyone dances. Oskar holds Tzofia tight in his arms, remembering a story he once heard—did Ciocia Agata tell him, or did he read it somewhere?—of a boy who, after much wandering, found his lost half when, finally, he found his love.

Tzofia keeps to her practice schedule, taking her violin with her on their honeymoon in Eilat. Oskar watches from the veranda as she works to perfect a piece, measure by measure, movement by movement. She places five one-lira coins at the end of a table. Playing the section through without mistake, she slides one coin across. Then she plays the section a second time, and slides the second coin. When she makes a mistake—something Oskar wouldn't notice in a million years—both coins go back and she begins again. She tells him that her first teacher, Pan Skrzypczak, taught her this way.

Oskar thinks, this beauty that Tzofia creates is a gift to the world and he ought not begrudge it. Yet it costs him. She is here with him; they are together. *Married*. But there is a part of her that is elsewhere.

25

ANA
1960

With Oskar's birthday approaching, Ana decides she'll make a copy of their parents' photograph and frame it for him as a gift. She's cherished having the photo back these past months, perched atop her bureau beside Oskar's carvings: Ari's lion, and a flower, new for Iris.

Gingerly, she rotates the frame's metal clips and seeks to lift away the leather backing. She doesn't want the photograph to rip or disintegrate. For a moment, she considers that she could photograph the picture *in* its frame, but she knows it won't look as good. She continues to pry off the back panel, releasing a sharp smell of hide. She comes to a layer of thin cardboard cut to size, then a small square of vellum. She lifts these out and finds herself staring at a different, smaller photograph, pressed behind the picture of their parents.

Ana is confused because it looks to be a photograph of *her* at fourteen or fifteen, which it can't possibly be. A girl with hair and eyes just like hers, holding a bundled-up baby. She turns the photo over. Written in script: *Elżbieta and Mira, 1935*. So, she's the baby.

She thinks a relative—a teenage cousin?—must have come through town near the time of her birth and her parents sprang for a photograph. Someone from her father's large, far-flung family, with whom Ana actually shared her appearance.

Before Ana can get to the darkroom, she comes down with

a flu, the two photographs stowed in the drawer of her bedside table. Over several days in bed, feverish, she is visited by long-ago memories, women with swelling bellies waiting on the garden bench to see her mother. Their shiny faces filled with worry, with hope. Now and then, while chopping vegetables for soup or folding the sun-dried clothes, Mama would say, "Sometimes it takes a miracle to have a family." Ana thinks of those words now with a start. What *kind* of miracle?

She reaches into her drawer for the little photograph, looking from one face to the other. *Elżbieta and Mira*. It doesn't fit: a relative with a name she can't remember her parents ever mentioning. Maybe Elżbieta was a Polish girl from the village who helped her mother as she juggled her midwifery practice and a newborn. But why wouldn't Aunt Freida have been the one helping? Jews and Poles didn't easily mix; that was clear at market. Maybe the girl knew her herbals, or maybe she was a neighbor? But none of this explains why they look so very alike. Or why her parents would go to the expense of having a photograph taken.

She stands up and circles the bedroom she shares with Boaz. Field boots huddled in the corner; a headscarf draped over the doorknob like a question mark. She reaches for the back of a chair, solid wood.

Before Bluma's truck came to take them to the Dąbrowskis', their mother stuffed the picture frame into their satchel. She must have placed the smaller photograph behind the one of her and Papa, so Ana would have it.

Ana looks to the bureau, the lion and flower carvings there. The picture frame, taken to pieces.

She lifts her eyes to the mirror. Her face, new. Like a stranger's.

Next morning, trembly, she boards a bus to see Oskar. Across the aisle, a mother snuggles her young son, nose to nose. Ana stares out the window at the sandy hills. Over and over, her thoughts lead her in directions she doesn't wish to travel.

She arrives at the woodshop, cheeks flushed, hair loosened from its kerchief.

"Is everything all right?" Oskar asks. He brushes the sawdust from his shirt and hair, and steps toward her.

She holds out the photograph.

"This looks old. When was it taken?"

"1935."

"I don't understand."

"It's the year I was born."

"But you're a teenager here."

"That's not me. I'm the baby."

"What? So who is *she*? She looks exactly like—"

Ana buries her face in her hands.

"Stazja?"

"I think maybe she is my mother," she bursts out. "I don't see who else she could be. Her name is Elżbieta." She shows him the writing on the back.

"But that makes no sense, our mother—"

"Was a midwife. What if this girl came to her for help, and. . . ."

They're both silent a moment.

"I don't know, Oskar. Maybe our parents couldn't conceive. Maybe *she* couldn't raise me—she looks so young—and they took me as their own?"

"No, they wouldn't. Anyway, they conceived me."

"*After*. That can happen."

"Stazja, maybe she's someone in our family. A relative."

"I wondered that, too, but I don't think so. She—and I—
don't look like anyone else in the family. Oskar, if she was
Christian . . ."

"If she was Christian, wouldn't she have gone to the church?
Brought the baby to the steps?"

"Not if they decided during the delivery—"

"Would our parents have taken a baby like that?"

"I don't know. The Dąbrowskis took *us*."

"But that was to save us."

"Yes, that's what I mean."

Oskar's eyes move from the photograph to Ana's face. "Where
did you find this?"

Ana thinks of how Chana pinned her wedding ring to Oskar's
diaper. Packed the satchel with Ana's spinning top, the picture
frame. "It was behind their photograph. I went to copy it as a
gift for you and—"

"Who put it there?"

Ana's face contorts. "They must have wanted me to know."

When she returns to Neve Ora, Ana closes herself off in her
room. Boaz comes in to find her crying.

"Chani, what's the matter?" he asks.

Her Hebrew name is no longer a happy echo of her mother's.
Her breath heaves, the room tight. "We have no privacy here. No
space," she says.

He pauses, looks around. "All the rooms are the same, I
think."

"And I want to see Ari and Iris for more than a few hours a
day."

"All right." He speaks as if soothing a child. "Do you want to sign up for additional caretaking shifts? I'm sure some will be in their houses."

"No. I want to spend time *just* with them. And I don't want other women mothering them."

"Everything is communal here, that's how—"

"I know, but it's not right."

"For them?"

"For them and for me."

"I've never heard you like this."

"I'm telling you, it's damaging not to know your mother."

"They know you!"

She begins to sob. "They get passed from lap to lap. We're *all* exchangeable."

"Please, tell me what's going on?"

She rummages through her purse, places the photograph in his hands.

"*No one* ever kept hold of me," she says.

Ana feigns a relapse of fever and stays beneath the bedcovers. Ida knocks on her door, but Ana sends her away. She stares again at the smaller photograph, searching for the truth in it. There is tenderness in Elżbieta's face, the soft cradle of her arms. Yet, at the same time, there is fear in her eyes.

How could she not have been terrified? She would have been disavowed by her parents, expelled from her village. Consigned to a life alone, no way to provide for the two of them. Maybe giving her baby up was a way to save them both. But Ana wonders what has become of her from all this saving.

Boaz comes, midday, to check on her. The faint scent of vinegar clings to him.

"Chani," he says.

She turns to him, the shutter of her eyes open, blank.

Chani. Ana. Anastazja. Mira. Probably she had a different name at the start. Each a lie in its way. Each a fake root, leading her to grow hollow.

26

OSKAR
1960–1963

Ana's discovery sends Oskar and Tzofia spinning, each in different ways.

After his sister left the woodshop, clutching the photograph of her as a baby—with *whom*? a different mother? some teenage Polish girl?—Oskar felt shaky, first in his arms and legs, then fully, head to toe, as if his body had become confused about the blood pulsing in *his* veins. The initial shock shifted to anger. Even as he felt it, he was surprised at its strength. All those times she was gruff with him. Walking past, arm in arm with Ida; ignoring him at the children's homes, caring more for Zissa than for him; hardly ever checking on him during the sea voyage or at the camp in Cyprus; critical of him at Neve Ora for not fitting in. He'd told her, over and over, that he did not want to be captive on Eva's journey, yet she had refused to help him get back to the farm. Instead, she'd insisted that it was right for them to be returned to their roots—roots that weren't even hers to begin with!

He paced circles around the woodshop. The others there watched him warily. Eventually, Shmuel ventured his name, softly, "Yossi." And he slowed, looking around the room. His latest set of nesting boxes perching in the woodshop window. Bits of rosewood, left over from the music stand project, waiting on his worktable to be carved into new chess pieces. His ragged breath grew steadier.

It took weeks for him to cool down completely, took

remembering what Agata had told him: Ana protected him. It took thinking what Szymon counseled: one move leads to the next. That all of this led him to Tzofia. That Stazja is central to him, regardless.

As for Tzofia's reaction, her buried yearnings to find her own mother broke the surface, moving her to sift through lists and registries, piles of records at Yad Vashem. To no avail. She wrote to the convent that harbored her, and to her violin teacher, Pan Skrzypczak. The return letter she received from him, full of relief for her survival and delight at her tremendous musical accomplishments, was a salve, calming her a bit. But soon after their renewed contact, she received word of his death.

Now, Oskar worries over Tzofia's continued agitation, her tumultuous moods. When she plays local concerts with the orchestra—of which she is now a member—Oskar reserves a seat for Szymon, who slips off his shoes unnoticed and presses his feet to the floor, feeling the vibrations. Her playing grows more beautiful every time—Oskar and Szymon both think so—and even she seems pleased with her meteoric progress. Yet her mood remains dark.

Finally she tells him: she is with child.

Joyful, Oskar hugs her tight, but she is limp in his arms. He steps back. "Tzofia?"

"I'm scared. I want to be a parent, but I don't know how—I lost my mother when I was five, my father before that—"

Oskar nods. At Neve Ora, he watched as orphans reared children, became parents. "We'll find our way. We both will."

Oskar remembers how, each day of his visit with Agata and Józef, the Nowaks' stripe-feathered chicken crossed the lane, preferring the Dąbrowskis' land. Agata and Józef stopped their work, and together they returned him. Józef's arm around Agata, Agata's

head bent to Józef's shoulder. A gentle steering of the chicken in
the spring sunshine, back to his flock, his home.

More than anything, Oskar wants to build a family.

Tzofia continues with daytime rehearsals and nighttime concerts
through the pregnancy, traveling between Tel Aviv and Jerusalem,
Haifa, Beersheba, and Ein Gev. She performs in a long, lacy black
dress that stretches as her belly grows. Her schedule includes concerts in Greece and Cyprus.

"After these, you need to stop. You need to *rest*," Oskar tells
her.

"I'm fine," she says.

Luckily Tzofia's last weeks of pregnancy coincide with the
orchestra's off-season; no concerts, no travel. Oskar builds a cus-
tom stool—a match for the music stand he gave her as a wedding gift—so that Tzofia can play, seated, *at home,* until the baby
comes.

Shoshana is born beneath a harvest moon. Together, Oskar
and Tzofia bounce her and cradle her and walk her up and down
the street. Oskar is the one who starts in with the telling of tales.

"Did you know, Shoshana?" he begins:

*Long ago, deep in the jungle, an elephant made a sound by beat-
ing a log with his foot. A monkey started dancing, which rustled the
leaves and made a rattling noise. A crane, landing on a crocodile's
back, ran its beak on the crocodile's scales, adding a new sound. All
the other animals joined in, except for the frogs. They believed their
short legs could not dance or play. This went on for days, the frogs
feeling left out. When, finally, a frog began singing, the other animals
happily matched their beats to the new song. After that they all made
music, together. . . .*

"And now that you know how music came about, let me tell
you how the first violin was made."

When Oskar tells Shoshana the story of "The Magic Box," Tzofia brings out the stringed box along with her violin. She plays animal sounds: a cow's moo, an elephant's trumpet, a donkey's bray, a cricket's chirp. Shoshana giggles and tries to imitate. At bedtime, Tzofia whispers a lullaby about baby chicks waiting for their mama to return home with glasses of tea to drink. Her mother's lullaby. Shoshana rubs at her eyes and blinks, trying her best to stay awake, drifting to sleep.

Tzofia returns to her busy rehearsal schedule. Their closest neighbor, Esther, a woman impatient for her grown children to give her grandchildren, watches Shoshana when she can. There are rumblings about whether Ana and Boaz will leave Neve Ora; if they move to Tel Aviv, the cousins can be together. This is how Oskar and Ana talk of it, "for the cousins," but it's strained.

Some days, Oskar takes Shoshana with him to the woodshop. Despite the loud sounds, the sawing and hammering, she is happy there. Oskar rigs up a curtain to protect her from the wood shavings that permeate the air. Her babbles soon become words, accompanied by signs for communicating with her uncle Szymon, who comes often to Tel Aviv to spend time with Oskar's family and a community of the Deaf.

Shoshana is just three when, entering the concert hall, holding hands with Oskar on one side and Szymon on the other, she lets go to sign "family," then takes both their hands again before weaving down the aisle and settling into her seat. Whereas she bounces and waves her arms to the cacophony of the woodshop, in response to her mother's music Shoshana grows wide-eyed and still.

"Shoshana is right," Szymon signs later to Oskar and Tzofia. "You are my family and this is where I want to be."

Oskar feels a deep joy, remembering the earliest days of their friendship, walking by the river, noticing every flutter of water and wing, Szymon with his sketch pad and he with his whittling projects; close ever since.

"Let me arrange for you to show Shmuel your drawings," he says.

Shmuel, who has met Szymon on various occasions, looks at his work and hires him on the spot. From then on, it's the three of them in the shop amid the whir of saws, the scents of wood and varnish, and an ongoing chess game, set up in the corner.

One day, perusing Oskar's station, piled high with his nesting boxes, Shmuel says, "This box business, Yossi. You must really miss her." He's standing there, stout and oxlike, but with an affectionate grin.

"Who?"

"Your mother."

"I don't understand."

"Well, what is a mother if not a nesting box?"

27

RENATA
1968

Renata and her team enter the nearby university's large auditorium to attend a public lecture. Posters have been up all over, announcing the talk, "On Extant Remains," by a prominent philosophy professor from New York. The first rows of seats are already filled with faculty and graduate students, so they take seats farther back. Settling in, Renata holds her bare arm up to Linda's—both of them tawny now. Robert pulls off his field hat and Margaret sends down a bag of pistachios. They each cram a few nuts into their mouths, and Ian tucks the crinkling bag into his pocket.

After an effusive introduction, the speaker steps up to the podium. He is youthful and hip, with a goatee, black jeans, and a black turtleneck. By way of a joking start he says, "Incidentally, I always wear black clothes; the outfit isn't because I'll be talking about death and dying."

Renata wasn't aware from its title that the lecture would be about death and dying. Ian throws her a concerned look. She adjusts herself in her seat, returns a tentative nod. "On Extant Remains" is surely of archaeological interest. Anyway, how painful could a philosopher's musings be?

"Is death a *harm* to an individual who has died?" he launches right in. "This is a question I'd like to explore today. And I'd like to begin with Epicurus, to whom I owe the title of this talk. Epicurus's commitment to intrinsic hedonism prompted him to say, in his 'Letter to Menoeceus,' that 'everything good and bad lies in sensation.' To quote:

> *'Make yourself familiar with the belief that death is nothing to us, since everything good and bad lies in sensation, and death is to be deprived of sensation. . . . So that most fearful of all bad things, death, is nothing to us, since when we are, death is not, and when death is present, then we are not.'*

"Focused on sensation as Epicurus was, he believed that, if a person's death is not an experience that they have, then it *cannot* be a harm. However," the philosopher says, looking around the room, "the same can't be said about *dying*."

Renata's pulse quickens. Her mum's last miserable months, wasting away in pain, regressing. In the front row, academics scribble in notebooks. One, in profile, isn't writing, but is clearly thinking, his forehead in furrows. A rogue curl sticks up at the top of his head and he has a pencil behind his ear.

The speaker delves into the logic leading Epicurus to his conclusion that death, if not experienced, is neither intrinsically nor extrinsically harmful to the dead. "On this same logic," he says, "if dying *is* an experience, a sensation, then the harm thesis would hold." He pauses dramatically.

"Now, coming back to the state of already being dead." Another pause. "We are deprived of life by its ending. But aren't we also deprived of life by its not *beginning* sooner? Notice, we don't ordinarily find it objectionable that we failed to exist prior to being alive. And it's most likely that the way things were for us prior to existing is how things will be after death ends our existence. So, *is* there harm in death?"

A few people murmur, impressed, but Renata bristles at the

reduction of human loss to some sort of mental game. The fact remains, her mum is gone, and they'll never be together in this life again.

When the lecture is over, she whispers to Linda, "I'll meet you by the door," and walks to the back of the auditorium to gather herself, her head in her hands. She hears, "I'm very sorry," and looks up. It's the professor with the pencil behind his ear. His eyes are wide with concern. "I doubt that our speaker has experienced the death of anyone close to him."

She gives a weak smile. "No, probably not."

He lingers. She senses that he, too, was upset by the lecture and is puzzled by his own feelings. "To come *here* and talk as if death may not have been a harm to all who perished . . ." He takes a breath. "Sorry," he repeats, and she gulp-laughs now, because, even in his accented English—Hebrew mixed with something else, she's not sure what—he apologizes like a Brit.

She rejoins the team and they walk back to the lab, but instead of going straight in, they take to the couches in the lounge area. After a while, Robert says, "I suppose the alternative to dying would be to live forever, and maybe that's not the best thing?"

"Not for the planet," Margaret says, "or the rest of creation."

"No, but it *would* be nice if we could freeze certain moments, at least make the best times last longer," Ian says.

"Let us see some of your frozen moments, Ian! You must carry photographs of Olivia and little Mark," Linda says.

Ian pulls a few photographs from his wallet and passes them around. Renata's eyes linger on the picture of him kneeling on the floor beside his son, working on a puzzle. She loved doing puzzles with her papa. Her favorite wooden one, each piece fitting sturdily in place, with a fairy-tale scene of a large stork delivering a white-bundled baby to a villager's arched door. ("That *st*ork *st*ands on *st*ick legs." "But its *b*eak doesn't *b*other the *b*aby.")

The next to come around is a picture of Olivia, her head resting on Ian's shoulder.

"You make such a sweet couple," Margaret says. "What about you, Renata? Anyone special in your life?"

"Well, Bertrand brightens when I come into the Ashmolean," Renata jokes, and they all laugh. The elderly curator of coins at the museum is an institution himself.

"He has a bow tie for every occasion," Robert quips.

"I am just not sure you're his type," Linda says.

They sit close, legs extended to the battered coffee table and ratty orange rug. Sunlight pours in from the side window, and the lab's glass door reveals its tall counters, cluttered with specimen trays, microscopes, and cleaning tools. Maybe this is what home is supposed to feel like.

28

ANA
1961–1965

Maybe there is no real home for a person who has been passed mother to mother to mother. It is Ana's impulse, since her discovery, to take her children into possession and raise them not communally, but intimately, as a family.

She doesn't want visiting hours with her children. She doesn't want their connection proscribed, finite, and she doesn't want to wait all day to see them. She spent her childhood waiting for her parents to come for her; then she waited as she was transferred, home to home, never landing. She doesn't want Ari and Iris to know that feeling.

Early morning, she and Boaz dress for the workday, planning to return in the afternoon for the children's visit.

"This isn't right for me anymore," she says.

Boaz brings her hand to his lips. "Your birth origins don't matter to anyone here. Besides, you've never cared what others think."

"It's not about my birth origins. I've realized what I need, and what our children need. I don't want us living this way, separated, the children reared by whoever is on the sign-up sheet. *I'm* their mother."

"We're building something communally. *Re*building—"

"We can build our family, raise our children together, just the two of us."

He lets go. "I'm speaking of something bigger, something we can depend on."

The kibbutz was a long-held dream for both of them; Boaz's, since his time in the Naliboki forest, and Ana's, since hearing Eva's stories in the Lodz children's home. Maybe Ana's was more fantasy than dream. Everything is different now. She wants to go, even if it means leaving Ida and her other friends here. "I have lost my foundations. I can't build something bigger until I build a small thing first."

"Chani—"

"Please, Boaz, say you'll think about it."

For the next several weeks, Boaz keeps his distance, staying away except for sleep and for the children's visiting hours, during which he fixes his attention solely on Ari and Iris. He throws himself into field chores, the darkroom, meetings he never used to attend. Ana leaves the room only when work demands it. He snipes, "If you want more time with the children, you'll need to get out of the room."

Oskar appears unexpectedly at Ana's door. She takes a step back, puts a hand to her unkempt hair. She blinks at him in the bright sun. Has he gotten taller? Is his hair a shade lighter?

"I thought I'd check on you," he says.

They stand awkwardly a minute, his calm disarming her.

"Let's take a walk, Stazja."

She hesitates but he coaxes her along the curving Neve Ora paths to the herb garden they used to tend together. A gathering wind rears up, causing the tall billowy plants to sway and bend. Oskar carefully steps through the garden, tamping at the base of each plant, reinforcing its place, rooted in the soil.

They sit under the sycamore tree, shelter from past storms.

Oskar stays quiet. Ana wonders if this, her *unmooring*, is what he has felt ever since being taken from the Dąbrowskis. If Chana and Zvi aren't her parents . . .

She's scared to look at Oskar. "It seems you're not my brother," she says finally.

"I'll always be your brother," he says.

She sways toward him, folds into his embrace.

She has almost nothing to go on to find out more about her mother.

A given name: Elżbieta. No surname.

An approximate birth date: 1920. Was she fifteen when she had Ana, in 1935? She may have been younger than that, or older. In the photograph she just looks young.

A possible location: Brzeziny. She gave birth there, but she may have lived in any one of the surrounding villages, traveling to avoid recognition.

Yet Ana wants to learn what she can. She photographs the small picture and heads to the darkroom to make copies. Boaz is there, silent at her arrival. She lingers awkwardly for a couple of minutes.

"Are you finished with the developing trays?" she asks.

"Yes, go ahead."

In the tight space, they'd ordinarily touch, but she steps around him. She knocks into the table. He put his hands out to steady the trays of shifting stop bath and fixer.

"I'll help you," he says.

They create duplicates of the photograph and Ana composes a letter, explaining her search and requesting any leads. She copies the letter on two separate sheets of paper, encloses a photo in each, and posts them to the Brzeziny town registry and the Saint Nicholas church.

With every piece of mail Ana receives hereafter, her breath snags momentarily on hope.

It's not Neve Oran in spirit, but Ana maneuvers child-caring shifts in *her* children's rooms, and now, seeing more of Ari and Iris than family hours provide, she lets herself fully feel what she couldn't before. She marvels when Ari clasps a thick book in his arms and settles in the corner to turn its colorful pages, and when Iris extends her pinky finger to feed "nectar" to a nursery room of pretend baby butterflies. She revels in Ari's love of stories, especially myths, and Iris's imagination, her nurturing instinct. She thinks to show Ari a myrtle bush, its leaves said to be favored by Aphrodite, and to show Iris field marigolds, beloved by butterflies (and birds and rabbits). She is still dismantled—the small photograph now leans beside the larger one on her bureau, her head a swirl of confusion—and yet spending this extra time with her children settles her. At least she knows she is theirs and they are hers.

Late one night in bed, Boaz says, "I've been going to weekly committee meetings."

Ana doesn't look over at him. She holds herself straight and still, staring into the darkness.

He rolls to face her. "We're not a true socialist democracy. We exclude those who can't work; we don't distribute resources in a way that's actually equal."

"I've complained that the domestic chores are still mainly assigned to women," she says.

"So, if we were to leave"—his eyes finding hers—"I would be all right with it."

Ana buries her face in his chest.

"Especially if we can live near Oskar and Tzofia," he adds. "Our families should be close by."

Shmuel passes a tip to Oskar about a job opening at a printing press, a good fit for Boaz. They pack up and move to a small Tel Aviv apartment. Ana strives to create a warm home, furniture courtesy of Oskar, coverlets and curtains sewn by her own hand. She pots lilacs on the patio and improvises a rock bench to sit by them. Herbs in planters span the entire length of the windowsill. She shops and cooks, and she mothers Ari and Iris, not by committee, not by collective, but directly and on her own.

Still, she misses the community of Neve Ora, misses her friends. The people in neighboring apartments here nod hello as they walk by with groceries, fiddle their keys into locks, then close their doors. She manages brief conversations with other mothers at the playground, but nothing comes of it. No instant friendships, as she had with Ida.

"It takes time," Boaz assures her, though he, too, is out of his element, puttering around in the evening, when he'd ordinarily be at council meetings.

In the park one day, Iris cries and cries, and though Ana holds her close, Iris doesn't stop. Ana checks her for cuts, bruises, wetness. She takes her up into her arms, suddenly unsure how to do this, feeling herself as helpless as a child. A woman passing by says, sympathetically, "Sometimes, all we can do is be there with them."

Eva comes for a visit, and she and Ana take a walk together. Ana says, "I didn't belong at Neve Ora anymore."

Eva is quiet, so Ana continues. "I think we've done the right thing for the children and for ourselves, but I wonder if there's anywhere I belong. I'm the daughter of three mothers." She looks sideways at Eva. "Four." She chokes out a laugh. It doesn't conceal the pain, the monumental effort she is making for the sake of her new family: to view her past, not through the lens of abandonment but through the lens of necessity.

Eva half smiles, that ever-present grief in her eyes. "Well. I believe each of your mothers dearly loved you. The love doesn't stop."

Now Ana is quiet.

Eva digs into her pocket and removes a tattered finger puppet, a frayed and rumpled sheep. "My mother knit this little ewe for my Rachela. Only neither of them survived."

Ana takes hold of Eva's hand.

"I've tortured myself over all of it. Leaving my baby buried there, bringing other children here—some who wished to come, some who didn't. I've had no choice but to believe in resilience," Eva says. "We will reroot, if given the chance."

Palm fronds rustle in the wind. Eva looks thin enough to blow away.

Ana considers her own circumstances. She was given up twice, but not to the earth. She was given up to live, to grow, to see children of her own.

"The love doesn't stop," Eva says once more.

When, in wintertime, Oskar is preparing a package to send to the Dąbrowskis, he asks Ana if she'll take a family photograph and develop it. She arrives with her camera, Boaz and the children, too. As Oskar, Tzofia, and Shoshana begin arranging themselves in a well-lit spot, Oskar interrupts. "Stazja, they'll want *you* in it, too. All of you. Your family." So they huddle together and Szymon, who is over, takes the photograph.

A few days later, Ana returns with the picture for the Dąbrowskis' package, and a copy of the old photograph, framed in a brushed silver casing, of Chana and Zvi. She hands it to Oskar, aware of the muddled connections between the four of them, aware that he doesn't share in the same memories. Yet she can't doubt that he is her brother.

Oskar places it on the living room shelf beside other family photographs. He has features like theirs but no remembered history. It is the same for Ana with Elżbieta. They have the same face, yet Ana cannot conjure a single smell, a look, a moment of connection.

"Can you include this in the box?" She passes him a card for Agata.

When Boaz is at the press, Oskar at the woodshop, and Tzofia at rehearsal, Ana spends her days with Ari and Iris and Shoshana. The play hopscotch on the patio and hide-and-seek. After a snack at the table, Ana brings out paper and colored pencils. Ari draws a picture of Zeus, thunderbolt in hand, atop Mount Olympus. Iris leans over Shoshana, helping her to grip a pencil in her fist, showing her how to form a *shin*, the first letter of her name, though Shoshana manages only marks and scribbles.

Ana commits herself to Jewish ritual because, whether or not it's her birthright, it's the ground where she's rooted. Boaz is displeased at first. He considers religion a bourgeois convention, inegalitarian and sexist. But Ana explains that fulfilling the customs carries her to a remembered place of belonging, of something shared.

She hosts Oskar's family on Friday nights, saving up for a small silver wine cup. She bakes a weekly challah and lights candles, the rhythm of it soothing, familiar, and warm. Closing her eyes, waving her arms before the flame, Ana thinks, Chana and Zvi could be here in the scents of yeast and fire, and her cellular origins don't have to matter, she is their child. She remembers standing beside Chana at the stove, adding teaspoons of honey into boiling pots of elixir; Zvi's praise at the steadiness of her small hands. She wishes Oskar remembered life with them, felt the same way; but at least he's here, Tzofia at his side, Shoshana in his arms.

She embroiders a matzah cover and afikomen bag in time for Passover, and other memories pull at her: Agata, teaching her to cross-stitch, a sampler with flowers and herbs; the gold-threaded rosary bag she carried on Easter.

At Hanukkah, Oskar arrives with three hand-carved dreidels, one for each of the children. Ana reaches for Shoshana's before she can put it into her mouth. It feels, in her hand, like her old spinning top, and now Ana considers the older girl at the market who gave it to her: darting through the Jewish section, shimmery hair and wide eyes like hers. Pressing the top into Ana's little palm, then holding for a beat, looking just a moment longer, before hurrying away. It was *her*.

In the course of years, the children grow as tall as the lilacs potted on the patio. Ari races around wearing an Olympic crown made of paper-cut leaves, while Iris carefully crafts a Pan flute from drinking straws. Ana develops a network of friends in the building and around the neighborhood. She and Boaz find their way to a close, settled happiness.

Still, she can't ignore the dangers of living here, old anxieties roiling her anew. Reports of an ambush on a bus from Eilat to Tel Aviv. A killing of hikers in the Judean desert. Ana has the same cramping in her stomach when she hears of Arabs killed in retaliatory fire, refugees killed in skirmishes at the borders. Fearful, she hesitates to plan adventures with the children.

"We have to go about our lives," Boaz says.

Ana sees in his eyes the wish that he could promise to protect them.

On Ana's thirtieth birthday, Ari and Iris present her with a joined box of burled acacia wood, engraved with flowers along the sides and a shiny gold clasp for opening and closing—clearly Oskar's work.

"It's for your treasures, Mama," Iris says.

Ana wraps both children into a hug. "You're my treasures."

"But we're too big to fit!" Iris says.

"Pandora's box had bad things inside," Ari says.

"I promise, I won't keep bad things inside *this* box."

"Except hope. Hope clung to the inside," Ari amends, exacting about his myths.

"I'll keep small treasures and hope."

"How can you keep hope inside a box?" Iris asks.

"Why don't we stop by the woodshop later," she says to their delight. "I bet your uncle will know."

29

RENATA
1968

Renata pops into a bakery to buy chocolate rugelach. The man who spoke to her after the death and dying lecture is there. He has the same rogue curl sticking up and, in the daylight, out of the dimness of the auditorium, she sees that his eyes are a deep amber. He nods his recognition and, looking around, says, "I always come, hopeful that they'll bake baguette." The cases hold pastries and cakes, no long loaves of bread.

"I'm here for the rugelach," Renata says. "You know what they say, *When in Rome* . . . And I'm an archaeologist, so I take that sort of thing seriously."

He laughs, a warm ringing. "Well, I'm a philosopher and I like rugelach, so I'll get some, too."

She buys a large box for the team to share. Back at the dig, they maul it.

Their work continues, early mornings on-site, followed by long afternoons in the lab. Several nights in a row, Renata returns to her room so tired that she practically pours herself, liquid, into bed. She wakes more than once to find her magnifying glass in the pocket of her pajama pants, and laughs.

She is energized being here. It is sunny and hot and people *communicate* with each other. Not the stuttering reserve of gray, rainy England. Even Margaret and Yonatan sorted themselves out when Yonatan apologized about taking Irit to Tel Aviv, saying he believed they had an open relationship, and Margaret accepted his apology, no hard feelings, and ended it. Best to know where things stand.

On her next day off, Renata decides to return to Tel Aviv. She has been thinking about the chess sets she saw there, despite knowing that (a) she doesn't need one, and (b) it's already going to be cumbersome, flying home with the nesting boxes she bought from the same shop. Still, the game boards were beautiful and the playing pieces wholly unique. Her father would have *loved* a set like that, and today, that's tugging at her.

As she finds her way back to the neighborhood, she thinks, at the very least, she can treat herself to lunch at the same falafel stand—the best she's had. She retraces her route, once again passing the market tables with bright jelly candies. She sees a florist's shop she didn't notice last time, a bouquet of lilies in the window. She keeps a lookout for the carpentry shop at the end of the block.

Just outside the door, she's caught off-guard by a scent. She knows it—a cooking scent from long ago—but she can't place from where or when. She closes her eyes, breathing it in. Is it coming from inside? She enters the woodshop, and rather than inquiring about chess sets, she asks, "Do you know what that smell is?"

The same man who helped her with the nesting boxes steps around his worktable, brushing the sawdust from his shoulders. He cocks his head and says, a bit embarrassed, "It's *knedle* with"—he searches for the English word—"plum? My sister is cooking upstairs."

"Knödel? A German food?"

"We call it *knedle*. Sweet dumpling, from Poland."

The aroma is even stronger than out on the street. She inhales, wondering if her parents had Polish friends in Tübingen who cooked something like it when she was a little girl. They never took her to Poland.

Renata eventually turns her attention to the chess sets, examining the expert carving and wood joinery. A woman, presumably the woodworker's sister, bustles in from the back stairs carrying a large covered baking dish. Her hair shimmers white and she has blue eyes—more the type to be Renata's sister than his. She is thanking another man, the shop owner, for use of the kitchen.

"It's good. We're drawing customers," the shop owner says, looking Renata's way.

Renata smiles. "It smells delicious."

"I can't take credit. It's an old family recipe," the sister says.

"Your mother's?" Renata asks.

"One of them," the sister answers, eyes on her brother.

Renata glances between the siblings, confused. "Well. Let me take this," she points to the chess set, "and leave before I purchase more than I can carry with me on a plane."

Outside the shop, toting her bundle, Renata thinks of everything she has to pack, all the stuff she's bought while here, on top of all the stuff in Oxford, her mum's things to be sifted through. Maybe she can just pile the boxes into a moving van and look through them later, when her feelings aren't so raw?

While crossing the street, Renata is almost hit by a bicycle. She jumps out of the way, her glasses flying. The rider, bushy-bearded, sporting his own pair of thick glasses, skids to a stop. A rabbinical type, without the garb. He leans down to pick up her glasses, intact, on the curb and hands them to her. She puts them on, still a bit disoriented. Before riding off, he says, "When your eyes aren't pointed in the right direction, no pair of glasses will help you see."

Early morning, the archaeologists working in the south quadrant discover a segment of First Temple wall directly beneath a segment of Second Temple wall. A surprise, given their elevation. The working theory had been that walls of the First Temple period would be built farther down the slope. But given the surrounding topography, maybe the construction in this area was higher?

Ian wonders if it's a boundary wall, or something else.

"It could be the foundation of a building," Linda suggests.

"Or a retaining wall," Robert says, surveying the hill they're on.

Later at the lab, looking with a magnifying glass at a burnished potsherd, Professor Shomron asks, "Renata, what do you think about that wall?"

Uncertainty snags in her throat as everyone looks over.

"Well," she says, "it was built into the hill at a sharp angle, right? That would have made it hard to destroy; yet we have evidence of destruction all around. It *could* be a retaining wall. My hunch is, it's what remains of a boundary wall."

Professor Shomron nods.

30

OSKAR
1965

With Tzofia away performing in New York, Oskar sleeps with the phone near the bed and now he wakes with a jolt, predawn, to its ringing.

"Tzofia?" He pulls the corded receiver to the bed, rubbing his eyes, readying to hear her account of the recital, her biggest solo yet, at the famed Carnegie Hall.

"I have news you won't believe. . . ."

Her excited voice, the words spilling out. When she stepped onto the stage and scanned the audience, as she always does before a performance, she *felt* something—a flutter at her shoulder, a tug as if on an imaginary string.

His brain is still foggy. "What? Are you all right?"

"Yes! My mother was there! All the way through the Brahms Scherzo, I kept thinking my mother was there somehow, in person or in spirit. And she *was*! While we were taking our bows I saw her, standing in the third row, arms reaching out to me."

"Your mother? In New York?"

"Yes, at my concert!"

Amid Oskar's shock, a clear thought: *this* is what Tzofia has always played for. Why she's said "yes" to every performance invitation, no matter where in the world, and assented to every recording offer. Why she's always practiced with the window open, if even just a crack. She's been sending her violin out singing, calling for her mother.

Before they'd been separated, they'd hid together in a farmer's barn, the days spooling out, perilous with Nazi danger. To distract her, her mother taught Tzofia the fundamentals of music. She used different lengths of hay to represent notes—wholes, halves, quarters, and eighths. She whispered about ties and flats. She hummed the Brahms Scherzo, its upbeat start, its swooping high notes.

Oskar's mind travels to a pile of burned barn beams near the Dąbrowskis'. He climbs out of bed and stretches the phone cord to look in on Shoshana, asleep in her room. A pink flush at her cheeks, hair pressed to her skin, damp like a seal pup.

At five years old, the age Shoshana is now, Tzofia was in a barn loft, listening to her mother's whispered stories of a girl and a yellow bird, music playing in her head. Until her mother sent her to the convent for safety, alone—

"When is your flight?" Oskar asks. "Will you see her again before you leave?"

"Yes! I'm going to meet her husband, Aron. They've been in New York for twenty years. Did I tell you, she teaches the cello?"

"This is all so incredible, Tzofia."

"Now that we've found each other, we don't want to lose any more time—and she wants to know you and Shoshana. She's coming to Israel."

Oskar promises that he won't say a word to Shoshana; they'll wait until Tzofia gets home to share the news. Returning to his room to hang up the phone, he's still incredulous. Was it luck, or fate, that brought Tzofia and her mother together? Was it the beauty of Tzofia's music? Atop the bookcase, carved birds, a garland of paper roses, the music box he made for Tzofia.

He imagines her mother here, at their table, Tzofia nestled close on one side, Shoshana on the other. His next thought is his sister. How will she feel, learning this news, after everything she's been through?

He decides to tell her at the soonest opportunity, that same day, before Tzofia arrives home, while Boaz takes the children for a race around the park.

"It's such a crazy thing, Stazja," he says. "One of her mother's music students had a spare concert ticket to Carnegie Hall. No idea of the relation."

"Her mother lives in New York City?"

"Yes." He waits for his sister to become angry or jealous; to say it's unfair. She's eerily calm. "I know you've been going through a lot," he continues, "and I'd understand if—"

"I'm happy for Tzofia."

Her face is open, her eyes steady on his. He nods, grateful.

"Of course I'm happy for her, Oskar. And her news gives me hope."

They prepare for a visit from Savta Róża and Saba Aron, transforming the sunroom into a small bedroom, decorating it with Shoshana's bright crayon drawings of flowers—roses mostly, because her name means rose and so does her grandmother's.

"It's an enchanted garden," Róża exclaims when she sees it. She has the same slight shoulders and soft almond eyes as Tzofia.

At first, it's a flurry of hugging and crying and telling stories over long meals. Oskar, elated for Tzofia, is surprised when, less than a week in, he finds her curled in bed, clutching the shred of blanket her mother brought, unearthed for her by a nun at Siostry Felicjanki. By the time her mother arrived at the convent to reclaim her, Tzofia had been moved.

"I spent so many years waiting for her, and she didn't come."

"But she told us how she searched for you," Oskar soothes. "How much she desperately wanted—"

"She let go of me."

Oskar takes her hand, kissing her wet cheek. "She's here now."

One evening after dinner, Róża takes out her cello, which she brought in lieu of most everything else. She plucks the strings, testing the notes. Tzofia remains seated, her feet knotted beneath her, but she leans forward, head tilted. Listening.

Róża plays the first bars of something.

"Does your song have a violin part?" Shoshana asks.

"Yes, it does," Róża says. She lifts a small pile of sheet music; at the top, "Ravel's Sonata for Violin and Cello."

Shoshana looks at it, not yet able to read the title or the music. She turns to her mother. "Mama? Can you play it?" she asks.

Tzofia doesn't answer. Oskar pulls Shoshana to his lap. Aron shifts his chair beside theirs. Tzofia leaves the room and returns carrying her practice violin, picking hard at the strings. The room buzzes as she plucks, rotating the tuning pegs. Shoshana's weight is uneven on Oskar's lap. When he shifts her, she looks up at him with a worried look. Seeing, Tzofia extends her bow, a fairy tap to the top of Shoshana's head. A giggle.

After a moment's quiet, Tzofia and Róża begin, spare melodies weaving together, two strands forming a single braid. Their notes curl around one another, whispering, pattering.

Oskar feels himself breathe, feels Shoshana settle into him— then the violin abruptly stops. Róża's bow trails off.

"I'm sorry," Tzofia says, red-cheeked, blinking at the floor.

"It's my fault," Róża says. "Duets take time. I was rushing us." Turning to her granddaughter, she says, "We'll have other concerts."

Shoshana nods, looking between them.

In the darkness, I try to pretend I am nested inside my mother inside her mother inside her mother. The space is big and rattly, and I don't fit snug and safe. I roll to a corner, thinking to burrow there, but I am curved round and it is angled square.

I no longer hear the girl and her "Mum" clinking their forks on plates, sharing their news of the day. I shift, feeling a sharp metal frosting tip at my side, a lump of papers beneath me. I find the edge of an old apron cloth faintly scented of cake. I wrap myself inside it, warm and tight.

I know, one day, the girl will come find me.

31

ROGER
1968

Early to meet Bennie near Lions' Gate, to pick up snacks in the market, then hike by the tombs in the Kidron Valley, Roger sees a crowd growing at an excavation site. It looks like reporters have gathered, with spectators flanking the area as well. He heads over. Journalists are asking questions of the lead archaeologist, as her team stands by. Roger makes out the slender figure and braided hair of the archaeologist who likes rugelach, standing a bit apart from the others. He approaches her.

"Hello again," he says.

She turns to him, her eyes large behind her eyeglass frames, a streak of dirt down her nose.

"What's going on here?" he asks.

"We've discovered a section of wall that we believe dates to the First Temple period."

"Ah, so you're bringing further intrigue to the debates on borders?"

"Exactly," she says.

"Where are you from?" He'd noticed her British accent earlier; it reminded him of the language tapes he used so that he could read the English-speaking early modern philosophers in the original.

"We're from Oxford," she answers. She gestures to some of the others on the team. "We were digging for evidence of Second Temple boundaries and found this."

Roger nods.

"And you?" she asks. "Where are you from?"

"Is it so obvious I'm not Israeli born?"

"I'm practiced at tracing origins." The warmth of her smile breaks off the spin of old insecurities, a boy who never fit in.

"I'm from France. But I've been here since I was nine. I'm Roger, by the way." He uses his first, given name.

"Renata. And now I understand your longing for baguette."

He smiles.

There is a pause, her eyes going to the pencil behind his ear. Roger reaches a hand to it, embarrassed. "Yes. Well. I . . . I'm meeting my cousin for a walk," he says, "and then I teach an afternoon class at the university. Perhaps I'll come back this way, to see . . ."

Roger returns after the hike, but the crowd has dispersed and there's no one at the site. Later, winding through campus, he brightens to see Renata walking in his direction.

"Hello *again*," she says. "We're presenting at a colloquium." She points to the archaeology building yet her eyes hold his.

"Would you like to meet afterward?" he blurts.

"Professor?" A student's voice. Roger turns to see a small group from his seminar, tentative in their interrupting, yet grave in their concern that Locke's theory of personal identity might be sunk by Reid's objections.

Renata stands by, watching. Her eyes may be the same blue color as Sister Brigitte's, and as kind.

"Let's talk during my office hours," he says to his students. "In the meantime, why don't you think carefully about the concept of duration, how that might help Locke?"

The students thank him and shuffle off.

"They find me everywhere," Roger says.

"Well, I have some philosophical questions of my own. Maybe I can ask them when we meet."

They walk along the Cardo of the Old City, amid the scents of cardamom and coffee, the tight bustle of people speaking Hebrew and Arabic, cats slinking by. When they pass several shops with wood carvings and cutting boards, Renata tells him of the wood-worker she found in Tel Aviv, the chess sets and nesting boxes made of beautiful, burled wood. Roger takes a chance, telling a joke: "Do you know why a tree can't answer your questions?"

"Why?"

He is pleased to see she is smiling.

"It's stumped."

Laughing, they pass a stall full of bright scarves. After a bit of quiet he says, "And what do you call someone who is *partly* from Britain?"

"What?" she asks, turning toward him.

"Brit-ish."

She groans and laughs.

"This last one you'll like, I promise: Where does a mummy go swimming?"

He stops walking. Her eyes, like sparkling sea glass, meet his, waiting.

"The Dead Sea."

She is smiling at him. "No jokes about France?" she asks.

"Never," he says, smiling, too.

A bit later, they climb the steps to the rooftop and sit together, looking out at the slopes of the Mount of Olives, the glittering golden Dome of the Rock. Roger asks about Oxford. He's heard of the legendary philosophy dons there. Renata tells him of some of her favorite places, including the Ashmolean Museum.

"I have to go back by month's end," Renata says. "My land-lady is selling the building and I have to empty out our flat. My mum's flat."

"Where will you go?"

"I don't know. I'll have to find something else."

A silence.

"When I first got here, I didn't think I'd ever feel at home," Roger says.

"This place grows on you," Renata says.

"Hmm?"

"There's something about the ancient land here, with roots for all people, if only we could share in it."

He likes how she thinks. He nods, feeling simultaneously grounded and floating.

They resume walking—it seems neither of them wants their time together to end. Nearing the Western Wall, unreachable just a year prior, now opening onto a makeshift plaza after the area was razed. *If only we could share in it.* They don't approach the prayer area but stand back, still and silent.

The setting sun casts a gold glow over the expanse of white. Roger feels holiness emanating from the stones here. A wholeness amid the fragments of temple walls, a place where belief and his questions of identity transcend religions' demarcations.

The air buzzes with chanting, moaning. Praying.

"I'm not Jewish," Renata says, as if on the same train of thought.

He nods. He's spent so long confused about the nature of his soul. "I was raised in a Catholic convent before coming here," he says.

"Really?"

"Yes."

"Whenever I see religious artifacts, it's the commonalities rather than the differences that seem most salient," Renata says. "But as for what or who I believe in, I just don't know."

"Not knowing what to believe in—now, that's my area of expertise."

Along with cheese, olives, dates, and rugelach, they pick up *ka'ak* (the closest thing to baguette) for their picnic the next evening. This time they climb the Mount of Olives, spreading out their food, relishing the panoramic view.

"It must be gratifying to dig for artifacts, find clues to lived histories," Roger says.

"I love it! But it can be frustrating when we unearth seemingly random objects with no clue as to how they fit together."

"I know all about that, in the conceptual realm. You try to formulate a theory but there are ideas that don't fit or are contradictory."

"Or some you never think of, like missing pieces of a puzzle."

"Yes. That's the worst. How can you find what you don't know is missing?"

Roger tells her of his curiosity about a person's persistent identity over time.

"Archaeologists look for clues to identity, too," Renata says, "through evidence of habitual behaviors. How a people worshipped, how they buried their dead, their cooking and drinking and work habits. These can give insight into what they believed in and valued, who they were."

"What about *changes* in habits over time? How would you account for those?"

"I guess we'd have to establish the changes as occurring within the range of datable contexts."

"But would they lead you to think a new population had arrived on the scene within that time? Or that the original one had morphed its behaviors? And how would you confirm either way?"

"I imagine it would depend on finding consistency in other areas, a variety of factors, really. And perhaps we'd do well to have a philosopher on our team," Renata says with that smile.

The moon rises, round and bright. They talk on and on, their conversation growing more personal. Roger tells Renata about Sainte Marie's and his time in Spain with Brother Jacques.

"The Church hid me. They said they were protecting me—and during the war, they were—but later, they wanted to keep me Christian. My friend Henri is still there, and a nun who looked out for me. But I am with family here. My aunt, my father's sister, had to petition the courts to get me back."

Renata nods. "My father died when I was young. He was an engineering professor." She looks over at him. "You remind me of him, actually. What I can remember."

"Really?"

"How your mind works—and plays."

Roger thrills to hear this. He dares to reach for her hand, soft in his.

"It was just me and my mum after that," Renata says. "And now she's gone."

Stars blanket the sky. As they continue talking, she leans against him. His arm wraps around her, and he pulls her closer, unloosing a flutter low in his stomach. Only once does he remember feeling like this, when he was on the plane in the clouds over the Mediterranean, halfway between an old life and a new one. Time suspended yet unspooling still.

The sky lightens—violet, pink, orange—and Roger thinks,

for the first time, that even when the sun's brightness obscures them, the stars are always there.

On Friday night, Roger shows up late for dinner at Aunt Sarah and Uncle Uri's. He rushes in and hugs them all, the cousins and the kids, as exuberantly as they hugged him upon his arrival here in Israel.

"What's with you?" Bennie asks, his youngest perched in his arms, waving a wooden spoon in the air.

"Why do you ask?" Roger is smiling a huge smile.

"Well, for one thing, your shoes are a matching pair, and for another, you came in here humming."

"Let him be," Aunt Sarah chides, but as soon as the meal is over, she pulls him into the kitchen and asks, "So, is anything new?"

Undeterred, Bennie follows them in, the spoon-conducting baby in his arms again. "*Is* anything new?"

"Can I borrow a sifter?" Roger asks.

"You're baking at your place?" Bennie asks. "I didn't think you could toast a piece of bread in that desolate kitchen."

"And also a rolling pin, *s'il vous plaît*?"

32

RENATA
1968

Sunday afternoon, Renata watches as Roger pulls a tray of macarons from the oven. Perfectly rounded and filled, alternating bright yellow and pale green.

"These could be sold at a French bakery!" she exclaims.

"You'll want to taste them before saying so."

She bites into a green one. Exquisite, with a subtle hint of pistachio.

"It's brilliant."

Roger beams. "Try the lemon."

They stand in front of the oven, eating the cookies off the cooling tray.

"Even my mum would've approved. You should see our kitchen, all her supplies—the piping bags and frosting tips, the spatulas and smoothers."

"Really?"

"Yes, and the reason I was buying rugelach that day is, I've set myself the task of tasting all of Jerusalem's bakeries. I should have started here."

"You should have." His eyes are pools of dark honey.

Renata feels shy all of a sudden. She's inexperienced in this—this flirting, this wanting. Ian was really more of a fantasy, off-limits. Now she's here with this smart, gentle, silly man, with whom something could actually happen. She wants it to.

Roger lifts her face to his.

"I've gotten sugar on your cheek," he says. He leans in to kiss her there, a soft brush on the curve of her face.

"Oh?"

"Also, on your neck."

He moves his lips to her neck. A flush rises.

Reaching for the counter, coating her fingers in the powdery sifted sugar, she touches his lips.

Later, they walk along the edge of a grove amid the occasional *pat* of a falling olive.

"You know, Britain has nice desserts," she says.

Roger gives her a look, eyebrows raised.

"Why are you making that face?" she asks. "France doesn't have a monopoly!"

"Doesn't it?" Roger asks.

"In England we have trifle and banoffee pie and sticky toffee pudding—"

"The names alone feel like lead weights in the stomach."

"I bet you've never even tried them!"

"Right, because no one outside England bothers to replicate them, while chefs the world over make éclairs, mille-feuilles, and macarons!"

If she could only freeze time, she would stop it now, Roger's arm tight around her, scents of eucalyptus and the pressed earth, sugar on her lips.

A breeze rustles the leaves. She leans into him, smiling. "Did you say . . . 'macarons'?"

"I did."

She can't believe how easy and natural it feels. She and Roger just fit. She adores so many things about him. His intelligence and curiosity, his kindness. He takes time to listen to his students. He takes care to skirt the flowers that grow into the walking paths. He bakes French pastries! He's serious yet funny—and honest about who he is. Why must she leave so soon, when she's only just found him?

Over the next several days, Renata arrives early to the dig site, smiling madly, unable to pull her face straight. No one lets her live it down. If she didn't love her team already, she loves them now.

"So, when are we actually going to see this guy?" Professor Shomron asks.

"*I've* seen him," Margaret says proprietarily. "He was in the crowd at the press meeting, and he's been outside the lab some afternoons, to meet Renata."

"So that's why you haven't been coming to the bar with us," Robert says.

Renata nods, her smile still stretching her face.

Ian says, "It's nice to see you smiling."

"And it's nice to see you wearing happy colors!" Linda says.

"I agree," Professor Shomron says.

Renata touches a hand to the bright scarf, patterned in reds and pinks, she bought yesterday.

As they work, the others dig for further details. The fact that Roger is a philosopher elicits a noncommittal mumble; that he's a good baker brings out some real excitement.

"He's going to make me a mille-feuille," she tells them.

"Sure, because he knows you have a thing for layers," Robert says.

Later, when she's walking beside Margaret and Linda on the way to the lab, they talk of how terrible the timing is, the current dig wrapping up and the next one, just a fortnight, before she'll return to Oxford.

"It's really too bad you can't stay on a bit," Linda says.

"I know," Renata says, thinking of the night she and Roger stayed up, watching the sky fill with stars, pinkening to dawn. "I can't imagine going back."

33

ANA
1968

Every Friday, Ana cooks dinner for Oskar's family, and she is especially pleased when Tzofia, thin as a waif, reaches for second servings, exclaiming, "It's so good, Chani!" She likes being the one to feed everyone; happy for Oskar to bring Shoshana early so the cousins can play, and if Tzofia's practice time runs late, happy to set aside a plate of her favorites for when she arrives. This Friday, though, Ana is stormy as she moves about the kitchen.

Until now, Tzofia's mother has come only for visits from New York, and Ana has managed to quell her pangs of jealousy over their reunion. But the news that Róża and Aron would soon make aliyah and move here to Tel Aviv is more than Ana can take. Realistically, how many more playdates and Friday dinners will their two families have together? Once her Savta and Saba are here, Shoshana will surely choose to spend time with *them* in the afternoons. And Friday nights, Tzofia may want just her family.

Already, tonight is going to be different, not because of Tzofia's mother but because Oskar has to stay late at the woodshop. He called to say that he won't be able to bring Shoshana to play before dinner; they'll arrive around the same time as Tzofia. In fact, Tzofia arrives first, tucking her violin safely out of the way, joining Ari and Iris in dominoes, chatting with Boaz. Ana holds herself apart, cooking—and chiding herself: How can she begrudge Tzofia finding her mother when it's the very thing she, too, wishes for?

Then Oskar arrives, Shoshana in tow, and everything about the night annoys her. The easy chitchat at the dinner table. Her own blustery silence. Spoiling a night they have together in anticipation of nights they won't have together.

Later, when the adults are cleaning up in the kitchen and the kids are in Ari's room working on a puzzle, she hears Tzofia say to Oskar, "We received next season's concert schedule; tell Szymon I'll reserve him a seat for the opening next to you and my mother."

At that, Ana blurts, "Do you realize you never offer *us* tickets? And we're your *real* family."

"Jesus, Stazja—"

Tzofia looks startled. "I'd be happy to set aside tickets for you, Chani. I didn't realize you'd want to—"

"We don't need her to save us seats," Boaz says to Ana. Then to Tzofia, "It's not a problem, we can buy tickets."

"That's not the point," Ana says. "It's *unfair.*"

"Is this about concert tickets, or my mother?" Tzofia asks, turning angry.

Oskar wraps a protective arm around Tzofia. "Stazja, please—"

Ana knows she's putting Oskar in a bad position but she can't stop herself. "Have you thought about the Levys, how they are going to feel when your parents get here?" she asks Tzofia.

"The Levys are happy for me," Tzofia says.

"Would you two check on the children?" Oskar asks Boaz and Tzofia.

"The children are behaving perfectly well," Tzofia says, but she turns to go.

When they've left the room, Oskar asks, "What's wrong with you?"

Ana feels herself deflating, but she goes on. "Maybe you're fine with it—Tzofia's all-consuming music, and now her mother moving here. But *I'm* the one who hosts every Friday night and—"

"And we love coming—"

"Well, what do you think is going to happen when Róża and Aron are here full-time? I bet you anything, you won't come anymore. Have you considered what that will be like for me?"

"I don't understand, I thought you liked cooking for Shabbat. If it's too much for you—"

"I'm not saying that. I'm saying, you're going to stop coming."

"No, that's not going to happen," Oskar says.

Ana shakes her head.

"Listen, if sometimes we don't eat at your house, then you'll eat at ours. And I'm certain Tzofia can get you concert tickets."

Ana swipes at her eyes, wishing not to cry. "They go on too late, Iris won't be able to stay up." Her tears are hot and angry.

"Stazja," Oskar says. "You're my sister. You've kept us together all these years."

He reaches for her arm. She pulls away.

"You didn't want to come here," she says.

Oskar shrugs, gently takes hold of her anyway. "But we're a set," he says.

34

ROGER
1968

Roger rises bright and early, catches himself humming, and smiles. As he buttons his shirt, he spies Henri's latest letter—including the news that Brother Jacques has started keeping bees at Sainte Marie's, Henri's fascination with the science of it, and of course a few riddles—folded up on the floor by his bedside. He picks it up, rereading.

And another one, *mon ami*—

Seeing the zen master on the other side of a raging torrent, a student waves his arms and shouts, "Master, how do I get to the other side?"
The master smiles and says, "You are on the other side."

Henri's prescience. Roger puts the letter in his pocket, giving it a pat, before heading out to meet Renata.

As he makes his way to their meeting spot by the New Gate, Roger thinks: he is going to ask her to stay. It's a bit crazy after such a short time together. But there are opportunities for archaeological work here, and with the attention her team is receiving, she'll surely have luck finding a position. If she can't, if she has to straighten out her flat, keep on with her postdoc work in England, maybe he can try for a semester's sabbatical in Oxford. One way or another, he wants to give their relationship a try.

He sees her approaching, wearing a sundress dappled with flowers, her hair loose around her shoulders. "I like seeing you with your hair down," he says.

"I brought a scarf, in case we go inside any of the churches," she says, taking hold of his hand.

As they walk again through the Old City, the Christian Quarter this time, Roger thinks of long-ago services led by Father Louis and Father Vicente; prayers said with Sister Brigitte on the garden bench and with Brother Jacques at the water's edge.

"Did you attend the famous Christ Church Cathedral in Oxford as a little girl? Or did you go to one of the smaller Oxford churches?" he asks Renata as they cross the courtyard to the Church of the Holy Sepulchre.

He's seen photographs of Christ Church Cathedral. He couldn't imagine what it would be like to attend Mass there. The chapel at Sainte Marie's was a quarter as grand. The most striking thing about the Basque chapel was its ocean view—and the smell of honey.

"We went to the Oxford Oratory."

"Oh, so you're Catholic."

"Well, I was never baptized. We were from Germany originally, but once we got to Oxford—"

Roger stops walking. "What?"

"I think we were Lutherans before that."

"No. You're from where?"

"Tübingen. My mother moved us after my father died, to Switzerland and then to Oxford."

"When?"

She looks at him, puzzled. "I was six when we left Germany, and nine when we moved to Oxford."

"What year were you six?" He tries to do the math himself but his brain is locked.

"I was born in 1940. So, 1946. Roger?"

Roger's face is hot, the back of his neck clammy. He drops Renata's hand and takes a step away.

When he raises his eyes to hers again, everything is different. She is different. He sees her features as if through a new lens: the blue eyes, the light hair. Germanic. Aryan.

"What is it?"

"What *is* it? My parents were killed by German soldiers. My grandparents, too. All of my family was murdered, except for my aunt's family. And me."

"Roger, I'm so sorry." She doesn't step forward. She looks frozen.

Roger stares at her, his head pounding. His mind conjuring the images not pressed into albums: his parents bone-thin, breaking.

He can't imagine how Aunt Sarah and Uncle Uri will react. Renata not being Jewish is an obstacle they'd have gotten around—as they did with him when he arrived, steeped in Christianity. But her being German?

Her family was there during the war. They must have adhered to Nazi rule, if not endorsed it.

As if reading his mind, Renata says, nearly inaudibly, "Roger, my parents weren't Nazis. My father was a professor. My mother decorated cakes."

His response comes out hoarse and overly loud. "Were they resisters?"

She looks at him, wide-eyed, the blood drained from her face.

"I don't know," she says.

He feels as if he could suffocate. He'd have to pick between her and his family. They could never brook this. He doesn't think that he can.

"Roger—"

All those years without a real home, until he arrived here. His aunt and uncle searched for him, petitioned for him, embraced him, raised him up. They gave him a place to belong.

"I don't see how this can work," he says.

ANA
1968

Oskar knocks, early morning, unexpected, his face ashen, a telegram wilted in his hand.

"It's Ciocia Agata."

"I'll go with you," Ana says.

After a flight and a series of connecting trains, they disembark, rumpled, and begin the walk toward the farm. Ana looks down the lane at the church, the neighbors' houses, and the fields beyond. She can practically see Oskar as a boy, his curls glinting in the dappled light as he collected branch after branch, a pile he carried in his arms. Taking him by the arm now, she says, "I'm a mess, Oskar. I didn't think it would feel like this."

He looks at her.

"Growing up, I believed we . . . I . . . was a Jew hidden among Christians. Now it turns out I'm likely a Christian among Jews . . ." She trails off. "Praying to a God that isn't mine."

"God is all of ours, if God is any of ours," he says.

"And my children—"

"Your children are growing up with their parents, who love them."

She nods, grateful.

After a while, Ana says, "I used to believe Eva saved us."

Oskar is silent, but he takes her bag, heavy, from her shoulder.

"Do you feel any more at home in Israel?" Ana asks.

"Tzofia and Shoshana are home," he says.

"I feel that way about Boaz and the children," she says. Still.

As they walk by the edge of a field, she picks dry lavender. "Do you remember hearing violin music as a baby? The sound came through our ghetto apartment wall, and you turned to it, every time."

"No, you've mentioned it, but I don't remember."

"Mama was sure it was a sign of your intelligence and sensitivity. She'd brag to Papa." She still calls them that.

"What else did they say about me?"

"I'll try to remember."

They continue past the bright-shuttered houses.

"I hope Tzofia is faring all right," Oskar says.

Ana shakes her head, knowing Tzofia is preparing for her mother's imminent arrival. She can't help the bitter thought: *I'm not a violin prodigy performing the world over, so I'll likely never find my mother.*

Oskar turns to her, reading her expression. "Stazja, you can keep looking for her."

She twists a lavender stalk between her fingers. Wispy, low passing clouds cast them in shadow. She hasn't received a single reply to her requests for information.

Józef greets them at the farmhouse door. Haggard. She'd been picturing him as he used to be, strong, his hair dark, those crinkly, smiling eyes. Now she flashes to the first time she saw Józef— pale and bleary, pacing their threshold—when Agata needed help and he came for her mama.

He wraps Ana tight. "Look at you."

He pulls Oskar in, too.

"How is she?" Oskar asks.

Józef leads them to Agata's bedside. She is chalky white and dull-eyed until she sees Ana's face and brightens.

"Oh, Anastazja." Agata clasps Ana's hand in hers.

"Ciocia," Ana says, tears welling.

"You came with your brother."

Ana looks over at Oskar, already holding a carved bird in his hands.

"Yes," she says.

Ana walks through the house, feeling herself large in the space, marking each remembered thing: Agata's embroidered wall hangings, the little tarnished cup tucked in the back of the dish cabinet, Oskar's favorite nesting boxes. The braided grass wreath, a gift she'd made for Agata, still hanging on the door. The small basket high on the shelf.

When she enters the room they slept in, she inhales dried wood and must. On top of the bureau, an assortment of Oskar's whittling projects: spears, a whistle, a spoon. Gingerly, she opens the thin, uppermost drawer and shakes it. A rattling sound. Heart pounding, she reaches into the far back corner, and her fingers clasp around the spinning top.

A neighbor drops by with a pot of beet soup. Ana puts it to heat on the stove and sets the table while Oskar follows Józef into the bedroom. Ana hears Agata say, "I'm coming to the table. I've waited so long for this."

"Here, take the pillow and blanket," Józef says to Oskar.

Together they prop Agata onto a pillowed chair and bundle her with the blanket. She's the size of a girl. *Was she always so small, or was it that I was small?*

They join hands. Agata's fingers feel thin enough to snap. Józef's are thick, calloused and warm, enveloping Ana's whole hand. She doesn't close her eyes but looks down, seeing the nick in the table that Oskar made, accidentally, whittling inside.

Józef gives thanks for Oskar and Anastazja's arrival. He prays for God's wisdom and for Agata's comfort. He says grace over the food. Before letting go of hands, Józef looks to Oskar, then to her, and asks, "Do you know what they call our group?" A dimpling at the base of his cheeks.

"What?" Oskar asks.

"A family."

Józef gets up to stoke the fire. Oskar reaches to the high shelf, retrieving the basket in which they placed moss and feathers, bark and lavender, all still there though faded now, placed around the stones. "Did you know?" he asks Ana.

She nods, regretful now that she'd kept him from adding a carved bird.

"I would have kept it for you forever," Agata says.

Ana takes the two stones in her hands, drops them in her pocket. She walks out at dusk and gathers late-blooming sage to steep into a tea that will comfort Agata. The air is cold, heavy. She kneels down, touching her palms to the chilled dirt. The stones press against her thigh. She thinks: *I don't need to find her.*

And then it is snowing. Large, soft flakes blanketing the field.

Ana walks back toward the lit house and sees Józef carrying Agata, still bundled, out into the snowy night. Oskar is moving beside them, a look of uncertainty on his face. But Agata is smiling, the flakes catching on her eyelashes, melting on her cheeks. The sky, gone inky, not yet many stars.

"We could use a birch branch," Oskar says. "Didn't it put stars in the sky?"

Agata reaches for his hand. Her fingertips are blue-black.

In the morning, Agata calls for Ana.

"Anastazja."

"I'm here."

"There's a silver baby cup."

"Yes, at the back of the dish cabinet. Do you want—"

"My sister gave it to me when I became pregnant."

Ana nods.

"I kept it, even though I lost the baby."

Ana puts her hand on top of Agata's blanketed arm. "That's all right."

"I was so weak from bleeding; it wouldn't stop. We ordinarily kept to ourselves, but our midwife was at a birth, so Wujek Józef called on your mother."

"I remember," Ana says. Chana rushing around, piling herbs into a basket. But there's something Ana hadn't understood: Christian midwives served Christians, and Jewish midwives served Jews, except—

"She saved my life," Agata says.

Ana leans in to kiss Agata. The skin on her forehead is dry, her scent sharp like turned apples. Her pale sea eyes, the same as ever. "And you saved ours."

One last day and a night. They gather around Agata's bedside. Her face is peaceful now after several hours of intensity, her vision turned inward, her labored breath stopped. From his pocket Oskar removes the smallest, innermost nesting box, carried back from Israel. He places it in Agata's hands, so it can be buried with her.

"What about these?" Ana asks. She holds out the two stones.

Oskar leads her to the set of nesting boxes on the low side table and opens them, one by one. The last remaining, the second smallest, has nothing within. "Can we put them in here?"

Ana nods, and Oskar snugs the two stones inside, then returns the boxes, one inside the next. Carefully, he closes the top, leaving the set there, where it's always been.

At the gravesite, they speak out Psalm 23 and Ana also silently recites the Mourner's Kaddish. They hug one another, and they hug Józef. They grasp cold clumps of earth in their warm hands, and gently form a mound.

*In the dark, echoey space, I grow restless among stuck-together photo-
graphs, wood-handled pastry cutters, and musty papers. I roll around
and dig. I find love letters tied in a pink satin bow. Wax crayon
drawings. Official correspondences. I read each, one by one. I read
this:*

22 March 1946

Dear Mrs. Neumann:
*The UNRRA Child Welfare Division is tasked with identifying
and repatriating children unlawfully removed from their families
and placed for adoption in connection with the Germanization
project of the Lebensborn Program. Subsequent to our home visit
of 4 February, investigations have led to a match of photographs
as well as the corroborating detail of a small mole at the left
earlobe, determining Renata—born Renia Kaczmarek—to be the
rightful child of Ola and Janusz Kaczmarek of Zabrzeg, Poland.
You will understand the family's eagerness for her swift return.*

    Enclosed, their letter:

Our beautiful Renia! We have prayed for your safety and
homecoming every day since you were taken from us. Finally,
our prayers are being answered.

Do you remember the song "Kosi Kosi" you loved to
clap to, and your favorite lullaby, *Oj lulaj, lulaj*? When we
lost hold of you, you were carrying your tiniest wooden doll.
All this time, the other dolls have waited for the little one to
return home, as we have waited for you. We are crying with

joy, hopeful that you will soon be with us. May our family be whole once again by Easter!

Your loving parents. (Dictated and translated)

From the interview notes, I understand that you were misled as to the circumstances by which Renia came into your custody and I recognize the difficulty this discovery must bring. Nevertheless, the rights of natural parents prevail in this matter. There is concern that repeated attempts to find you at your Tübingen residence have been unsuccessful. I ask that you please contact our offices at once.

Sincerely,

G. S. Bauer, Child Welfare Investigating Officer, Central Tracing Bureau, United Nations Relief and Rehabilitation Administration

The page is yellowy, crinkled and old, yet I know its truth persists: they are there, still, one inside the other, inside the other, inside the other.

I hope the girl will hurry and find me so that I can tell her: all this time, they, too, have waited.

36

ANA
1968

Agata's death pounds Ana like a tidal wave, knocks her off her feet. Back home, she takes to bed, barely able to turn her head to acknowledge Ari and Iris. They round the bed holding aloft her treasure box, her spinning top. "Mama, would you like to play with this? Or this?" trying to cheer her, but she's drowning in grief. And regret. Why didn't she see? She could have had Agata as a mother; she was there all those years. Amid the childhood ruptures and hiding, the truths and lies of her origins, the complete scrambling of her sense of self, Agata was there.

No matter how many times Boaz gently leads the children away from Ana's bedside, they return, vying for her attention, willing her to focus on them. Instead: the creak of the ghetto stairs beneath her feet. Chana's hand tight at her arm, propelling her toward Bluma's truck. Eva's slight frame jostling against hers. The hard bed of the truck, swerving amid shadows. Away, away. Ana's arms splay out to the edges of the bed, reaching for something to hold on to. She shivers, cold. How *long* was she held warm in Elżbieta's embrace before being handed off, then handed off again?

She feels the magnetism of perilous objects everywhere in the house: the kitchen knife, a bottle of aspirin, Boaz's leather belt, a shaving blade. What would it be like, a single deep slit of the wrist? A dry swallowing of pills, a rope to the rafter. What would it be like, oblivion?

Never before has she had such thoughts. She is a wife and mother. She has a brother.

Oskar begins showing up before and after work. She stays in bed, face to the wall.

One morning, after conferring with Boaz, Oskar says, "Stazja, I'm taking you with me to the shop."

"I don't want to."

Ari, in the doorway, fear in his eyes. She extends a hand, shaky with guilt.

"Okay. I'll go," she says, and she allows Oskar to drive her there.

Oskar sets her up in a chair at the back corner of the shop. She closes her eyes, blocking out the commotion around her. The woody scents evoke something Eva shared with her not long ago, a dawning thought: as she hustled children through forests, outrunning the cries of other mothers, the roots she could not see were *as* tenacious, *as* entwined, as those she had to leap over.

Ana burrows beneath Oskar's coat and lets herself drift to sleep. When she opens her eyes, the light has shifted. Szymon is sitting in a chair nearby.

She nods off several times. Each time she wakes, he is beside her, still.

She agrees to go again, the next day. Szymon takes up his place next to her. The others pick up his work orders, and Shmuel doesn't raise objections. Szymon stays, constant and unmoving. Ana thinks, *Maybe he's here more for Oskar than for me, but he is here all the same.*

At home in the evening, propped on the living room couch, Ana sees Iris carefully walk toward her carrying a drink, bright green leaves swirling in a tall glass. Boaz and Ari watch from the kitchen.

"I made it with herbs, like you do when *we* are sick," Iris says.

Ana can taste mint and lemon balm. It's refreshing and the

smile she shares with her daughter shifts her from deadwood to a wobbly spinning top.

"Thank you. It's helping me already."

Despite Boaz's wary looks, Oskar speaks of Agata: the way her voice lilted when she began a story; how she gave a quick squeeze to their toes after tucking them in for sleep; how she buttoned their coat collars to ensure they'd be warm.

Ana remembers the soft fur. A way of saving them.

The flowers in the garden bloom purple and pink and send a sweet scent through the open windows. The sun presses in, beaming rectangles of light across the floors. Slowly, Ana grows stronger. One Friday night, after an early dinner prepared by Boaz and the kids, with Oskar's family partaking, Ana asks Oskar if he'll take her to the Western Wall so that she might pray for Agata.

"Are you sure?"

"Yes, I want to place a message in the stone there."

37

RENATA
1968

At the lab, Renata can't concentrate. She dodges cheer-up invitations—Ian and Robert, getting falafel; Margaret and Linda, heading one last time to the rooftop bar for drinks. She even begs off the dinner marking the end of the first dig, arranging to say her goodbyes at the lodging house. She's too gutted for company—and too furious with herself.

What kind of archaeologist fails to learn the basic facts of her own origins? Why didn't she confront her mum about the war, ask how they'd navigated it, whether she or Papa were pressured into complicity? Her mum, who clearly kept secrets, is gone now, and Renata is left wondering: What was all that British assimilation about, if not a cover for German shame?

In her airless room, sprawled across the swaybacked bed, she turns her anger on Roger, too. He's being illogical and unfair. She was five years old when the war ended, and no matter what her parents did or didn't do (no matter what any Germans did or didn't do), he can't hold it against *her*.

Yet, over and over, her thoughts return to the anguish on Roger's face before he turned away. He lost both his parents. His aunt Sarah lost nearly all her family. Tears run down Renata's cheeks and fog up her glasses.

Then, the worst thought:

Could her parents have been Nazis?

She climbs under the bedcovers, shuddering. The possibility of it is paralyzing. All she wants is to block it out. To sleep.

She spends the next several hours shifting and tossing, in and out of disturbed slumber. When she opens her eyes, a different resolution: she *can't* block this out. She *won't*. She needs to learn what role her parents played during the war.

She'd lacked courage in her relationship with her mother. She wasn't brave enough to ask hard questions, dig for answers, push against her mum's defense walls. Maybe, deep down, she'd feared what she would find. But she's determined now. She will scour historical records and question Tübingen neighbors (Gisela, to start); she will turn the Oxford flat upside down, sifting through every personal scrap her mother has hidden away. She will uncover the truth.

She yanks off the tangle of bedsheets and blankets. From the phone in the hallway, she books her return flight, two Saturdays from now, after the second dig is completed.

Early mornings at the site, Renata tries to stay focused on the ground in front of her, seeking evidence of First Temple boundary construction at this higher elevation along the slope. Still, whenever a figure walks by in the near or far distance, she thinks of Roger. She wishes she could show up at his apartment, or his office, or the library where he has a carrel. She can't.

She wishes he'd come find *her*. Each afternoon at her lodging house, she checks if anyone has called or come by. No.

The dig wraps up, and then it is the last night before her scheduled flight. She heaps her things into her suitcases, careful only in the repackaging of the nesting boxes, one inside the other. She's not tired, and can't bear to stay in her cramped room, so she pulls her satchel over her shoulder and heads out into the sticky night, walking in the direction of the Old City.

She thinks about the hope that moves people to bare their hearts, to pray. She wonders how Roger would feel, knowing that she's resolved to unearth her past and to understand her place in the history that has so deeply affected his family. Would it change things between them? Would he reopen himself to her? They had been happy. They had *fit*. Could they somehow get back to that?

Renata weaves through the narrow streets to the area of the Kotel. She crosses the plaza, the Wall immense before her, its stones cleaving to hundreds of folded notes.

She pulls a bit of paper from her satchel.

38

ROGER
1968

Alone in his apartment, grief pins Roger to his bed. Since he left Renata standing outside the Church of the Holy Sepulchre, he can't think straight. Can't read or write. His teaching has been an utter disaster. Whatever past struggles he's endured, he's never felt so hollowed out, so hopeless. He finds no solace at all in philosophy. His sorrow lives in his *cells,* which apparently connect him, still, to his lost mother and father. His hunted, slaughtered *mère et père.*

He drags himself to Aunt Sarah's Friday dinner because otherwise she will worry. Uncle Uri is there, along with Bennie and Chasia and other cousins, with their roosted broods of five. They exchange glances at the sight of him. He hasn't shaved or changed his clothes.

"Why do you look like that?" asks Zev, Avi's oldest.

"Finish setting the table for Savta," Aunt Sarah says.

Chasia puts her arm around Roger as the conversation swells and everyone takes seats around the table. He moves his food around, no appetite, incapable of engaging in any discussion. When the others finish, he apologizes for not making dessert. Ordinarily he takes time in Aunt Sarah's well-equipped kitchen to bake something, *navettes* or *calissons* or else *palmiers*, which he serves with brushed cinnamon sugar, *exactement*. Not today.

"It's all right," Aunt Sarah soothes. After the meal, she pours coffee, and Bennie brings out cookies from a tin.

"What's going on with you?" Bennie mouths as he passes, but Roger doesn't answer.

"Is Rami growing a beard?" Zev wonders aloud.

The littlest kids pull on Roger's sleeves, oblivious to his low mood. He helps them with a grandparent prank, lifting them halfheartedly to perch small paper cups of water atop the swinging kitchen door before Sarah or Uri rise from the dining table to clear the last of the plates.

Aunt Sarah feigns surprise at the dripped water and chases the children with mock outrage. Then she pulls Roger aside. "Let's take a walk."

They step outside into the warm night and weave down the wide, open street.

When Roger finally forces himself to say what he's learned of Renata's German origins, that her family was *there* during the war, Aunt Sarah stills.

"Oh, God," she says.

"I know." His head feels like it could burst.

"Rami, I—"

"I know," he says again.

She takes his hand. "Why don't you stay over with us?"

"I think I need to be alone."

He moves through a blur of days. A knock at the door and it's Bennie, holding a bag of Roger's favorite foods—stuffed vine leaves, *ka'ak*, white cheese, and honey cookies. Roger unpacks the food in the kitchen, no thought of eating. The apartment is largely unfurnished other than his study, with a solid desk and chair, and floor-to-ceiling bookshelves crammed with books, so he leads Bennie there, motioning to the chair. Bennie sits, swiveling away from the desk, his long legs sprawled out in front of him. Roger begins to pace and talk.

Her family lived under Nazi rule but she's unsure of their involvement. How could she have not asked, probed, *demanded* to know? What does her reticence say about who she is?

Yet maybe, as a child, she *did* ask and was quieted. Roger knows as well as anyone that children don't have control over what happens to or around them. She didn't choose her origins, did she? It *can't* be fair to lump her in when she had no agency, and it may have been difficult, later, to pry. Still . . .

His thoughts circle like his steps; yet no matter where he lands, Roger feels disloyal—to his parents and family, to his devotion to reason and logic, to his connection with Renata.

His body starts to shake. He is helpless in the face of what is visceral rather than rational. His parents were taken from him, murdered, and all his life he's been consumed with uncertainty; not knowing who he is, or what he believes, or where he belongs. Then Renata showed up and they could talk endlessly, and they were happy. She seemed to understand him, to be *like* him, only—

His voice cracks. Bennie stands then, wraps him in his arms.

Aunt Sarah drives over the following afternoon, stocks Roger's refrigerator, and hugs him breathless. She returns two days later with more food, but Roger has barely touched the first delivery. Uncle Uri comes with her, taking a glass from the sink to water the wilting plants while Aunt Sarah talks and hugs and hugs and talks.

The days stutter past. Roger finds himself wanting to see Renata, wanting it more than anything. He holds himself back because: What has changed? Even as his thoughts grow clearer—*she* bears no responsibility for what happened, and it's not right to blame her for her German descent—there's no hope because he won't ask his family to open to this. They took him in, took care of him.

Like the wolf pack curling around the fallen boy in his childhood story.

He is surprised when Aunt Sarah shows up, late Friday, walking straight into the kitchen where he's standing, pointlessly, having forgotten what he came in for.

"Doda?"

"Do you love her?" she asks.

"Yes." He says it without hesitation.

"Well, then you'll need to figure it out." She's leaning against the counter, arms crossed.

"How?" he asks.

"You're the thinker."

"You'd accept her?"

"We accept *you*, Rami. We want you to be happy. What else is there in this life?"

"I told her it couldn't work."

"See if you can fix it."

Roger hugs his aunt as tightly as she has always hugged him. He doesn't bother to shower or change. He reaches for a piece of notebook paper and a pencil. Before he goes looking for Renata, he wants to write something, a message to place between sacred stones.

One might call it a prayer.

OSKAR, ANA, ROGER, RENATA
1968

In Jerusalem's Old City, at the site of the Western Wall, Oskar and Ana arrive together, then part for their respective prayer sections. They walk solemnly forward, past those who stand huddled or alone, covered heads bent, lips moving, to reach a place where they can touch the wall, lean their faces to it. The stone is cool on their cheeks despite the night's gathering heat, and it holds them, the scattered pieces of their hearts, their thoughts, their loves, their hopes, seeking a place to grow whole. Oskar prays for Ana's safety and rootedness, the same for the others he loves. In Agata's memory, Ana asks for forgiveness, and for guidance in her wish to bring Józef here, nearer to his daughter, his son.

Roger closes his eyes and bows his head, a melded hum of chants and pleas mixing in the air around him. The moon is full and bright, reflecting gold, the Dome of the Rock. Roger prays that he will find Renata, have the chance to lay bare his ever-changing self to her and beg her to join his family. Easing his words into a crack between the stones, he takes a step back, his eyes sweeping to the Mount of Olives, their picnic spot. It's when his gaze returns to the holy fragment of wall that he sees her through the lattice partition that separates the men's section from the women's. Renata. Standing there, as if in answer to all the questions he's ever asked.

Renata rests her forehead on the ancient wall, her blue glasses in her hand. The limestone emits a faint scent of sulfur, mixing with the smells of wool and leather and sweat. She joins with all who have stood in this place before her and all who will stand after, and she prays, not for a nice flat, as she once thought she might, but for true home, belonging, a life with the man she loves and with whom she fits. She presses her wilted piece of paper into a crevice between the stones; her deepest hope for honest connection, here, with Roger, no buried secrets. She is wiping her eyes, wishing never to leave but turning to go, when she hears him say her name. She puts her glasses on, looks in the direction of his voice.

EPILOGUE

At the Western Wall, nestled among its ancient stones, the notes placed there, one beside the other beside the other, wait, until one day they are gathered up, ceding room for those to come.

A woman, part of a team of collectors, works with her cleaned fingers and also a delicate narrow branch, carefully coaxing the folded papers from the cracks and placing them inside a box. As she dislodges each message, at a height high or low, pressed deep into the wall's fissures or so close to the edge as to flutter with a passing breeze, she treats it as holy, sanctified and private. She presses it in with the others, gives it a pat.

Paper by paper, the box fills. When she folds the top closed and carries it to the edge of the plaza, to be buried at the cemetery on the Mount of Olives, the notes layer, longings mixed together and shared. Collective. Collected. Not lost or forgotten, no longer alone, but gone to ground, to meld with soil and rainwater, to nourish the entwined roots of old and newly planted trees.

AUTHOR'S NOTE
AND ACKNOWLEDGMENTS

This story took root when I interviewed a woman who, in the years after World War II and in the wake of the lost millions, worked as an operative for the "redemption" of Jewish children, removing them—sometimes secretly, sometimes forcibly— from their Christian rescue homes and securing their passage to British-mandated Palestine with the help of the underground organization Brichah (meaning "flight"). She herself characterized her work as kidnapping; yet, in her mind, it was necessary work to save the children—and thereby save Judaism's future—after so much annihilation.

I later learned of a case in which Jewish boys, placed in a Christian institution for safekeeping during the war, were illicitly baptized and taken on the run after surviving Jewish relatives petitioned to reclaim them. The Church officials in this case also believed they were saving the children, saving their Christian souls.

Such cases of kidnapping occurred postwar. During the war years, a Nazi-sponsored Lebensborn program for Germanization was put into motion, involving the abduction of non-German (yet Aryan-looking) children. Mainly from Poland and the surrounding areas, the children were taken from school yards, park benches, medical appointments, or simply ripped from their parents' arms. They were brought to reception centers to undergo a selection process, whereby they were measured (in sixty-two places) and compared with diagrams based on an ideal "Nordic appearance"—elongated, narrow head; oval-shaped face; blond hair, blue eyes; pinkish-white skin. Of those disqualified, only the very youngest were returned to their homes. The older children, if physically fit, were sent to Germany for labor, while those unfit and deemed "racially tainted" were put into the children's concentration camp, Litzmannstadt, where most of them died. It should be mentioned that a large-size mole would have likely disqualified a child for Germanization.

Of those who were selected, the youngest were placed with German families. To qualify to receive a Lebensborn child, the parents would have to have been registered members of the Nazi Party. However, there is no evidence that these fostering and adopting families were aware of the methods by which the children came to them. After the war, UNRRA workers sought the return of the Germanized children to their birth parents, only to find themselves party to the further rupturing of attachments and sense of home.

I owe debts to many who helped me create this story with veracity. Thanks to Emunah Nachmany Gafny's careful research and generous consultation, Eva's route for Oskar and Ana is (loosely) based on a route used by an operative who smuggled children from Poland to British-mandated Palestine under the auspices of the Zionist Coordination Committee for the Redemption of Jewish Children (Koordynacja). Dr. Nachmany Gafny's book, *Dividing Hearts: The Removal of Jewish Children from Gentile Families in Poland in the Immediate Post Holocaust Years,* is an invaluable resource for anyone wanting to learn more about the efforts to reclaim Jewish children, the organizations that forwarded this work (often amid disagreements and rivalries that were political, financial, philosophical, and religious), as well as the complex and varied viewpoints and emotions of the field operatives and the children taken. Nachum Bogner's *At the Mercy of Strangers* also provides great detail. Bogner estimates that, of the thousands of Jewish children saved by non-Jewish families, convents, and orphanages in Poland, approximately six hundred were ransomed, mainly in the years 1946 and 1947, by Koordynacja and by Yeshayahu Drucker (of the Council of Religious Communities). Other child removal operations were conducted by Poalei Agudath Israel and the Rescue Committee of the Orthodox Rabbis of the USA.

David Kertzer's excellent reporting on the Finaly Affair shed light on the role of the papacy in baptizing and concealing Jewish children within Church structures, and informed my development of Roger's story. *In the Shadow of Vichy*, by Joyce Block Lazarus, was instructive as well. Though without clear figures as to how many Jewish children, hidden and saved by Catholics, were baptized and affected by the 1946 directive from the French Apostolic Nunciature stating that "children who have been baptized must not be entrusted to institutions that would not be in a position to guarantee their Christian upbringing," French historian Catherine Poujol provides a nuanced investigation into this postwar Church policy.

An estimated two hundred thousand Polish children were kidnapped during the war for the purpose of Germanization. Postwar aid workers from the United Nations Relief and Rehabilitation Administration (UNRRA) were tasked with identifying these children, locating them, and returning them home. In light of the sheer numbers, many of the children never learned of their true origins and lived out their lives believing they were German. Gitta Sereny's writings about Germanization and its aftermath deeply moved me and shaped my thinking about Renata. Also of great value was Willa Smith's *They Must Be Germans*.

The significant work of Boaz Cohen and Joanna Michlic on memory, identity, and testimony gave me insight into the experiences of child survivors of the Holocaust. Thank you to Eva Fogelman and Sharon Kangisser for connecting me. Consultations with Yuval Marcus, David Ilan, Elizabeth Klarich, and Lynn Dodd helped me immensely with the archaeological details. (Any missteps remain my own!) Efrat Ben-Ze'ev generously commented on the manuscript, deepening my sense of historical perspectives, and with the understanding of a writer's interest in tastes and smells, introduced me to apricot *leder*. Aleksandra Wolnicka helped me with Polish grammar—and curse words!—and Vera Vaidman led me to Tzofia's stretchy black performance dress.

Travel to Israel proved essential to my understanding of the complex, ever-shifting political circumstances and its ripples into archaeological programs there. Eitan Shomron answered every question I could think of, and he and Shula Shomron treated me to a wonderful day that brought the settings of my story to life. Roy Talmor revealed a rich history, punctuated by bells and chants and a perfect picnic spot—and the fact that Uri and Yotam Yakhini came along made it that much sweeter. Tamar Naor orchestrated every aspect of the adventure lovingly and with perfection, as she does everything.

Iris Berkman and Moi Wurgaft shared their personal kibbutz experiences with me, for which I am most grateful. Moi and Nina Wurgaft led me to greater accuracy and subtlety in my account of Israeli life—along with new friendships I deeply value. Emunah Nachmany Gafny and Margie Serling Cohn set aside chunks of their time to translate and read this novel, providing careful feedback on every aspect of the history and heart contained within it.

I am so thankful for their generosity and hope to clink glasses in person one day soon.

The stories of "The Magic Box" and "Sister of the Birds," as told by Agata to Oskar and Anastazja, are based on Gypsy tales collected by Jerzy Ficowski, translated by Lucia Borski in the volume *Sister of the Birds and Other Gypsy Tales*. Roger's "Naked Truth" parable borrows from that of the Maggid of Dubno. The story Oskar tells Shoshana about music's origins has its inspiration in Dylan Pritchett's *The First Music*.

Though deeply grounded in history and research, my work is entirely fictional, and I am beyond thankful for the extraordinary team that supports me in my writing life. I couldn't ask for a more terrific agent than Gail Hochman, nor a more brilliant editor than Caroline Bleeke. Amelia Possanza, Katherine Turro, Megan Lynch, Bob Miller, Malati Chavali, Kerry Nordling, Marta Fleming, Sydney Jeon, Jeremy Pink, Shelly Perron, Vincent Stanley, Sue Walsh, and Guy Oldfield are the best people to give a book wings.

I am incredibly thankful to those who have delved caringly and repeatedly into the emotion and logic of this story, pinning moments big and small with great astuteness and perception: my late, beloved mentor Kevin McIlvoy, Tanya Krim, Catherine Newman, Britt Shahmehri, Kate Moses, and Carrie Frye. (And to Catherine, again, for assuring me I could actually submit it!) Deep adoration and gratitude for early (and also late) draft comments and encouragement: Marilyn Abildskov, Caryn Brause, Jennifer Einhorn, Anna Eisen, Shari Fox, Becky Michaels, the late Ruth Salton, Missy Wick, Gideon Yaffe, and Jean Zimmer. For cherished friends, near and far, who have supported me, walked by rivers and meadows with me, poured tea with foamy milk for me. For the Rosners, Corwins, and Malinas, and Rosebud, my love.

Finally, I couldn't have written a word about finding home if it weren't for my wonderful husband, Bill Corwin, and our wondrous daughters, Sophia and Juliet—whose love and support (*and* intricate plot twist suggestions!) buoy me, and to whom I belong.

RECOMMENDED READING

Andlauer, Anna. *The Rage to Live*. CreateSpace Independent Publishing Platform, 2012.

Appelfeld, Aharon. *The Story of a Life*. Schocken Books, 2004.

Bauer, Yehuda. *Flight and Rescue: Brichah*. Random House, 1970.

Ben-Ze'ev, Efrat. *Remembering Palestine in 1948*. Cambridge University Press, 2011.

Block Lazarus, Joyce. *In the Shadow of the Vichy: The Finaly Affair*. Peter Lang Publishing, 2008.

Bogner, Nachum. *At the Mercy of Strangers: The Rescue of Jewish Children with Assumed Identities in Poland*. Yad Vashem, 2009.

Borggräfe, Henning; Akim Jah; Nina Ritz; and Steffen Jost, eds. *Freilegungen: Rebuilding Lives—Child Survivors and DP Children in the Aftermath of the Holocaust and Forced Labor*. Wallstein Verlag, 2017.

Clifford, Rebecca. *Survivors: Children's Lives After the Holocaust*. Yale University Press, 2020.

Cohen, Boaz. "The Children's Voice: Postwar Collection of Testimonies from Child Survivors of the Holocaust." *Holocaust and Genocide Studies*, March 2007.

Dwork, Deborah. *Children with a Star: Jewish Youth in Nazi Europe*. Yale University Press, 1993.

Epstein, Helen. *Children of the Holocaust: Conversations with Sons and Daughters of Survivors*. Penguin, 1988.

Ficowski, Jerzy. *Sister of the Birds and Other Gypsy Tales.* Translated by Lucia Borski. Abingdon, 1976. Selected from *Gałązka z drzewa słońca*, Nasza Księgarnia, 1961.

Gigliotti, Simone, and Monica Tempian, eds. *The Young Victims of the Nazi Regime: Migration, the Holocaust, and Postwar Displacement.* Bloomsbury Academic, 2016.

Grossman, David. *The Yellow Wind.* Picador, 2002.

———. *To the End of the Land.* Vintage Books, 2001.

Izhar, Neomi. *Chasia Bornstein-Bielicka: One of the Few: A Resistance Fighter and Educator, 1939–1947.* Yad Vashem, 2009.

Kamenetzky, Christa. *Children's Literature in Hitler's Germany.* Ohio University Press, 1984.

Kangisser Cohen, Sharon; Eva Fogelman; and Dalia Ofer, eds. *Children in the Holocaust and Its Aftermath: Historical and Psychological Studies of the Kestenberg Archive.* Berghahn Books, 2017.

Kertzer, David. "The Pope, the Jews, and the Secrets in the Archives." *The Atlantic,* August 27, 2020.

Kofman, Sarah. *Rue Ordener, Rue Labat.* Translated by Ann Smock. University of Nebraska Press, 1996.

Küchler-Silberman, Lena. *My Hundred Children.* Laurel Leaf, 1987.

Lauer, Betty. *Hiding in Plain Sight: The Incredible True Story of a German-Jewish Teenager's Struggle to Survive in Nazi-Occupied Poland.* Smith & Kraus Global, 2004.

Lukas, Richard. *Did the Children Cry? Hitler's War Against Jewish and Polish Children, 1939–1945.* Hippocrene Books, 1994.

Macardle, Dorothy. *Children of Europe: A Study of the Children of Liberated Countries; Their War-Time Experiences, Their*

Reactions, and Their Needs, with a Note on Germany. Hassell St. Press, 2021.

Meyers, Odette. *Doors to Madame Marie.* University of Washington Press, 1997.

Michlic, Joanna. *Jewish Families in Europe, 1939–Present: History, Representation, and Memory.* New England University Press/Brandeis University Press, 2017.

———. *Jewish Children in Nazi-Occupied Poland: Survival and Polish-Jewish Relations During the Holocaust as Reflected in Early Postwar Recollection.* Yad Vashem, 2008.

———. "'Who Am I?' The Identity of Jewish Children in Poland, 1945–1949." *Polin* 20, 2007.

Nachmany Gafny, Emunah. *Dividing Hearts: The Removal of Jewish Children from Gentile Families in Poland in the Immediate Post Holocaust Years.* Yad Vashem, 2009.

Neeman, Yael. *We Were the Future: A Memoir of the Kibbutz.* Overlook Duckworth, 2016.

Nicholas, Lynn. *Cruel World: The Children of Europe in the Nazi Web.* Vintage Books, 2005.

Oz, Amos. *A Tale of Love and Darkness.* Harcourt, 2005.

Patt, Avinoam. *Finding Home and Homeland: Jewish Youth and Zionism in the Aftermath of the Holocaust.* Wayne State University Press, 2009.

Sereny, Gitta. *The Healing Wound: Experiences and Reflections, Germany, 1938–2001.* W. W. Norton, 2001.

Smith, Willa. *They Must Be Germans: The Nazi Germanization Program and the United Nations Relief and Rehabilitation Administration, 1939–1947.* Barnard Thesis, 2020.

Stone, I. F. *Underground to Palestine.* Pantheon Books, 1978.

Szabo, Magda. *Abigail.* NYRB Classics, 2020.

Valent, Paul. *Child Survivors of the Holocaust.* Routledge, 2016.

Wylie, I. A. R. "Returning Europe's Kidnapped Children."
Ladies' Home Journal, 1946.

Zahra, Tara. *The Lost Children: Reconstructing Europe's Families After World War II.* Harvard University Press, 2011.

Other resources:

Jewish Historical Institute Archive

Ghetto Fighters House Archive

Yad Vashem Archive

USC Shoah Foundation, Visual History Archive

Western Galilee Holocaust Studies Program Website: Children of Holocaust, War and Genocide: The Relevance of Post WW2 and the Holocaust for Today's World, https://cwg1945.org/

https://www.yadvashem.org/articles/general/difficulties-in-rescue-of-children-by-non-jews.html

Amalia Margolin and Oshra Schwartz, directors. *My 100 Children,* documentary film, 2003